DARK CORNERS
OF THE OLD DOMINION

A VIRGINIA HORRORS ANTHOLOGY

EDITED BY

JOSEPH MADDREY & MICHAEL ROOK

DEATH KNELL PRESS

DARK CORNERS OF THE OLD DOMINION
A VIRGINIA HORRORS ANTHOLOGY

DEATH KNELL PRESS

All proceeds of this book are donated to
SCARES THAT CARE®
a 501(c)3 charitable organization.
For more information, visit
www.scaresthatcare.org

Dedication:

This book was born in 2015, when Dee Southerland had the idea to stitch together a literary Frankenstein's monster from the words of her fellow Virginia horror writers.

In 2022, the dream was revitalized with the help of six co-conspirators: Querus Abuttu, Red Lagoe, Joseph Maddrey, Bryan Nowak, Michael Rook, and D. Alexander Ward.

One year later... It's Alive!

Thanks, Dee!

DARK CORNERS

MAP OF HORROR CONTENTS

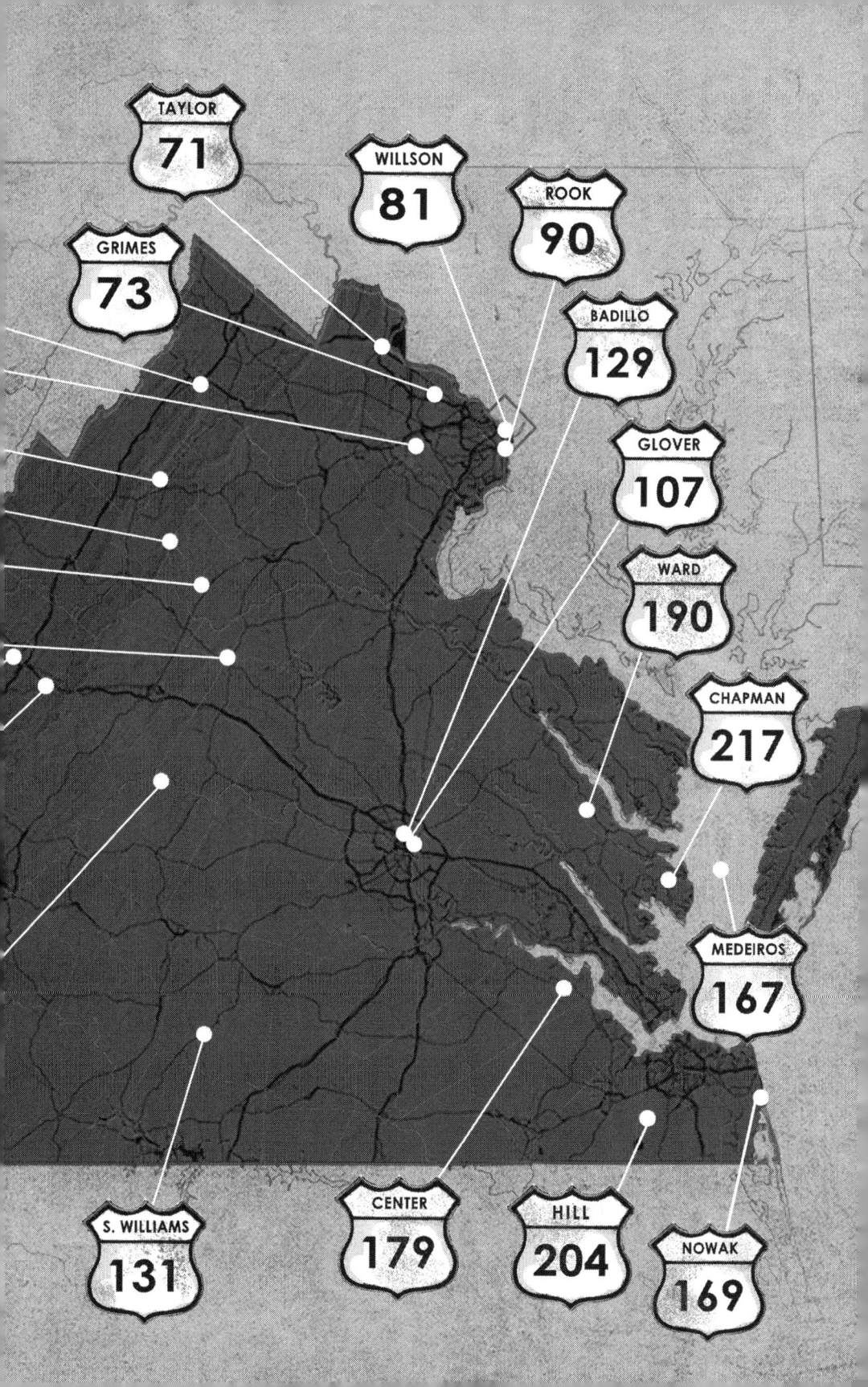

TABLE OF CONTENTS

PIEDMONT

COASTAL VA

FOREWORD

Brian Keene

In 1969, the Martin & Woltz advertising company, led by George Woltz, was hired by the Virginia State Travel Service to come up with a new slogan to drive tourism to the state. They discussed how Virginia was for history lovers. How Virginia was for mountain lovers. Beach lovers. Wilderness lovers. Fishing lovers. Hiking lovers. Camping lovers. All the lovers. Eventually, they decided upon 'Virginia is for lovers' as the state slogan—a somewhat provocative statement given that 1969 was also the Summer of Love, and the generational socio-political controversy that went with that. Regardless, the slogan stuck, and here in 2023 Virginia is still for lovers. You see it emblazoned on highway billboards, t-shirts, coffee mugs, keychains, and more. It's repeated in television commercials, radio advertisements, and podcast bumpers. It's a frequent pop culture reference. It's even been a question on the long-running game show *Jeopardy*.

I would argue that horror, as a genre, is also for lovers, and that we—the creatives who work in the field and the fans who enjoy our endeavors—should adopt the slogan posthaste.

Horror, after all, is only at its most effective if the reader or viewer feels empathy with the characters. We don't care if Jason Voorhees is carving up surplus teenagers unless we empathize with those teenagers. We don't care if Pennywise is menacing a group of children unless we're invested in those children. The best way to build empathy for your characters is through love. Horror fans come from every imaginable background, and they have a diverse litany of differences, but they also have commonalities that untie them, and the biggest commonality of all is love. Everyone, no matter who they are, loves something or somebody. Put that love in danger, and your audience will be immediately invested.

Horror—be it in fiction, film, comics, or gaming—is most effective when love is involved.

Which brings me to the point of this Foreword—the reason for this anthology, and the love that went into it. As you may have guessed from the title, this is a book about stories set in Virginia, written by authors who are either residents of the state or have deep ties to it. They are lovers, one and all. I say that because they are donating their time and their talents to this book in order to benefit another act of love—the Scares That Care charity.

As I write this, Scares That Care—a 501c3 charity—Is seventeen years old. I've been officially involved with it for about twelve years and have served on the Board of Directors for about a decade. Founded by former police detective and indie horror filmmaker Joe Ripple, and staffed by fellow board members, state representatives, and volunteers—all of whom are either horror fans or horror professionals—our mission is simple. Each year, we select three beneficiaries: a child suffering from an illness such as cancer, a woman battling breast cancer, and a burn victim. Then, we raise a minimum of $10,000 for each of those families. We also financially assist others throughout the year, often within the horror family—be it an author with a GoFundMe for medical expenses, or the funeral costs for a deceased horror fan. To date, we've raised over $600,000 for our beneficiaries. We do this in various ways—our popular AuthorCon expo, our former Scares That Care Weekend media convention, silent auctions of horror memorabilia at other conventions and events, crab feasts, holiday dances, online donations, telethons, 5K runs, film festivals, and more.

Our secondary goal is to show the world that horror fans, and the people who work in the industry, are normal, productive citizens. That we help our community and the other communities beyond ours. That we—just like everybody else—love.

Our slogan is "We fight the real monsters."

It has been my distinct honor to serve in this capacity. Sometimes it is difficult. It is emotionally harrowing to hear from the parents of a terminally ill child, and to then race against the ticking clock in order to raise the money they need to make that child's final months better. It is gut-wrenching to meet with those battling breast cancer and hear the fear and uncertainty in their voices. And personally speaking, as a burn victim myself, it is utterly brutal to talk to other burn victims, and relive the experience together, as a form of shared post-traumatic stress.

But it is also uplifting and satisfying to stand beside these people and face down those very real monsters with them. And when we ultimately help them defeat those monsters? Well... there's not a better feeling in the world.

Forget about silver bullets, crucifixes, holy water, head shots, garlic, wooden stakes, circles of protection, fire, daylight, or banishing spells read aloud from some moldering old leatherbound book. The best weapon against life's real monsters is love.

Horror is for lovers.

Okay, I'll get out of the way now, so you can get to the stories. You're in for a good time. There's one hell of a line-up ahead—legendary veterans like Stephen Mark Rainey, current stars like Clay McLeod Chapman, promising up-and-comers like Querus Abuttu, Bryan Nowak, Nicole Willson, and Paul Michael Anderson, and my fellow Scares That Care board member Sonora Taylor. And a bunch of other great writers, as well, many of whom are new to me—a problem that has now been corrected, upon my reading an advance copy of this book. Hopefully you will find some new favorite writers, as well, and will enjoy the stories as much as I did.

On behalf of the Scares That Care charity, and our beneficiaries past and present, a sincere thank you to all of the authors and editors involved in the production of this anthology, and to the publisher and cover artist, and especially to you for purchasing it.

You are loved.

— Brian Keene
Somewhere along the Susquehanna River
June 2023

All proceeds of this book will be donated to
SCARES THAT CARE®
a 501(c)3 charitable organization.
For more information, visit
www.scaresthatcare.org

IT HAD TO BE SHENANDOAH

THE BRIDE OF DREAM LAKE

Catherine Kuo

"Do you think it's going to rain? The weather forecast said there was a fifty-percent chance."

Jonathan didn't answer, too preoccupied with his phone. He smiled at something on Instagram.

"Sudden rain was what trapped those Thai kids in that cave, remember?" Bianca continued, craning her neck to squint at the gray sky through the backseat window. She cast a quick sideways glance at Jonathan's phone. A voluptuous woman in a bikini flew by as he scrolled.

"Jonathan?"

"Hm? What's up, babe?" he said without taking his eyes off the screen.

"I don't know if it's a good idea to take our wedding photos in the caverns today if it's going to rain."

"Don't be silly, it's perfectly safe," said Jonathan's mother from the passenger seat. "The Luray Caverns are a tourist trap, they wouldn't let millions of people in every year if there was any sort of danger."

"I guess you're right," said Bianca, adjusting her lace gown. She let her hand brush against her almost-flat belly. Bianca had sometimes fantasized about having a more hourglass-shaped body, but at that moment she was glad for the lack of curve.

The photographer in charge of their wedding photoshoot met them at the entrance to the caverns and ushered them down into a dimly-lit passageway. Bianca hitched up the skirt of her wedding dress and wobbled after Jonathan and his parents, her white Louboutin heels striking the manmade brick path with painful sharpness. Jonathan's mother didn't bother to hide the way she hungrily stared at the designer shoes.

Countless pale stalactites and stalagmites glowed with a sulfuric-yellow light and encircled them like rows of shark teeth. The air was still and damp, yet crisp at the same time. Mildewy without the unpleasant bite. The sound of water dripping from the stalactites onto the ground gently punctuated the looming silence, icy beads occasionally baptizing Bianca's head and shoulders as she walked under low-hanging arches. The caverns were massive, but she still felt herself getting claustrophobic. She stumbled forward and slipped her hand into the crook of Jonathan's elbow, but he slid out of her grasp effortlessly.

"Let's get some pictures in front of Dream Lake," called the photographer, waving them over to an expansive pool of water that perfectly reflected the ceiling and walls like the clearest mirror she'd ever seen.

The path did not extend to the edge of the lake, but the photographer insisted they clamber over the guardrail and make their way across the rocky, uneven floor of the cave to get a better shot. By some miracle, Bianca reached the water's edge without twisting an ankle and she leaned forward, peering down into the still waters. An eighteen-year-old black girl in a white dress looked up at her with large, pleading eyes. For one second, she didn't recognize the girl in the pool and jumped back from the edge.

"Bianca, what are you doing?" Jonathan's mother snapped. "If you fall in, you'll ruin your dress. Thank goodness I'm not paying for it, you're so careless with your things."

"I'm sorry," she said.

The photographer ordered them into several poses and Bianca politely obeyed, resting her lips against Jonathan's, putting a hand lightly on his chest, stretching her mouth into a wide smile. Once, she looked up into Jonathan's gorgeous brown eyes and almost remembered why she had been attracted to him in the first place. The moment passed as quickly as it had come and she immediately felt nauseous.

After the photographer had his fill of Dream Lake, they began navigating their way back to the main path. Bianca took a few cautious steps forward when she heard a rounded, wet plop behind her. Careful not to overturn, she looked back at the lake. A few quiet ripples flowed toward the limestone shore. She looked up at the jagged ceiling and then back down at the water.

"Bianca!" called Jonathan's mother.

She gathered up her skirts and hurried toward them, eager to put Dream Lake behind her.

Next, they descended into what was known as "Giant's Hall," the towering ceiling of which somewhat eased Bianca's claustrophobia. Two stone columns the size of redwood trees stood in the center of the path, allowing visitors a three-hundred-and-sixty-degree view of the massive natural wonder, but a smaller column off to the side caught Bianca's eye instead: a thinner, tiered formation crowned with a spike that stretched toward the ceiling, reminiscent of Rapunzel's tower or a wedding cake.

"Want to take a picture in front of the Empress Column?" said the photographer, following her gaze.

"No, that's okay."

It reminded her of her mother. Tall and narrow but with delicate layers of loose skin and fat cascading from her armpits to her thighs. The housewife to a wealthy hedge-fund manager, her main obsessions were see-saw dieting and overseeing her daughter's public image. They hardly spoke anymore, ever since her mother caught her in the bathroom with a clothes hanger a few weeks ago.

Bianca shook her head.

"They should definitely take pictures in the Cathedral," said Jonathan's mother.

Bianca tensed. "The Cathedral?"

"Great idea," said the photographer. He turned to Bianca. "It's a big open area where people held balls and stuff back in the day. Oh, and there's the Stalacpipe Organ, but we don't need to include that. Tacky, if you ask me."

Bianca nodded, but she wasn't really listening. She followed them down the wide path leading to the Cathedral and stopped at the edge of the circular dance floor. The others looked back at her, waiting for her to take the stage with the tuxedoed Jonathan. Normally, she had no problem being centerstage because it meant she could be with her beloved cello, but for some reason her feet wouldn't move.

As if to mock her lack of mobility, a staccato of light footsteps rushed past to her left. She turned just as a pair of bare, brown feet disappeared behind a thick stalagmite formation.

"Bianca?" said the photographer. "You good to go?"

"Um...Yeah," she replied, and finally joined them.

As they pretended to dance under the spiked fresco, Jonathan bent down to whisper into her ear.

"You think your daddy will give us a house as big as this?"

Bianca suppressed a shudder. Big enough for them to have separate bedrooms, she hoped. They had only done it the one time at that party, she had been a little tipsy, but she remembered it had been rough and unforgiving. She remembered him tearing off her dress and shoving it in without warning. She remembered asking if he had a condom. He hadn't answered. Afterward, she'd seen him at Tyson's Corner with another girl on his arm and thought she'd never see him again once she graduated high school. She had been wrong.

"Let's have you two toss coins into the Wishing Well," said the photographer, interrupting her thoughts. She had been so lost in her own head that she hadn't realized they'd left the Cathedral and arrived at a spot on the brick path overlooking a beautiful aquamarine pond.

"Wow," she whispered as she leaned over the railing to gaze at the foggy water.

"Here," said Jonathan's mother, handing them each a penny.

Bianca stroked the copper-plated coin with her white-gloved fingers, the dirt rubbing off on the sleek satin.

"At the same time now," said the photographer, lifting his camera. "One. Two. Three!"

Jonathan flung his coin toward the back of the pond and it submerged with a faint, distant splash, but Bianca brought the coin to her lips, closed her eyes, and kissed it before letting it drop into the water below.

"Um, let's try that one more time," said the photographer.

She didn't make another wish the second time. She only needed the one. The one that wouldn't come true, no matter how hard she tried.

Please make it disappear.

Without it, her parents would discard Jonathan like an old pair of shoes, her mother wouldn't force her to get married to save face, and she wouldn't have to be surveilled twenty-four-seven to make sure she didn't visit any clinics not approved of by the political circles her father belonged to. Without it, her father would keep his promise to send her to her dream music school, and maybe when the time was right for her, she could get married and have children with someone she loved. But now, at eighteen years old, what could she do? Even if it was possible to run away, where would she go? She was just a kid.

Bianca swallowed the tears that threatened to well up in her perfectly made-up eyes.

They continued on into the caverns in search of more photogenic rock formations, Bianca trailing in the back. As the others rounded a corner, she heard a familiar set of footsteps slap across the damp stone behind her. She whirled around too quickly this time and rolled her ankle, falling onto her ass with such force that she felt all her organs jolt upward.

"Oh, no," she moaned, not looking forward to what color the seat of her dress would be when she rose.

Movement about ten feet in front of her caught her eye and she looked up. A young brown girl with long, straight black hair peeked out from behind a stalagmite. She wore traditional Native American clothing, though from which tribe Bianca wasn't learned enough to know. The girl's charcoal eyes were filled with innocent concern.

"Hello?" said Bianca.

The girl didn't move, nor did she speak.

"Are you lost?" Bianca tried again.

"Hey, what are you doing?" barked Jonathan.

Bianca looked over her shoulder at him. "I'm sorry, I tripped."

"Well, get up then," he said, grabbing her upper arm and pulling hard. She winced.

"Wait, there's a little girl."

"What? What girl?"

"There," she said, pointing, but the girl had disappeared. "I swear, there's a girl wandering around by herself down here. She might be lost."

"We have this place to ourselves today, no one should be in here."

"Yeah, but—"

"Come on, everyone's waiting for you," Jonathan sighed.

With one last glance behind her, Bianca let him drag her back to the group. His mother and the photographer scolded her for ruining her dress, but they carried on despite the setback.

"Here, you guys might enjoy this," said the photographer, stopping near a seemingly inconsequential mass of rock and gesturing downward. "They look like fried eggs. Weird, right? The stalagmites broke off that way."

Bianca bent forward and made out two white, mishappen blooms of limestone sitting atop a rock shelf, each with a smooth, pearly center that resembled the yolk of a sunny-side-up egg.

"What's that in the middle?" said Bianca, squinting.

"The yolk part?"

"No, inside that." She leaned in closer. There was a dark, curved shape beneath the surface of the yolk with a stringy tail coiled under one end. She brought her face even closer. It had legs, tucked against its torso, and arms. And a head. A tiny, round, smooth head.

Bianca's vision swam and her stomach surged, emptying itself of the fettuccine alfredo she'd eaten earlier.

"Goddammit, girl!" shouted Jonathan, jumping backward to avoid getting vomit on his shiny black shoes.

"Good lord!" Jonathan's mother shrieked.

She felt someone slap her across the face, she wasn't sure who, but when her vision returned, she saw between the forest of black-clad legs the little Native American girl watching her farther down the path. Bianca pointed wordlessly at the girl, but no one paid any attention.

The girl motioned for Bianca to follow her before turning and ambling away. Without thinking, she slipped off her heels, staggered to her feet, and ran after the girl. The shouts of the others faded away as Bianca limped off the path and through the maze of stalagmites, her dress catching on the smaller protrusions, tearing the delicate lace. The girl ducked under a massive formation of flowstone, a spectacular cream curtain formed by years of flowing water and layers of calcite deposits. She waited for Bianca to catch up before disappearing into a low tunnel behind the flowstone.

As soon as Bianca got down on her hands and knees and crawled into the tunnel, she felt a blanket of comfortably warm air envelop her. A soft and low thumping echoed throughout the tunnel as she dragged herself forward, and she could feel her own rapid heartbeat slowing to match its steady rhythm.

When Bianca emerged on the other side, she found herself back on the shore of Dream Lake, but somewhere deeper within the cave than before. The ceiling was much higher here and the stone walkways framing the lake were more spacious. The Native American girl waved at her from a spot a few yards away, next to two ghostly-white columns framing another tunnel. The opening was oddly oval-shaped and only slightly taller and wider than Bianca. She would have to turn sideways to get inside.

Just as she took a step forward, something grabbed her wrist and yanked her backward.

"What the fuck is wrong with you?"

It was Jonathan, his starched white collar damp with sweat and his face lined with rage.

"The girl..." Bianca said, her voice smaller than ever.

"You're crazy, you know that! If your daddy wasn't rich, I wouldn't give a shit about you, but since you decided to get knocked up, I did your parents a favor so they wouldn't have to explain to all their friends why their kid's a single, teenage mom."

"Please stop," whimpered Bianca. His nails dug into her arm.

"*You* stop! Ever since we got here, you've been acting like a weirdo and I put up with it, but enough's enough. You come back right now and pull yourself together, or else!"

"You're hurting me," Bianca cried. As soon as the words left her mouth, his fist slammed into her left cheek and she fell to her knees.

"Get up!" he shouted, reaching for her again, but this time her flight response kicked in and she flailed her arms and legs, keeping him at bay until she could get back on her feet and run to the girl, who was standing in the mouth of the oval tunnel, her arm outstretched and hand upturned toward Bianca.

"Where're you going!" yelled Jonathan.

She could hear his leather shoes pounding the stone floor behind her and she poured all of her strength into one final sprint. Her hand found the girl's and they darted into the tunnel together. Jonathan crashed into the wall, his muscular frame too large to fit through the opening.

"Bianca! Bianca!"

She didn't look back.

As they journeyed farther into the tunnel, the light from the entrance disappeared and she could only trust the girl to lead her on through the darkness. But she wasn't afraid, the girl's hand was gentle around hers, a guide rather than a towline. The same rush of heated air arrived to greet her once more, caressing her frigid skin and soothing her wounds. The tunnel pulsed with the same low, steady drumbeat, bringing her a sense of calm she hadn't felt in a long time.

After a while, the tunnel floor began to slope upward, and a thin stream of warm water flowed in the opposite direction, splashing softly against her battered feet as they ascended. The tunnel leveled out again, but the stream remained, and Bianca felt the water rising as they went, going up to her ankles, then her knees, then her waist. Somewhere in the back of her mind, she knew she should be frightened, should be panicking, but she wasn't. The girl continued to hold her hand, even as the water rose above their heads and all Bianca could feel was the muffled drumbeat of the tunnel. Memories, worries, and feelings floated away on the current as she walked, until she was merely a body, and then, not even that. Just a swarm of mindless cells and strands of DNA, and then, nothing at all. Only darkness.

When the police arrived, they found her lying in the middle of Dream Lake, her face bloated with water and swollen bruises, her shredded dress billowing around her like the frilled tentacles of a jellyfish. Based on the photographer's testimony and the bruises on her wrist, her fiancée was eventually charged with her murder and sent to prison for many years after. A quiet, closed-casket funeral was held for the bride, and the news of her grisly death inspired an urban Virginian legend that would last longer than the memory of her own name. The only one who would remember her as a girl and not a ghost was the coroner who performed the autopsy. The girl's parents had bribed him to leave the fetus out of his report, but when he'd opened her up, her uterus had been completely empty. Scratching his head, he'd pocketed the five-hundred dollars and sewed her back up without a word to anyone.

A HOLLER YOU CAN'T CALL HOME

Paul Michael Anderson

Danny manages to rise with the sun, and packs his bookbag in the thick gloom that lays low like fog in his room. The sounds of the twins' asthmatic snoring in the bedroom to the right, the toilet tank that keeps running to the left, stepping to either side of the hallway's middle section to avoid creaks, he enters the living room/kitchen area that dominates the double-wide, a no man's land. Momma sleeps on the couch, light from the wall-mounted television playing over her moon-shaped face. The television is a flat-screen, but a knock-off, and the televangelist coaxing insomniacs to "give seed" sounds tinny and alien.

Momma shifts on the couch, and Danny jerks. He hadn't expected it to be like this: every nerve firing, aware of every inch of skin and ounce of weight. He thanks a god he tells everyone he still believes in that he swept the floor last night. Otherwise, he'd stumble over one of Mina or Melissa's toys, or Rodney's work boots, or Momma's stack of magazines she filches from the recycling bins over on High Knob, and there goes the entire ballgame in the bottom of the first inning.

He reaches the kitchen's lumpy laminate and steps on a dip in the floor, the creak like the roar of a landmine explosion. Momma mutters, "Rodney... ?" before it turns into a snore and Danny can breathe again. He reaches the door and winces at the suction of air pressure, but then he's outside, fingers of cool air creeping up his skin. He's okay. He tells himself this. His clothes are clean and feel it. The bookbag over his shoulders—carrying a couple of textbooks from the community college, an old Louis L'Amour western, about a grand he's managed to sock away for the past three years—rests comfortably against his back.

"I got this," he breathes, and his soft words feel like a violation of the quiet. He thinks of a line from a movie or show: He's white, eighteen, and living in America—what did he have to worry about? Actually, the line probably came from a book, but he would never admit it. Aside from Momma's dumpster-dive magazines, the only books in the house are his, and everyone reminds him of that.

Danny looks down to the carport, where the 1978 Pinto is tarped, surrounded by rusting tool chests and barrels. Ostensibly the car's his, but Rodney's always tinkering with it ("Tuning it, Danny," Rodney says, after a few beers. "Gotta have a proper chariot to ride like a king, y'know?"). Danny's driven it three times in as many years, always to make sure something about the engine worked, and only around the mountain. He's never gotten off the mountain on his own power.

He looks away, through a break in the sloping forest, and sees the green and furry slump of mountains across the valley. High Knob over there. Apple, too. Geographic markers that are as much a part of his world as his hair or his eyes. There's a stirring in his gut and he thinks with a mixture of excitement and fear that this'll be the last time he sees them.

Something reflects amongst the trees. The rising sun bouncing off a summer house's wide windows, maybe. He blinks at the twinkle, which grows into a spear, zapping right into Danny's eyes—

There comes a moment—not for everyone and not at the same time in a person's life—when the world seems to expand beyond their own provincialism; when they can, briefly, see the world from new angles, new contexts, and it is an awe-inspiring moment, akin, one thinks, to how it would be to actually see a god if one existed, as they see how others see them—

—and he staggers against the Pinto, the gas pump's nozzle going slack in his hand as he blinks away the sun-brilliance and vertigo stomps his brain.

"Dan?" a man's voice calls. "Dan Ritenour? You okay?"

Brisk footfalls against tarmac. "Dan?" the new man calls. His voice is familiar. "Hey, kid—you okay?"

Danny goggles at everything, but the world's a flaring pastel blur.

The dark shape of a man rises on his left. "Whoa, easy there, Dan."

Danny forces his eyes to focus and sees Mr. Christman, his old social studies teacher, standing near the hood of the Pinto, hands raised as if to catch Danny. "You okay? Looked like you were going to eat pavement."

Danny feels the solid ground beneath his feet, unlike the heaving front walk. He can't feel his bookbag on his shoulders and turns to see it through the passenger window, resting comfy in the bucket seat.

"The *hell*..." he mutters, widening his view, taking in the busy pumps of the Sheetz on Shenandoah Avenue, the four-lane a-bustle with traffic. *I was just at my house,* he thinks and then winces as pain flares in his temple.

"Dan..." Mr. Christman says.

He shakes his head. "Hey, yeah, sorry, Mr. Christman. Got dizzy for a second."

"You looked it," Christman says.

"I got this. Thanks, Mr. C."

Christman hooks a thumb at the Pinto. "Your car?"

Danny follows his gaze. It's the kind of car that looks good from a distance, but the imperfections creep in the closer you get. The red paint is aged, dried-blood, and the sun heliographs over the bumpers where rust hasn't eaten through. The tires are balding. The ceiling upholstery is detaching, creating an upside-down vista of hills and valleys.

"Yeah," Danny says, his throat dry.

But Christman grins. "I didn't even get my license until I was eighteen," he says, and something in Danny's chest lightens. Yeah, this new feeling says—he has his own car. Is it perfect? Christ no, but it's *his*.

The hell—, he thinks, and the vertigo stirs ominously.

"Where you off to on this fine summer day with that sweet summer ride?" Christman asks.

Where *is* he off to? He thought he knew, back at the house, but now that Christman's asked...

He swallows. "I'm just...off, Mr. C. I'm out."

"Off into the wild blue yonder? Strike out west, like Horatio Alger,

Davy Crockett, the Donner Party?"

Danny grins and the vertigo abates somewhat. "Well, not like that last one."

"Had a kid once, graduated before I had you. He hitchhiked west. He wound up working at a touristy surf shop in California, I think? I forget what his mom said." He studies Danny. "What does *your* mom think?"

He's tempted to lie, but Christman's eyes, that same hard gaze Danny remembered from class, say Mr. Christman knows half the answer already. "I left before she woke up."

Christman crosses his arms, shirt sleeves pulling up to reveal the scars, fading zig-zags that reminded Danny of chalk lines on bumpy hot top, kids would ask about in class. "Uh-huh." Danny knows Christman's going to tell him it's fucked, sneaking off like this, how could he do that to his mother— and the vertigo sloshes some more. Danny puts a hand on the Pinto's roof.

But Christman says, "That makes sense, doesn't it?"

Danny blinks. "What?"

Christman sighs. "You graduated last year, Dan, so we can put away the teacher-student dynamic. I'm glad, out of all of your siblings, that it's you getting out."

Again that strange lightness in Danny's chest. "What do you mean?"

"Shit, Dan, I've taught all your brothers. What have they done? They live up on Blue Mountain, dug in like ticks. A part of that—" He shrugs. "—that's just *people*, and I see that all the time, but that's not *everything*, y'know? I mean, your brother Jack. He wanted to join the military, right? I can't remember what branch—"

"Navy."

Christman snaps his fingers. "Right. But he never did."

Danny can picture Jack working with their oldest brother, Van, in Van's garage, tinkering with trucks and four-wheelers other mountain folks bring in, maybe with a forty-ouncer on a tool chest nearby. He remembers Momma and Jack's fights that would make the entire double-wide pulse. Jack waving the brochures and release forms like weapons, Momma wailing her children are abandoning her while Danny and the twins hid in the bedrooms, wincing if something hit a wall, and Danny wondering if Jack was going to leave, was going to *escape*, that was the word, *escape*, because that's what you had

24

to do with Momma's love—

"Your mom didn't want Jack to go, right?" Christman says, bringing Danny back. "I remember that, him meeting with recruiters, but your mom used to email us, tell us not to give him hall passes because she didn't want him going to their office."

"I remember," Danny says.

"You have to do what's right by *you*," Christman says. His old teacher's eyes are still hard but now they remind him of how they looked when he was helping a student. "Van was a mess all through school, Nate couldn't figure out what he wanted to be besides angry, but you and Jack? It was sad, the last time I drove through Linden and saw Jack sitting in front of Van's garage, y'know? That kid had a dream. You do, too, by the look of it, even if it isn't all that solid yet." Christman grins and shakes his head. "Shit, and that's your last teacher lecture by me, kid."

"You left home, too, right? When you were my age?"

Christman tilts his head. "Well, college and student debt, but, yeah— that was the only way out when you're a city kid."

"And you ended up *here*."

Christman laughs. "It worked out all right." He puts out his hand. "Good luck, Dan."

Danny shakes with him. That lightness has returned to his chest, sending tendrils of energy through his limbs. His teacher is *glad* he's getting out. He's *excited*. "Take it easy, Mr. C."

Christman snorts as he walks away. "You've had my class. You know that's not how I do things."

Danny looks out at Shenandoah Avenue, the twin bridges to the right. From here, he can see the junction signs for I-81 and Route 522 and 340. The lightness still fills his chest, an excitement, although it's febrile and vibrant.

Christman drives by in his car, tapping the horn.

"I got this," he says, and lets that lightness carry him back to the driver's side, sliding in to his seat and slamming the door—

—and recoiling when Shelley touches his shoulder.

"Shit!" he yells, and Shelley's hands spring off like they've touched a

stove.

"Danny?" she asks, her voice cracking on the last syllable. "The *hell*?"

The vertigo expands like a water balloon in his skull and he lowers his head to the steering wheel. His gut sloshes, and he grinds his teeth together. Shelley's hands flutter like startled birds over him and he thinks, *Home, the gas station with Mr. Christman, now Shelley...?*

The vertigo throbs, and he can only groan.

"Danny, *Danny*," Shelley says. "What—"

Didn't even think about her a second ago, he thinks, and a dagger of guilt, all serrated edges, slides into his gut.

"Danny, you're scaring the shit outta me."

He raises his head. Through the windshield, he can see Rural King, four-wheelers and mulch and miniature windmills scattered around the massive doors like the redneck Walmart had vomited during the night. The sun is rising now, and they are sitting in the middle of an empty ocean of parking lot.

"What the hell's wrong with you, Danny?" Shelley asks. Her curly dark hair frames her face like wings, her skin pale and eyes wide.

He swallows spit as thick as glue. "I'm sorry, hon. Dizzy spell. Bad one."

"That's not a good sign, getting dizzy for no good reason."

He can feel her anxiety working through him, making his muscles twitch. "Yeah, I know. What were we talking about?"

She cocks her head. "Does your head hurt? Maybe it's a tumor, y'know, like what happened to Craig Wolffart? He lost all control of his actions, and his sister told me—"

Her speech is speeding up, and he puts a hand on her forearm. His heart is racing. "Easy. I'm fine. Haven't been sleeping well."

She snorts, but her eyes are hard. "No surprise, dealing with your family all the time. That's what we were talking about, Danny. You needing to get away from your family." She lets air out through her teeth. "Your family's got you all wound tight, hon. You *know* that." She jerks her thumb between them, at his bookbag in the backseat. "My god, the tantrums your mom pulled at you just taking a few *classes* at LFCC, not even going to a regular *college* like *normal people*—"

"I told you about that?" he asks, honestly curious, and the vertigo pulses once as he feels a gritty, heavy settling in his chest.

Shelley looks at him levelly. "You didn't need to, Danny. It's how you act. Always late for study sessions at the library or the Daily Grind. Always in a sour mood when you arrive at class. Never inviting me over to study because your mom or your brothers or your step-dad would be around—"

That pussy must be grand if she's convinced you that college is a good idea, Rodney snorts in his head and Danny's face warms.

"—all because none of those rednecks did anything with *their* lives," she says. "Fuck, Danny, it's *normal* to go to college! How much more of this shit can you take?"

He thinks of Christman, of not having an answer when asked where he was going, and pain flares in his head. "But how do I do that? Where do I go?"

She hugs his arm. "Where do *we* go, you mean."

He manages a smile. "Of course. Where do *we* go? Do you wanna go to Loudoun County, or the coast? One of the cities—"

"Oh, god no. I'm too country for that, even a little *townie* like me." She leans her head on his arm. "I dunno, Danny, but we're old enough to start branching out a little bit. Maybe Strasburg? Or Middletown, so we can be closer to campus. Get a cheap place, save up money, get our associate's degrees..."

Danny's nodding along. The lightness in his chest has returned. The idea of a little apartment hovers tantalizingly in front of his eyes, highlighted by the grimness of being closer to D.C., where all he can picture is concrete and compacted traffic and no trees.

"You'll be far enough away so that you'll know whatever decisions you make will be your own and not just you parroting whatever your asshole brothers spout."

He frowns. Isn't he just in a way parroting what Shelley's spouting, and before that Mr. Christman? The vertigo digs at that and he looks at the parking lot in front of Rural King. He wants to never look at it again; he's *exhausted* from looking at the same things over and over. He knows why he's in *this* parking lot and not the Big Lots parking lot on the edge of town, which is where all the rednecks from up in the hollers come to hang out, like they're dipping their feet in the water without worrying about diving in, a middle ground for the townies and the mountain kids.

He thinks of Christman, who had gone to tons of places before *choosing* Front Royal. Danny wanted *that* kind of option.

"You okay?" Shelley asks.

"Yeah. Just thinking."

She's rubbing his arm while leaning against it. "About what?"

He sighs. "About how Van's asked me to come work for him, but other than doing a day here or there I can't do it." He clears his throat. "I don't wanna end up like Jack. He wanted to get out, y'know, but he... he couldn't take leaving Momma."

"That's why you take baby steps, babe."

"Shit, Shelley, the difference between me and Jack is I *can* take leaving. I know I *have* to." He unclips his seatbelt. "Legs are asleep. Gimme a sec."

Pins and needles in his thighs and calves turn his walk bow-legged as he steps out. How long had they been sitting there? In his head, he just sat down.

The vertigo pulses, once.

He looks back and Shelley's watching him through the open door and he thinks, pushing the vertigo back, that this is pretty much perfect. A start of a new adventure. He's ready for it, and so is she, and he can *feel* it, can't he? It's in his chest, lightening him up.

Danny turns away, towards the rising sun, and—

—the morning sun arrows into his eyes. He cries out and drops hard to the uneven front walk.

"Shit," he mutters. He throws a hand behind him and blinks out at the world, but it's hard—vertigo swims like an Olympian through the soft meat of his brain. In his mind's eye, he sees glimpses of Mr. Christman standing next to the Pinto and Shelly sitting *in* the Pinto, but it makes his temples pulse with pressure.

"What in the hell just happened?" he asks.

He hears the *shhh-thump* of the house's door, the creak of the screen door. "Oh, fuck," he says, and he can feel a new emotion zipping up the base of his skull like a firework to explode in his aching mind: anger, mixed with disgust and impatience.

"Danny?" Momma calls. The screen door creaks louder, at a pitch designed to burrow into his ears like a knife. "What are you *doing* sitting there? Do you know what *time* it is?"

Danny clenches his teeth and focuses on his heartbeat, the steady lub-dub like a two-fist combo. "Yeah, Momma. I do."

"Where are you *going*, Danny?"

He has to get away from Momma. He *has* to. He can feel his thoughts sinking into an acidic stew that, when finished, will dissolve whatever good feelings he has left.

He stands, digging in his pockets. "Going out, Momma."

"Where? How? You don't have a *car*."

He whirls on her and she cringes. *Good*, an alien-but-undeniably-*his* voice says.

He jabs a finger at the Pinto. "*Yes*, I *do*, Momma. Or are we all done pretending that Rodney bought that fucking car for me?"

Her lower lip quivers and the urge to shriek boils up his throat, begging him to loosen his jaw so he can let it out.

"How can you *say* that?" She's holding onto the screen door like it's the only thing keeping her upright. "Of *course* that's yours! It's just Rod, he's still fixing it—"

Danny digs around, feeling his pocket knife, a pen. Every scrap of linen he feels that doesn't cough up his keyring makes him burn hotter. "Rodney's been 'fixing' it for three fucking years—"

"Why are you using that *language*, Danny—"

He whips his head up. "Fuck, fuck, *fuck!*" He's forgotten his keyring. All his preparations and he didn't fucking remember to grab the *one thing* he needed most.

Danny stalks up the walk and Momma recoils back into the house. The screen door manages to crack hard against its aluminum frame before he rips it back open with a hollow metallic scream. Inside, Momma stands next to Rodney's recliner. On the television, the televangelist has given way to the NBC news affiliate. Light reflects off of Momma's wet eyes. Her hands knead each other over her stomach.

"Why are you so *angry*, Danny?" she asks. "What did I *do*?"

And a part of Danny almost wonders that too, but the anger itself crushes the thoughts. He's angry, furious, and has been for some time. He finds a part of him *hates* her: hates the way she stands there in a thrift store tank top that's been washed out of shape and hangs like a badly-built tent; hates that all of his siblings are only half; hates this double-wide with its moldy smell and rotting foundations; hates that he knows tomorrow's garbage day and she's going to take her dented Toyota with the illegal inspection sticker over to High Knob to dumpster dive through rich folks' garbage, all while sneering at the poor townie folks if they use EBT cards in Martins or Walmart; hates that he knows when Rodney will be home with Van, Nate, and Jack along from their own shitty trailers soon after, a big family meal those four will drink through, nitpicking Danny for actually eating or reading a book to avoid the insipid mountain gossip; hates knowing that they don't know what *insipid* means and that the fact he does is a source of derision for them; hates knowing all of this.

But... a part of Danny *doesn't* hate that. He's exhausted by it, he needs to get away from it, but he doesn't *hate* it because they're all aspects of his family. This stew of contradictory emotions swirls through Danny's chest and head.

"I forgot my keys, Momma," he says. He gets his feet moving, forcing himself not to stomp, feeling robotic as he heads toward the back hallway.

"I don't know why you *hate me so much!*" she cries.

Because you think I do, he thinks, but the vertigo yanks that back into the darkness before he can consider it fully.

"I just love my children!" she yells. "Is that a *crime*? Because I wanna keep you close and *safe*?"

He whirls. "You refuse to let any of us *go!*" he barks and then runs to his bedroom; oh god, the anger and disgust is overriding everything and he's turning into Nate and he can't be Nate, he can't be Nate or Jack or Van. He needs to be *Danny* and Danny *gets away*...

He bumps into his doorframe, and there they are—his keys on his dresser. He grabs them, an exalted *yes!* surging through him, and he turns to see Mina and Melissa in their doorway. He takes in their disheveled blond hair, in need of a wash; their pale faces smudged with dirt they didn't wipe off properly the night before; their faded nightshirts. They're almost stereotypical ragamuffins, just what people expect to see when they imagine poor holler kids. The anger takes a backseat, replaced by a gestalt of love and affection, but the emotion threaded through is the need to get *away*— away from the stereotypes and the derision and the boxed-in nothingness that comes when you know you have options but they're laughably impossible to use.

"See you, girls," he chokes out, and he turns away. He *has* to turn away, oh, he's drowning here and if nothing else epitomizes that feeling—not the house, not Momma, not Jack drinking at Van's fly-by-night garage—it's looking at his sisters and *knowing* they'll be on the mountain ten, twenty years from now. If they live that long.

He sees Momma at the end of the hallway, and like a cataclysmic earthquake the hate and anger punch through the crust of his despair.

"I just love you, Danny!" Momma cries. Danny laughs, and it's like grinding broken glass. "Haven't I always taken *care* of you? Kept you *safe*?"

Every question like a nail she expects him to hammer through her wrists on the cross she's built. "How is this *safe*?" he says. " How is this *love*? Nate's a nutcase, Van's dealing dope out of his garage, and Jack—how the *fuck* is *Jack* safe? He wanted to join the Navy, and you *badgered* him numb."

She blinks at that, but he sees something shift behind her eyes, a truth she's hidden from everyone, maybe even herself.

"That's not *love*. That's not *safety*. You fall in with whatever drunk fuckhead comes along, collecting kids the way those douchebags on High Knob collect baby dolls." He straightens, looking down at her. "I am not some toy you keep on a fucking shelf, Momma. Van and Jack and Rodney and all of them, they always ask me if I think I'm better than them. I *don't*. they'd never believe that, because *you* think anyone who tries something different is putting on airs."

He brushes past her. He hears her first sob as he reaches for the screen door and he sneers. "Pathetic."

There's no great lifting of weight when he steps outside. He strides grimly down the walk, eyes locked on the Pinto. He'll feel better once he's gone. Once he's off the mountain, he'll feel better.

The screen door screams behind him and Momma wails, *"Danneeee—"*

Something explodes behind his eyes and he hears the hatred and anger say, clearly, *That's it.*

He turns—

—and stumbles as his center of balance shifts. Then he's on his hands and knees on the walk, vomiting onto the dead grass. Pressure pulses behind his eyes as he heaves and hacks and coughs. He falls back and whoops in great gusts of morning air, sniffing back snot. "Oh shit. Oh fuck."

No more vertigo. No more weight in his chest or roiling in his gut. Just the morning, still cool, still silent. He looks out over the valley, but there's no winking light of reflected sun now.

He plants his elbows on his knees, holds up his head by the temples. He tries to think of nothing because he knows nothing makes sense, but he remembers the excitement Mr. Christman had bestowed, the confidence Shelley had infused, even the hatred Momma was convinced he felt. He wonders where Shelly and Mr. Christman are at the moment.

He feels nothing but exhausted, a deep weariness grafted to his bones, holding him down. Why shouldn't he? He's lived three days in the span of five or ten minutes.

He stands, looking to the Pinto, then the gravel lane. A right takes you up to the rest of the family: Van, Nate, Jack, Uncle Larry. A left on the gravel lane takes you down.

Danny frowns as he starts down the walk. Why phrase it like that?

Adrenaline seeps into his system as he goes to the carport. The tarp's not hooked, so it's a matter of brushing it off. Danny moves jerkily, swiping at the tarp, kicking it aside. He has to go *now*. He's started to feel the natural suction of this place, the pull that kept all his brothers nearby, the pull that rubs away any independent inclination one might have. The... flashes, hallucinations, whatever the fuck... had stopped his forward motion and now the need to *catch up* fills him.

He tosses his bookbag onto the bucket seat. It looks like it did when he saw it in Sheetz. He moves around to the driver's side, opening the door and reaching into his pockets—

—and doesn't find his key ring.

It brings no surprise but it does bring him to a dead stop. "Shit."

He heads inside, blinking at the dimness. On the television, the televangelist has given way to the NBC affiliate. Momma snores. He swallows, avoiding all the same creaks again. At his doorway, he sees the keys, just as he had before, but grabbing them doesn't bring the exalted *yes!* back.

When he turns, Melissa and Mina are standing at their door, watching him.

"Where are you going?" Melissa asks.

Danny swallows and something in his chest breaks until he feels only sharp edges. He hunkers, thinking he's going to be the only one who gets away; thinking one or both of them are going to be pregnant before they finish high school, just like Momma was with Van; thinking they looked the stereotype because they *were* the stereotype. Shouldn't he stay, or at least stay close, so he *can* protect them?

"I—" His voice cracks. "I'm going out for a while, okay?"

"When are you coming home?" Mina asks.

He pulls them in for a hug, a head on each shoulder. "Love you girls," he says. "I love you."

He lets them go and they retreat to the doorway.

He stands. "Let Momma sleep, okay?"

He has to turn away, has to do it *now*, and he does, not looking back. His steps down the walk reinforce the sounds of cracking in his chest.

He slides into the Pinto's driver's seat and starts the car. Its engine roars. "Okay. I'm okay."

He rolls the Pinto forward, then stops, eyeballing how to navigate around Momma's Toyota in the driveway. He makes the mistake of looking up at the house. The girls stand at the kitchen window. He thinks—

And it feels like a Great Truth, with intended initial capitals, that washes over him: It's not just what people do to hold you in place, but what you do yourself, what you hold onto to justify staying in a situation. All the what-ifs in the multiverse, all the ways other people see you, can't hold a candle to how you see yourself, what you use to keep you stagnant. It's not home, but it's where you live, just the same. It'd be easier, better, to believe that it's other people, to paraphrase Sartre, but he realizes it's just him, his own actions—or inaction. And it's possible to go in a loop about this, to ask what causes him to feel this way, to act this way, but what would be the point? He's here, and he has to make a decision. And, of course, live with it.

The girls look down at him, ready-made victims of a destiny they will never realize they have control over.

Danny pulls his eyes away and sees the break in the trees again. His eyes strain to see the flash of light again, to jump back into those other perspectives where he can feel the excitement or the confidence once more, even the hatred, *anything* to stand up against his own fading motivation. I'm ready, he wants to yell. The Pinto is poised perfectly on the level driveway, no need for his foot to rest on the brake—all he needs to do is put it on the gas and *go*. Everything waits for him to decide, because he *has* to. He can't rely on anyone to do it for him, but it's hard, so goddamned *hard*, even as a part of him mentally screams, I have my hand on the steering wheel, my hand on the gear. I'm *ready! I'm ready!* But the girls are watching, waiting without knowing for him to make his move.

He's still looking, still *ready*, when Momma opens the front door.

He sees her step outside, and heat rushes to his face. "Please," he begs to someone, to himself, and moves his foot to the pedal.

THE GIRL WHO SLEEPS IN THE ROOM NEXT TO ME

Charles E. Wood

October 17, 1934. Mother gave me this book to write in. She said it would help pass the time. I've been here for a week, but it seems longer. Everyone says I'm getting better, but it's not true. Last week, when mother found me coughing with blood on my hands and mouth, her eyes got really big. Soon, my room was full of people. "Don't worry," Mother said later while they packed my things. "DeJarnette in Staunton is the best place in the entire world for children." They took me away from my room and my sister. I don't like it here. The rooms are dark and smell strange. "That's the special cleaner nurses use," Mother said. They call it a children's hospital and I hear voices, but I haven't seen any other children.

October 19, 1934. I'm still alone in my room, but they've moved the other bed to sit beside me across the room. Mother says I might get a roommate soon. Nurses give me an elixir to help me sleep. I told mother I felt better, but she said I needed to stay a while longer.

October 20, 1934. Last night was chilly and my new roommate arrived. Her long hair covered her face. She climbed into her bed and went to sleep. She wore stained night clothes, and she smelled like the mold in our bathroom back home in Fairfax. This morning she was gone. Mother frowned when I told her about my roommate, and she whispered to the nurse.

October 21, 1934. Something's wrong. My roommate climbs onto her bed at night and sits with her legs dangling over the side. I think she's looking at me, but there are only pitch-black holes where her eyes should be, so it's hard to be sure. Something's wrong with her mouth. It's all crooked and dark and I can't see any teeth, but it's hard to get a good look peeking from under my covers. She sits there like a statue, and then after a long while, she turns and lies down. I guess she tires of staring. Does it hurt to stare with no eyes? I wonder if she gets cold lying there without blankets. I'm stuck to the bed and too scared to move, so I lie there under the covers and stare back at her. I can't fight the nurse's elixir, and I fall asleep. When I wake, she's gone. Why can she move so freely? I mentioned my new roommate again today, and the nurse told me I was dreaming. "It's a side effect of the elixir," she said. "You don't have a roommate."

October 22, 1934. It was a quiet night, except for the usual noises outside my room. My roommate didn't come.

October 23, 1934. Last night, the girl didn't lie on her side. She just sat there with her legs hanging over the edge and stared at me with her empty black holes. Somehow, I found my voice and screamed, but nurses here ignore screams at night. I tried to stay awake under my covers to watch her, but I fell asleep, and she was gone in the morning. I wonder if she wants something. Her mouth opens sometimes, but nothing comes out. It's like a giant black yawn, too big for her face, but it's somehow familiar.

October 24, 1934. I reminded Mother that my coughing has stopped, and I want to go home, but she doesn't listen. I asked if I could walk around, but the nurse said I need to stay in bed "for your own safety." I asked if my sister could visit, and Mother ran from the room crying. The nurse gave me more elixir.

October 27, 1934. The last few days the nurse gave me extra elixir, and I slept a lot. My roommate's here every night now. Last night she got off the bed and stood there watching me silently, her moldy left hand stretched out as if beckoning me. I pulled the covers over my head and shivered until I fell asleep. Mother and Father are worried because I keep asking for more blankets. Parents aren't allowed to stay overnight. I need extra blankets when she comes, but I can't tell Mother and Father.

October 29, 1934. Each night she's moved a little closer to me, stretching out her smelly gray hand. I'm scared of what she might do when I'm sleeping, but I can't fight the elixir. No matter how many blankets I have, I still shiver. Why is her face familiar, and what does she want?

October 30, 1934. Tonight, I made a mistake. She was standing only a few feet from me, almost close enough to touch me. I panicked and threw a blanket at her, but the straps made it hard. The blanket went right through her and landed on the floor. Her face twisted angrily, and she screamed at me, but there was no sound. Then she vanished.

October 31, 1934. Something's different tonight. It's almost midnight, and she isn't here. Maybe I scared her away, and she's gone for good. Maybe it's because it's All Hallows Eve and she's with all the other black-eyed children. Whatever the reason, she's gone. I'm using my favorite crayon to write this now instead of waiting for tomorrow. My eyes are growing cold. I remember where I've seen that face. I remember the night I carved her face with a knife from the kitchen. I only wanted a little piece of her tongue, but she wouldn't share it and it was harder to cut than I expected, so I took her eyes instead because she needed to learn to share.

A chill slowly crawls like fingers up my back. I feel the cold move across my shoulders and curl around my neck. Cold hands fumble for my face from behind. Sister wants her eyes back.

CAVE KISSES

William R.D. Wood

The wasp was really digging in.

"Hold still. Almost got it." Madison was lying. She didn't almost have it. The little fucker had wormed itself into Aubrey's hair good. The sun had yet to crest the mountain peak above the old train tunnel entrance, so the overgrown rail bed was more shadow than not. That wasn't helping and Aubrey's thick, luscious mop was probably the only thing protecting him from a righteous sting.

She sorted through the strands of hair, pinching the tip of the dirty blonde lock the wasp was entangled inside. She pulled it straight out from his head, giving the hair a good shake. Aubrey squealed, but whatever programming evolution had built into the wasp did not respond. Instead of flying to safety and freedom, the bug moved deeper, toward Aubrey's scalp. Its tiny abdomen convulsed as a droplet appeared at the tip of its stinger.

They were out of time.

She snatched the knife from her belt, snapped it open and swiped it through those glorious tresses and slung the clump of hair to the ground, wasp and all, bringing her foot down again and again on top of it.

The wasp spiraled in the air around her foot before disappearing into the late autumn camouflage of yellows, reds and lingering greens. How the hell was the thing still active this time of year? Shouldn't it be hibernating or whatever bugs did when it got cold?

"Close one." Her breath formed a cloud before dissipating in the chill morning air. She turned to Aubrey, feeling quite the mighty huntress and savior of fair prince in distress.

"You cut my hair." His voice trembled. For Pete's sake, was he about to cry? He cupped the side of his head with both hands where she'd cut as if he were concealing his sudden nakedness before an angry god. "You cut my freaking hair, Madison."

She moved in close and coaxed his hands down, placing them on her shoulders instead. Now that she got a good look, it was a bigger chunk than she meant to take, and way closer to the scalp than she thought. She repressed the smile at how freaking sharp she kept her knife.

"Do you have a mirror?" Aubrey asked.

He was a funny one. What did she see in him, exactly? "It's not that bad."

It kinda was.

"Why did I let you talk me into this, anyway?" Rummaging through his backpack, he produced a Virginia Tech ball cap and pulled it down as low as it would go. He looked both ridiculous and adorable.

That was why, wasn't it? He was gorgeous. He was smart too, even funny, at least when in the safety of his natural environments, namely coffee shops and libraries. He'd moved from Richmond to Dooms with his mom last year and still referred to living in small town Virginia as "roughing it." Like he was camping or something. And that made him exotic.

Really, though, it was the hair. "That's on you, big guy. You're the one who wanted to check out the tunnel."

"Before I knew how hard it was to get to—and before a wild animal tried to kill me."

To coddle or not to coddle? To be honest, he needed to be a wee bit stronger for her tastes, a little less whiny. Oh, but the hair. She sighed. Ducking away from his hands, she took in the gaping tunnel mouth.

He'd been right about that much.

"Now that's fucking cool," she said.

Long ago, a gap had been blasted into the mountainside and the rock walls to either side of the muddy rail bed rose sharply, framing the entrance, a square of brick and masonry barely wider than the mouth. The face stretched upward thirty feet or more. At the bottom, fifteen or twenty feet wide and maybe a hair taller, the entrance was creep factor ten. She loved that. Stones lined the edge like ancient arches she remembered from history class — she couldn't remember what they were called, except for the keystone at the top from which hung a twist of old vines, making it look like a single dripping fang. A grid of welded steel struts overlaid by chain-link fence attempted to secure the opening, but she could see at least three places to squeeze through.

Aubrey pulled out a laminated cross-sectional drawing of the mountainside—because, you know, Aubrey. *The Blue Ridge Tunnel. 1850 – 1858. Also known as The Crozet Tunnel*, read the header.

Madison slipped her arm into his and leaned in, letting the side of her breast push against his arm as she stole a quick glance up. He didn't look at her, but he un-pursed his lips at least.

"How far in does it go?" She knew the answer, but he needed maybe just this one more little feel-good to break down his funk shield.

"All the way, silly," he said. "The tunnel's over three-quarters of a mile from one end to the other, but there's a concrete wall a little less than halfway where they closed it off back in the fifties."

"That's so cool." She could tell by his tone she had him. "Let's do this shit."

The chain link fencing at the bottom right pulled away just enough for her to slink through, but Aubrey had to squirm and twist for a full minute to join her. Shadows from the metal grid fell across his grimace that gave way to a look of childish awe as they both peered into the blackness ahead.

Madison took the little Maglite miner's headband he offered her and twisted the lens until it lit up the first twenty feet into the mountain's gullet. A pungent earthiness oozed up, carried on the merest suggestion of a breeze. Where was that coming from if there was a wall? The tingles washed through her head-to-toe and she started walking.

"Madison, hold up." He was inspecting the brickwork that started at the floor on both sides and met overhead. Dozens of gaps marked missing bricks that had dropped out over the years. Gray moss clung in some of the cracks, but mostly they were bare. It looked like someone had gone cobblestone-happy, but instead of the floor they'd covered everything else. The pattern continued back as far as her light reached, which was far less than she expected, like the tunnel was absorbing it, feeding on it. "This is really cool. People scratched messages into the bricks. You can almost read some of them."

Fascinating. She just saw all the spray-painted graffiti. The larger work was artsy, letters interconnected and woven together, basically illegible. The smaller stuff, the legible bits, were primarily claims of sexual exploits punctuated with a disproportionate number of poorly rendered penises. If she'd wanted to see that shit, she could have visited the men's room at the gas station at the bottom of Afton Mountain. "Let's go. I want to see the wall."

"Right, right."

The floor was uneven, riddled with puddles, ruts and fallen chunks of brick. Every footfall bounced softly off the walls and ceiling. Madison had to pan her light at the floor every few steps to avoid turning an ankle, either in mud, loose gravel or occasional smears of dead moss.

"There's actually two walls," said Aubrey. "The second about a quarter mile beyond the first. Can you believe some dude planned on piping natural gas into the cavity between the walls, like storing it there."

"Bullshit."

"Seriously."

"To what? Make his own personal volcano?"

Aubrey laughed. He didn't do that often. Madison felt a little tug in her chest. He was pretty cool.

"I'm guessing that didn't work out."

"All I could find at the library was—shit, shit, shit!" Aubrey's light partially blinded her, but she could tell he was swatting madly as his face. He stumbled, one foot coming down in a puddle and sliding out from under him. He slammed into her and knocked them both to the floor. "It's on me, it's on me!"

Righting herself, Madison pulled his hands from the side of his face, the same side she'd butchered outside. For god's sake. She pulled his ball cap off and used it to wipe off the streak of water still running down his cheek. "Cave kiss."

He squinted as her own head lamp illuminated his face. "Cave what?"

"Cave kiss." She pointed her light at the ceiling. The gaps between the bricks were getting wider, the moss more prevalent, reflecting tiny pinpoints of light. That shit had really gnawed away at what had likely been years of hard overhead toil. Aubrey looked up and got a perfectly timed repeat drip from the tunnel ceiling. "It's what they call it when a cave drips on you."

He wiped his face with the back of his hand and took his cap. "I thought the wasp…"

"Followed us into the cold, dark cave?" She panned her light back up at the ceiling. This time there were no glittery reflections though, and the bricks were far more bare than she'd thought.

He put on the cap and pushed to his feet. "It's a tunnel, not a cave."

Beyond Aubrey, daylight was a tiny half ellipse in the distance. How far had they walked already? She twisted the lens of the Maglite until the light went out. Aubrey, taking her cue, did the same. Another cave kiss plipped into a puddle in the distance. A second one farther away, as if a single droplet were skipping from puddle to puddle, racing to escape the darkness. Creepy was her go-to word, but it was inadequate. Had the workers who dug out this tunnel ever felt this way? Hell, was this how ancient people felt when they decided what they found inside caves was less scary than what was outside? She shuddered.

Taking Aubrey by the collar, she pulled him down into a kiss. He seemed lost for a second, but quickly found his place. She pushed against his chest a minute later, separating them. "Cave kiss."

"…fine," he mumbled. "Fine. Let's get to that wall so we can get back to the car. I feel a coffee coming on."

"Mister adventure."

The brickwork gave way to craggy chiseled rock, great gouges in the natural diagonal ribbing of the rock. Foliation the geologists called it, if she remembered right. Now it was becoming as much cave as it was tunnel. Occasionally, looking back at the ever-dwindling entrance, they trudged on. Eventually, she couldn't really tell if the opening was getting smaller. Only when she forced herself to remember how long they'd walked, did the distance sink in. They were deep into the mountain. Maybe too deep. Now she was spooking herself.

"Here it is."

Madison stopped. Aubrey was a few steps ahead. The last ten feet of the tunnel floor in front of him was a mirror reflecting the headlamp beam in watery ripples across the ceiling and the concrete wall. It seemed so out of place, like they'd come upon an ancient ruin from time immemorial. The tunnel entrance had been weird, but this was…yeah, creepy. She really needed a new word. The floor clearly dropped away beneath the water, though only a few inches if you could trust the refraction.

Seams ran up and down, left and right across the wall along with a couple of graffiti tags from those brave enough to come this deep. But what was that?

A circular opening centered at the base of the wall? The hole, maybe two feet across, was framed by a circular ring with smaller holes, like empty bolt holes. A pipe flange, the bottom of which was underwater an inch or two, allowed water from the floor to drain into the brand-new darkness inside the pipe. The breeze was stronger with a metallic tinge, like ozone or acid. She bent over and tried to aim the light into the opening, but couldn't get the angle.

"Culvert. To run the gas through, I guess." Aubrey put his arm around her and took a deep breath, letting it out slow. "This was fun. Ready to head back?"

"What?" She glared up at him, causing him to turn away from her light. She stepped into the water, gasping as the icy wetness flooded into her shoe like an electric shock. "We just got here."

She took another step. He tried to pull her back, but she was free. The water was mid-calf by the time she got halfway to the wall and Aubrey was pacing back and forth at the edge like a water-shy dog on a lakeshore.

"Relax," she said. "It's not that cold and I'm not leaving without at least touching that wall and getting a better look in there."

Each slippery step took her deeper and came with an involuntary gasp as fresh skin met icy tunnel water. The cold was seeping in fast. The car was not close and even when they got there she did not have a change of clothes. What was she thinking? This was once in a lifetime shit, though, right? The bragging rights alone were worth a trip to the ER. A little hypothermia never hurt anyone.

"You're freaking crazy," said Aubrey, but he was smiling and that was all she needed.

The water reached her crotch and then her belly button before she smacked her palm on the surprisingly warm surface of the wall. Grit, broken down by the moss and freed by the impact, sprinkled into the water. She gave Aubrey a whoop and leaned her headlamp into the open pipe. The inner surface was fairly smooth but completely rusted. In the gloom on the other side she could see posts, or brackets, mounds of sand or more moss maybe. It was hard to tell. Even holding the light at arm's length inside the tube didn't improve the view. "How thick is the wall?" Her voice wavered, reminding her, despite her overabundance of adrenalin, her body was going to pay a price.

"Ten feet, I think. Why?"

No guts, no glory. Just the sort of shit all dads tell their preschool daughters before they ship out to Iraq, right? Madison bent at the waist and plunged headfirst into the tube. Aubrey was going batshit crazy behind her, but the pipe distorted his voice, transforming his protests into feline yowls. His screeching, her own scuffling through the pipe, the trickle of water beneath her, and the pounding of her heart combined into her own internal battle cry. Full fucking speed ahead. She couldn't get fully up onto her hands and knees, but every awkward step brought her closer and closer.

She reached the end suddenly. The swath of light was hard to direct and her neck would only bend so far from inside the pipe. Leaning out without fear of falling wasn't working, and she wasn't small enough to flip over and descend feet first.

Fine. The ground was sandy, mostly smooth and higher than the other side by about a foot, except directly below the pipe. The flow of water struck there, hollowing out a small section before following the concrete wall off to the right and down the side of the tunnel. There was no grabbing the edge of the pipe either.

Gymnastics class don't fail me now. Pushing forward, she dropped and rolled, but failed to plant her hands properly. They sank into a foot of icy water and her momentum flopped her onto a shoulder before she stopped in a graceful sprawl flat on her back, wincing and spitting sand. Could have been worse. Aubrey could have seen it.

She got to her feet and swung her light around. A lot like the tunnel on the other side. Clumps of moss hung from the walls and formed mounds on the floor, all still gray but shinier. It glistened, speckled with tiny pinpoints that caught the light like little diamonds, but only for an instant, and not when she swept the light back across the same pieces. Weird shit.

Aubrey was still yelling but she had no idea what he was saying. The far end of the pipe was a mile away and his face was perfectly centered as they illuminated one another.

"What the fuck are you thinking?"

Whoa! The boy had used the f-bomb. He *was* scared.

"You get back over here right now."

And he was getting all bossy, too. Hmm. Madison kinda liked that, but he needed to realize she had as long as she damned well wanted. And just what was Mister Adventure going to do about it, anyway? Of course, she didn't want to ruin a good thing. The hair was a work of art, after all. "In a minute, *Mom*. I'm gonna look around."

Her voice was even weirder in the new section of the tunnel, like it was on reverb. Each echo shifted up and down the spectrum as it repeated, louder, softer, then louder again, over and over until it eventually died away. Aubrey had said the two walls were a quarter of a mile apart and they were creating some truly eerie acoustics. That was a lot of volume for sound to get jumbled up in. Taking a few steps deeper, she saw rusted metal cradles and brackets sunk into the floor. Further down at the extent of her light, another bracket jutted upward from a puddle. At some point, workers had been realizing that crazy dream of pumping the mountain full of flammable fucking gas. The present certainly didn't have a monopoly on stupid.

A clump of moss struck the bracket next to her with a *slock,* startling her. It shimmered the same as the rest of the stuff under the light. The ceiling didn't have a definitive bare spot the moss had dropped from. In fact, the ceiling was a lot barer than when she first looked a couple of minutes ago.

Kneeling by the freshly fallen clump, she poked at it with the blade of her knife. The size of a dinner plate, thin and stringy, the tendrils interwoven like coarse fabric. Was that normal? Cooler still was the tiny mouse skull entwined in the shit. What did she know about normal, anyway? Moss, lichen? Some other things she hadn't paid attention to in biology class?

A loud grunt filled the cavity.

She spun in time to see Aubrey drop unceremoniously from the pipe, half landing in the puddle and half in the grit, just like she had. Holy shit.

He'd followed her. She rushed to his side and helped him into a sitting position.

Without a thought, she swiped gunk from his face and kissed him.

"You weren't listening," he gasped, when she finally let him go. "We gotta get out of here."

"Are you kidding?" She felt so, well, alive. It was amazing.

"The moss, Madison," he swung his light around. "It's not right."

Figures. He finally impresses her and immediately loses his fucking mind.

"No, listen." He pushed to his feet and pulled her back toward the pipe, nervously swinging his light across the ceiling, walls and floor. "It started disappearing."

She tried to follow where he was directing his light, but his movements were jerky, plus her view was jostled as she resisted being pulled toward the culvert. Was he right? She'd just noted herself there was less than when she got into the chamber.

"It like melts back into the walls—I don't know." He gave her arm another tug. "Seriously, and there's little bones stuck in it too."

Okay, but that was just because mice died sometimes and the moss grew over it. It was just because—

Aubrey leaned in and forced her to make eye contact. "We've got to go."

A glob of moss dropped from the ceiling somewhere farther down the tunnel in the darkness, then another. Then more.

The ceiling was coming down, a wave of moss dropping and rolling toward them like an oncoming storm, points of light twinkling in its midst like flashes of miniature lightning.

She dove into the culvert, hands scraping as she scrabbled across the rough, rusty surface. The arc of the pipe made the process painful, the process at speed, a hundredfold. Each strike of her palms like razor blades and each blow to her knees like a hammer. Behind her, Aubrey screamed, the sound magnified by the pipe this time instead of muffled. The wave had come down on him, it must have. Was he okay? He had to be okay.

She launched from the mouth and into the water, sputtering as she came up, spitting out the muck she'd stirred up only minutes before. Before she'd sloshed about in cave water. This time, the thought of what was in the water—and in her mouth—made her gag.

The culvert was empty. Where was Aubrey? She splashed to the mouth, her headlamp dropping into the water. She could see the light under the surface, but the refraction kept her from being able to grab it as she collapsed at the mouth. His light was swung wildly a few feet inside as his screams bellowed out of the tube.

Thank god.

"Madison—"

She saw his face, the pained smile that meant freedom, and then it was gone. His face sucked back, replaced by the diminishing light.

She dove at the opening, bent at the waist her torso in the tube, arms stretching. His fingers clawed at hers and she grabbed a wrist. Then he grabbed hers. She pulled, bloody knees digging into the concrete wall beneath the culvert, icy water lapping around her.

He came through on top of her, and they were running. Her supporting him, then him supporting her, as they tripped and fell, moving down the tunnel toward the microscopic light in the distance.

Her heart pounded and her breath fogged her eyes. There was cold and pain, but it was on the fringe, beneath her notice. She knew only they were getting closer, that his hand was in hers, and they had to reach the light.

At the mouth of the tunnel Aubrey tore back the chain-link, widening the hole, and pushed her through as she dragged him with her. He hoisted her up, carrying her but only a few yards before collapsing to the ground, her on top of him.

"You...okay?"

Panting, she flopped onto the ground, ignoring the rocks and dead brush digging into her ass. Every part of her was ringing with all the signs of pain except the pain itself. It was all going to hurt something fierce in a few minutes. Worse tomorrow. At least there was a tomorrow. She nodded. "You?"

He looked like someone had dumped a bag of shit on him, doused him in water and then beat him with a stick. She probably looked worse. "I think so."

The keystone of the tunnel loomed over them. Shadow dropped across the mouth in a sharp line like a curtain just inside the welded steel grid.

"Jeez," he said swatting at his neck. "Freaking wasp."

She batted his hand away and pulled a tuft of his hair clear. A hundred tiny eyeballs in the gray patch on his neck squinted in the sun, then closed as tiny tendrils began to sink into Aubrey's neck.

"Hold still." Madison reached for her belt and did not repress the smile at how fucking sharp she kept her knife.

IN MOUNTAIN MIST

Margaret L. Carter

"**S**low down, for heaven's sake." Judith gritted her teeth to keep from yelling when Don cruised around another curve as if driving in clear daylight.

In the fog, or possibly a low-lying cloud, the headlights illuminated only a yard or two of pavement. Otherwise, just the silhouettes of roadside trees stood out from the backdrop of featureless gray-white. *And nothing else, no matter what some people claim.* It was one thing to study and write about legendary monsters killing hikers and other tourists. Buying into the tales herself would be taking research too far.

Grumbling under his breath, Don eased off the accelerator. "At this rate it'll be midnight when we get back to the campsite."

"If it weren't for you, we wouldn't have to go through this in the first place."

"How is it my fault? This afternoon the weather app didn't say a thing about fog."

"We wouldn't be out here if you hadn't insisted on camping instead of spending the night at the lodge." After a meal in the lodge dining room and an interview with a desk clerk for an article Judith was working on, they'd hung around for two more hours to listen to an Appalachian folk singer in the bar. "It'll be fun, you said. Just like a second honeymoon, you said." *Cool it, sarcasm won't help,* she admonished herself, but she was too annoyed to soften her tone.

He relaxed and glanced at her with a fleeting smile. "Well, that is literally how we spent our honeymoon."

"Yeah, twenty-six years ago. And in case you've forgotten after all this time, we camped out because we couldn't afford a week in a hotel. We're not young, energetic, or broke anymore." Her back already twinged in anticipation of a night in a sleeping bag on a thin air mattress, if they managed to reach the campsite safely in the first place. "Not to mention that you didn't have a-fib and high blood pressure then."

"You'll notice I didn't drop dead from assembling a tent."

At least they couldn't possibly get lost, even without a functioning GPS. Although wireless reception at this altitude in the Blue Ridge Mountains was erratic at best, all they had to do was drive directly along the Skyline Drive back to the campground. The main hazard they had to worry about—as long as they didn't slip off the shoulder or crash into a car heading the opposite direction—was overshooting the turnoff into the woods. She kept an eye on the mileage indicator, ready to alert Don if he seemed about to miss the narrow side road.

Reverting to a conciliatory tone, he said, "You got your first interview done, anyway. How'd it go?"

"Fine. She's lived around here most of her life, long enough to know the difference between bears, deer, and legendary beasts, so she comes across as an intelligent witness. Not that I believe she really saw one of the alleged local cryptids, but deciding if the reports are factual isn't my department."

To fit her article into a journal of contemporary folklore, as she planned, she'd use a cautiously objective tone. If that plan, her first choice, didn't succeed, she could revise the piece for a popular magazine that had published her writing in the past. Then it'd be all about a slant towards the "maybe real."

"If something's out there eating people," Don said, "I'm confused about how you've got witnesses."

"When the victims are in pairs or small groups, some have managed to escape after their friends got killed. And they're not eaten, just mauled to death, which is kind of…strange." After another nervous glance out the window, where there was still nothing to see but fog, she added, "The weirdest part is that survivors claim to have seen different creatures. You'd expect the local consensus to settle on one beastie and stick with it."

"Different like what?" Don looked away from the road to glance at her.

She choked down the impulse to nag at him again. Sure, if she'd talked him into renting a room, they wouldn't be risking disaster now, but it was a bit late to insist on turning back.

"At least four types mentioned in the past year." She ticked them off on her fingers. "Wampus Cat, Devil-Monkey, Snarly Yow, which is a kind of Black Dog monster, and Sheepsquatch."

"You've got to be making up that last one."

She laughed. "Nope, there really is a Bigfoot-type cryptid that looks like a giant, bipedal ram. Allegedly."

"You think the victims were killed by bears, right?" Don leaned forward to peer over the steering wheel as they crept up on another curve.

"That seems most likely, unless a cougar has wandered into the area, which sounds pretty farfetched. There's never been a confirmed sighting around here in this century or the last. And again, according to reports from the rangers, you'd expect predators to feed on their prey. Anyhow, it's an unusual cluster of animal attacks in such a short time. That is, if the incidents are even connected. I can hardly wait to hear what the guy I'm meeting tomorrow will have to say."

"If we ever get back to the campground tonight at this speed." He revved the engine but slacked off again when she glared at him.

Too tense for further conversation, she clutched the armrest at every bend in the road. She couldn't help visualizing the drop-off on their right, invisible in the fog just beyond the trees, with no barrier except a knee-high stone wall, and only at some points. She stared into the mist ahead, as if she could extend the range of the headlights by straining her eyes hard enough.

At the next tight curve, Don cast a sidelong look at her and slowed down before she could snap at him. Just as the road straightened, something dark loomed ahead.

"Don, look out!" She grabbed for his sleeve with her left hand and the armrest with her right.

A hulking shape, at least man-height, blocked their path.

Don slammed the brakes. The car swerved onto the narrow shoulder with a screech. Judith's fleeting glimpse of the...animal...showed her something black on two legs with the torso of a woman but the head of a cat. She stifled a scream, heart racing.

The passenger-side door scraped a tree before the vehicle jolted off the pavement with a succession of jarring bumps over loose rocks. Finally they slid to a stop. Her head banged into the window frame. When the momentary pain faded to a dull ache, she scanned the road for the thing, but it had vanished into the fog.

A bear, of course. I imagined a cat-woman because we were just talking about that.

A groan drew her attention to Don. He'd slumped sideways, his head against the window, eyes closed.

"Are you all right?" She gave him a gentle shake. *Stupid question.*

To her relief, his eyes opened, though he met her gaze with a blurry, heavy-lidded stare. "Hurts." He slurred the syllable and clutched his left shoulder. "Here…" He ran his hand down his upper arm. "Chest, too." He gasped between the words.

She reached for his wrist to hunt for the pulse. When she found the spot, the beat seemed abnormally rapid. *Not that I'd necessarily know what's normal.* His skin was clammy. Even more alarmed, she felt his forehead. Cool and damp. *Damn, it's got to be his heart.*

"Don't move. I'm calling for help." A stray thought popped up. *If he has to spend the night in a hospital, I'll have a valid excuse for checking into an actual motel in the valley, with WiFi.* Appalled by what had erupted from some layer of her brain, she mentally babbled: *Please God, no, I didn't mean that. Make him be all right.*

She dug her phone out of her purse. No bars, of course. She stepped out of the car in the faint hope of getting reception. The headlights showed that by one small stroke of luck they'd ended up on a gravel-surfaced trailhead parking lot rather than the verge of the road.

I hope that bear has moved on.

Her cell still didn't get a signal. She shook it, the next second mentally deriding herself for the ritualistic gesture. A dripping noise interrupted her focus on the tiny screen. With the light from the phone, she inspected the car and noticed a steady stream of water leaking from under the front. *A chunk of gravel must have bounced up and hit the radiator. Can't drive.*

Her heartbeat sped up. She swallowed, trying to stifle the panic. She walked back to the door she'd left open, drawing slow, deep breaths to appear calm. In the glow of the dome light, sweat slicked Don's face. "My phone doesn't have a signal," she said, "and something's broken under the car. I'll have to walk back to the lodge and call for help on their landline."

"Dangerous." His breathing sounded labored.

"Not really. I can't get lost, I'm not going to fall off the shoulder, and if another car comes along, that would be a plus. We haven't driven all that far yet, so I should be able to make it to the turnoff to the lodge in less than an hour. There it's more likely a car might come along and give me a ride." *Hope he buys this. I can't let him see I'm scared to leave him alone.* Reaching into the back seat, she retrieved a bottle of water for him, then switched on the emergency blinkers.

She dug a flashlight out of the glove compartment and slung the strap of her purse over her shoulder. Squeezing his hand, she said, "Hang in there. I'll be as quick as I can."

"Not quick, careful."

She nodded and shut the door. If she lingered any longer, her calm façade might disintegrate.

The cool night air, typical for June in the mountains, made her skin prickle, but she knew she'd warm up within a few minutes of brisk walking. After the first hundred paces, she realized how optimistic her time estimate had been. Instead of hurrying, she had to pick her way gingerly along the shoulder, the flashlight illuminating no more than a few feet ahead. Shining the beam into the fog only made her eyes hurt and worsened the dull headache. Her leg muscles grew sore from the slight but steady upward incline. Every couple of minutes she checked the phone again with no luck. Listening and watching for rescue in the form of a passing vehicle brought only disappointment too. *Everybody else has better sense than to be out in this.*

She glimpsed motion from the corner of her eye. The bear? Stomach churning, she peered into the mist to her side. Nothing. *Imagination. Nerves.* The woods on her left, opposite the drop-off into the valley, could hide anything. *Any ordinary animal, that is. Definitely not something unnatural.* She forced herself to concentrate on the ground underfoot. The last thing she needed was a twisted ankle.

Something rustled in the trees, different from the muffled chirps of insects and night birds. In the fog, she couldn't pinpoint the direction of the sound. She glanced from side to side. Did she see a shadowy form keeping pace with her? But focusing on the spot where she thought she'd noticed movement, she didn't find anything. *Of course not. Optical illusion. The eye wants to fill in the gaps.*

Out here alone, she could sympathize with people who imagined seeing monsters. But why so many conflicting reports? Regional lore included lots of half-beast, half-man cryptids and some that could change between animal and human. None had the power to assume multiple shapes, though.

When she checked her phone yet again five minutes later, it still had no signal. Almost slipping on the wet grass at the edge of the pavement, panting from effort and alarm, she looked up.

And stopped short.

The dark thing loomed less than three yards ahead. Bipedal, about a foot taller than her, blurred around the edges, it had a feline-shaped head, a vaguely female torso, and a languidly lashing tail. In the flashlight beam, its eyes glowed crimson.

Judith took one step back, struggling for balance. *Not real, no way. I must have bumped my head harder than I thought.* She blinked at the apparition as it turned amorphous and dissolved.

The next second, it re-formed. A man stood before her: Don, in his jeans, T-shirt, and denim jacket, immobile and silent.

"You're supposed to be in the car. You shouldn't be walking." She gulped for breath. "And how did you get here ahead of me?" *He couldn't. He'd have walked right past me. This is impossible.*

He only gazed at her without speaking.

Her head buzzing, she edged toward him, tucked the phone into her purse to free her right hand, and reached out but didn't quite touch him. He still didn't stir or blink. "I don't believe this either. You can't be here. You're another hallucination. Brain damage from that bump." *He's in the car, maybe in pain, maybe dying.* She must have a concussion, or something worse, though she hadn't thought she'd hit the window frame that hard.

The figure evaporated and solidified again. It coalesced into a recognizable shape, covered with shaggy, black fur. It stood on four legs, its head level with her chest and its canine muzzle gaping to display a mouthful of fangs. The eyes shone red. For the first time, it made a noise, a rumbling growl. The primal part of her brain screamed, *Monster! Run!* The more rational top layer countered. *Worst thing I could do. And there are no such things as monsters.*

Not a giant dog. A bear, that's what it has to be. Backing up step by step, careful not to stumble, she stared into the thing's eyes and willed it to be a bear. A few seconds later, its body bulked up, and its muzzle shortened. *Definitely a bear. Take that, hallucination.*

It lumbered toward her. The pulse pounded in her temples. She continued to retreat, struggling to remember the experts' advice for dealing with bears. *Don't run. Stand your ground, act calm, make yourself look big.*

She halted, praying the animal couldn't smell her fear. *Can't let it attack me. I have to get help for Don before it's too late.* Waving her arms, she tried to sound calm while shouting, "Leave me alone, bear. Go away!"

It kept coming. At arm's length, its cold breath blasted her like the odor of rotten meat in a refrigerator. *Cold? Not hot?*

This isn't in my head. It's real! A wave of vertigo swamped her, as if the world were tilting underfoot.

The thing shapeshifted yet again, into the giant dog disguise. Whatever its true nature, it was solid enough to breathe on her. *It wants to terrify me. It must thrive on fear. Well, it's succeeding.*

She couldn't let the terror paralyze her. *Stand your ground, act calm,* she reminded herself. *I have to escape and get help for Don.* If the monster had a solid body, could it be hurt?

Fighting to control her shaking hands, she groped in her shoulder purse for the hair spray she carried. She'd never needed it to fend off a mugger, but would it work on this beast? The creature lurched still closer. She squirted hair spray directly into its face.

With a howl, it backed up, pawing at its eyes. After a sideways glance to get her bearings, she switched off the light and sprinted into the trees, barely visible in the fog. She crouched down and froze in place. Would the creature give up and go away? Or, no matter how quiet she remained, could it track her by scent?

She heard it panting and snuffling along the road, first near her hiding spot, then becoming fainter as it moved farther away. *Is it actually losing interest in me?* Holding her breath, she strained her ears until she couldn't hear it anymore.

I've witnessed an authentic cryptid attack firsthand. Hope I live to write about it.

If the monster was a genuine shapeshifter, that fact explained why all the surviving witnesses reported something different. *How long has it stalked these mountains, feeding on people's fears? It makes everybody see what they expect. I didn't have any firm expectation, so it picked a bunch of images from my brain.*

On hands and knees, not daring to turn on the flashlight, she crept to the edge of the road. As far as she could stare into the mist, the area looked deserted. What now? Turn back or continue in the direction of the lodge? Since she couldn't tell which way the beast had gone anyway, she had only one reasonable choice. *I have to call an ambulance for Don. That hasn't changed.*

After returning the spray can to her purse, she picked up a thick fallen branch from the ground. Not much of a weapon, but better than bare hands. She rose to her feet and started up the road at a painfully slow pace. Not seeing or hearing any threat after a couple of minutes, she risked the flashlight, pointing it at the ground directly in front of her.

A shadow loomed in her path. Heart pounding, she brandished her improvised weapon as the thing coalesced into a cross between bear and giant dog. With a wordless yell, she swung the branch at its head.

It vanished. *That easy?*

A deep growl behind her answered the question. Whirling around, she confronted the monster, now at least eight feet tall. She took a step back, stumbled and recovered, then tried to turn and flee. It shifted position to block her.

It's been playing with me this whole time.

Trembling, she dropped everything she was holding, sank to the ground, curled up, and wrapped her arms around her head. A huge paw raked her exposed forearms. The momentary sting of its claws morphed seconds later into searing pain.

A wave of icy cold enveloped her. Not wind, a sensation as if she'd been shoved into a walk-in freezer. Undulating blue light penetrated her half-closed eyes. Rolling onto her side, she risked peering up at the beast crouched over her.

It no longer resembled an animal of any species.

The electric-blue glow that made her head swim emanated from a cloud that detached itself from the mist, sparks igniting inside it like miniature lightning bolts. Eyes, teeth, pseudopods, and claws formed, dissolved, and reappeared. At its center, a dark core swirled. It floated toward her. She scrambled to her hands and knees but didn't bother with a futile attempt at flight. The thing was already encircling her. No wonder none of the survivors had described its true form. As the darkness expanded and the shimmering light faded, she thought, *If they saw this, it was too late to escape.* And then, *I'm sorry, Don, I failed you.*

The dark engulfed her.

DOOM AT DRAGON'S ROOST

Stephen Mark Rainey

"We've found it!" Dan Foard pointed to a twisted piece of metal lying at the bottom of the rocky ravine, some thirty feet below. "That's a piece of Spencer's plane."

His partner, Natalie Maddox, leaned over the edge to catch a glimpse of the section of wreckage. "I can just barely make out some numbers," she said. "You sure?"

"Yeah. The registration number was N2903J. I can see '903J' from here."

Just over a year ago, Todd Spencer's Cessna 172 Skyhawk had vanished, by all indications in this area of the Blue Ridge Mountains, and a half-dozen search parties had failed to turn up any trace of it. On that tragic night, Spencer, a private pilot from Browns Summit, North Carolina, had taken off from Greensboro's Air Harbor Field bound for Charleston, West Virginia. Thirty minutes after take-off, just north of Aiken Mill, Virginia, a near-hysterical Spencer reported seeing "something huge" in the sky. Moments later, Air Traffic Control lost the plane's transponder signal and then radar contact.

A genuine unsolved mystery. Foard and Natalie had long hoped to find solid evidence of a crash. Now they had.

Natalie pointed to the shallower end of the ravine, a hundred or so feet down the slope. "If we go down over there, we can make it without rope. I don't see any other pieces of the plane. Do you?"

Foard scanned the steep sides of the chasm; the autumn-dressed woods, colors dulled by late-afternoon shadows; the highest reaches of the ridge above their heads. Almost a mile up that incline, half-hidden by forest, the craggy—reputedly "haunted"—rock formation known as Dragon's Roost rose like a medieval fortress. Nearby, he saw plenty of fallen trees but no path of bent or broken trunks that might indicate a crippled aircraft had hurtled through them.

"No, I don't." With his phone camera, he took several photographs of the remains of the Cessna's fuselage. "Okay, let's go check it out."

They threaded their way down the slope, clambered into the shallow end of the ravine, and then backtracked toward their target. Roots, hidden rocks, and slick leaves made the going difficult, though they were well-accustomed to rugged terrain. They both lived in Aiken Mill, a once-prosperous hamlet that nestled in the valley between Copper Peak, Mount Signal, and Thunder Knob, some thirty miles southwest of Roanoke. Foard taught U.S. and world history at nearby Beckham College. He had met Natalie almost a decade ago, when she was the college president's new administrative assistant. Since then, they'd become fast friends. They loved exploring together these seemingly endless miles of forestland that—almost miraculously—remained free of civilization's encroachment.

Many times over the past year, he and Natalie had hiked into the darkest reaches of the forest, more than half-hoping to turn up some sign of the downed aircraft. Today's discovery felt like striking gold.

On his phone, Foard opened his local map and dropped a pin at their precise coordinates. He took several close-up photographs from different angles before kneeling to examine the piece of wreckage.

Odd, he thought, that it didn't lie half-buried among the branches, brush, and detritus that littered the ravine's floor.

Natalie clearly shared his surprise. "Does this look over a year old to you? It might have just fallen here yesterday. Or today."

"Yeah. You'd think it would be at least partially buried."

"We'll need to report this," she said. "We can't just remove it."

He looked around the ravine again. "My question is—where the hell is the rest of the plane?"

A moment later, he heard heavy crunching in the leaves above their heads, and a deep, grating voice rumbled, "You people are on private property. Some consider that a killing offense."

Foard jerked his head up and saw, standing on the edge of the drop-off, a burly, bearded man in a camo jacket glaring at them from beneath the brim of a dirty cap. A shotgun—a 12-gauge, from the looks of it—rested in the crook of one arm.

Shit! A moonshiner, almost certainly.

In all his ramblings, Foard had never happened upon an illicit still, but he knew plenty must hide in these woods. Not without reason did Sylvan County bear the semi-official title "The Moonshine Capital of the World."

"Sir," he said, doing his best to keep his voice level, "I'm quite certain this is all national forest land." He saw that Natalie's face had gone pale, her emerald eyes wide. "I can assure you neither of us would willfully trespass on private land."

"Oh, I can assure you this is private land. What the hell are you doing out here?"

He gestured at the hunk of aluminum. "This is a piece of a plane that crashed out here over a year ago. We're investigating it."

"Who is 'we'? Who are you with?"

"We work for Beckham College." Before he thought better of it, he added, "But this is a private investigation. And this is a valuable piece of evidence."

"Just so you know, sir," Natalie said, "if this is private land, it should be marked with purple—"

The man cut her off. "Purple tape don't mean shit. And I don't give a rat's ass about your 'investigation.' Tell you what, you two come on up out of there. And if you don't do exactly what I tell you to, I'll blow your fucking heads off."

Foard's heart slammed into overdrive. "Sir, we are not looking for any trouble. We'll be more than happy to just leave."

The man hefted the shotgun and aimed it at Natalie. "You try to leave, you're gonna be shy one lady friend."

Natalie took an involuntary step backward but in a steady voice said, "Sir, I don't think you understand—"

"One more word and you're both done."

Defeated and disgusted, Foard shot a last look at the piece of fuselage before starting toward the shallow end of the ravine, with Natalie close behind. He took a mental inventory of anything on his person or in his backpack that might facilitate self-defense: a very sharp military folding knife clipped inside his right front pocket; a fifty-foot coil of rope in his backpack, for all the good that might do; and a small tool kit with several sharp implements. He owned a 9mm pistol, but he'd never felt inclined to carry it into the forest. Natalie always packed pepper spray wherever she went, but bringing it to bear against a man with a shotgun might prove slightly problematic.

Basically, we've got nothing.

Neither of them dared reach for their phones with the shotgun trained on them. Anyway, there was no service out here. Still, if one of them could start a video going…

Nope. The motherfucker's eyes weren't missing a movement.

Yeah. Motherfucker.

Once they reached the top and stood before the glowering stranger, they kept silent, hoping to avoid riling him. After studying them for a moment, he motioned toward the top of the ridge with his gun barrel. "All righty. We're gonna walk up that hill, y'all in front of me, single file. And you're not gonna so much as look around. Are we clear?"

They both nodded.

"Move."

Foard took the lead as they started. His heart clanged like a sledge on steel, and his legs felt like jelly, but he managed to walk without stumbling. Now and again, he glimpsed the distant contours of Dragon's Roost through the dark foliage. The rock formation lay far enough off the Appalachian Trail, which cut through the northwestern corner of the county, that relatively few hikers made their way to it.

Aptly, a dark legend dating back at least a century surrounded Dragon's Roost. As it was told, a mad musician who lived on nearby Copper Peak once summoned a winged demon by way of his music, and the demon took up residence on Dragon's Roost. According to the legend, if you ventured there after dark at certain times of the year, the demon would claim you.

If we die tonight, I suspect it won't be at the hands of a winged demon.

By the deepening shadows, Foard realized how late it was getting. If they hadn't been so intent on checking out their find, they would have already started back to his SUV, parked on an old utility road about three miles south of their present location.

Was the man actually taking them to Dragon's Roost?

The incline grew steeper and rockier as they ascended. They were maybe a quarter-mile shy of the summit. Now, to Foard's surprise, he heard a low, erratic thumping; percussion, of some kind. And as they continued onward, he made out other, sharper sounds: twanging strings, rumbling bass notes, keening woodwinds. All dissonant, arrhythmic, as if a bunch of unskilled musicians had gathered to produce random, raucous noises.

From behind, Natalie's whisper barely reached his ears. "Dan. To your left."

He glanced left and spied a number of pale, twisted objects scattered among the trees. He recognized the partially crushed wheel cover of a Cessna 172. A piece of the vertical stabilizer. A small, bent rectangle of aluminum—an aileron.

Todd Spencer's Cessna.

How the hell? He could understand the searchers failing to locate a single fragment of wreckage, like the one in the ravine, but not a cluster of them so close to the summit of Dragon's Roost.

Behind him, heavy footsteps crunched nearer, and then the gruff voice said, "Hold up."

Foard drew to a stop, and Natalie took the opportunity to move a few steps closer to him.

Motherfucker ambled forward, his eyes roving over the debris that had fallen from the sky. For fallen it had; this was not the plane's point of impact. A rain of wreckage. And no way could it be over a year old. By all appearances, it might have just happened.

A different plane? No, not possible.

Motherfucker pushed up the brim of his cap and gazed at Foard. One corner of his mouth lifted into a crooked leer. "That's some shit, ain't it."

Foard couldn't stop himself. "Sir. I have to ask. What were you doing down in these woods? You couldn't have known we were there."

Motherfucker seemed to debate with himself before answering. At last, he pointed to Dragon's Roost. "Naw, I was up there. I saw you."

"We were only there a few minutes. You could not have seen us a mile away and then gotten all the way down there."

The man's voice came out soft. "It fucks everything up. It fucks up time."

Natalie sent Foard a puzzled glance. "Tell me, sir. What is that music—that noise—coming from up there?"

Instantly, the big man recovered. "All right, shut the hell up. We almost there. And then you gonna see. You gonna see the last sight of your lives."

Shit. They'd pushed too far. At least he hadn't shot them. Still, if they could make some connection with the man, they might induce him to lower his guard.

As they continued their ascent, Natalie managed to cling closer to Foard's side without angering the man. And now he noticed that she cupped a small object in her right hand.

Her canister of pepper spray.

She must have drawn it from her pocket when Motherfucker turned his attention to the airplane wreckage. But this could be dicey. She'd have to be in just the right position to use it, and if she missed, that would be it for them. Still, the man had as much as told them they would not leave Dragon's Roost alive. This, their slimmest of chances, had to be better than no chance at all.

The racket from above grew more abrasive to his ears. Good god, how many people were up there? And what the hell were they playing—or trying to?

He had to do something, say something to capture Motherfucker's attention. Occupy his mind with something other than his designs for them.

So risky.

"Sir. My name is Dan Foard. Why don't you tell me yours?"

"Do you remember what I told you? Talking is a bad idea. If you speak again, one of you ain't gonna make it to the top. I think you know which one."

Damnation. For himself, he might take the risk. But he didn't dare endanger Natalie.

Shortly, they broke through the trees and found themselves facing a solid wall of rock that rose a good twenty feet above their heads. From the summit, the instrumental cacophony echoed down the stone, flowing like magma to scorch their eardrums. To their left and right, flanking the central wall, two massive, arrowhead-shaped points of Tuscarora quartzite protruded high into the deepening blue sky. Seen from a distant vantage point, the multiple points capping the ridge resembled a rough crown—or a huge stone nest, hence the formation's name.

Foard had hiked up here many years ago. Unless you were an experienced rock climber—and he wasn't—spectacular views from the top didn't exist. In the center of the Roost, precariously piled rocks and gaping pits posed threats to life and limb if one wasn't careful. After his lone excursion here, he'd felt no compulsion to return.

"Now," Motherfucker growled. "We gonna move to the right until we can get up on that next level. Go."

With Natalie close behind, Foard began skirting the long, high wall. As he drew nearer to the huge, towering "arrowhead," he saw a gap between its leading edge and the end of the wall. Between the two formations, piled slabs of broken rock created a crude, natural staircase that ascended toward the heart of the Roost.

"Go on."

Foard started up, picking his steps carefully, for a fall could spell his end as surely as a gunshot. Natalie came next, then Motherfucker. Here, their captor's position was as precarious as his captives'. Still, Foard was too far ahead to attempt a move against him, and Natalie couldn't possibly spin around, maintain her footing, and pepper spray the bastard before he brought his shotgun to bear.

The raucous "music" grew damn near deafening here.

A long, difficult step onto a broad, flat rock; a shorter step through a V-shaped opening between two boulders; and Foard found himself standing in a wide, arena-like bowl, surrounded by jagged stone walls. The "floor" was pitted and cracked, and in the wall at the opposite end of the bowl, a ten-foot-high gaping maw revealed only blackness within.

The awful noise was blasting from that featureless opening.

He remembered this place, and he knew the opening didn't go very deep—maybe fifteen feet. It certainly wasn't large enough to accommodate a band of "musicians."

A massive sound system and a recording, maybe? But why?

Behind him, Natalie and Motherfucker clambered up from below. As the godawful noise washed over him like a caustic wave, his balance wavered, and he threw out a hand to brace himself against the nearest rock wall. Whatever the hell was happening, Motherfucker's shotgun seemed less of a threat than this relentless assault on his senses. Natalie stumbled up beside him, a bewildered grimace on her face.

Motherfucker's voice reverberated from miles away.

"Pretty fucked up, ain't it?" He pointed to the dark maw. "Now, I'm afraid you two are gonna have to step on in there."

Beyond the stone parapets, the sun's last rays withered and died. Like a cold shroud, darkness fell far too quickly over them. Stars suddenly glimmered in a midnight sky.

Jesus, how…?

What was it the man had said?

It fucks up time.

With difficulty, Foard turned around, his body seemingly entombed in frigid tar. "Tell me how you found us. You couldn't have known we were out here."

"I saw you long before you got out here," came the echoing voice. "I saw the pieces of that plane fall out of the sky, and then I knew you were coming. From up here, I can see through time. That devil, he does fuck it up in funny ways."

Natalie called, "And this noise?"

Beneath the starlight, Motherfucker's proud smile shone in the darkness. "That's the echo of the music my Great Grandaddy John and his bunch played to call up that devil. My name's John Gray Eubanks—the fifth, I think—and I been the keeper of the Spheres Beyond Sound since I first come up here. That's what they call this devil's homeplace—the Spheres Beyond Sound."

"What about the airplane?"

Eubanks's bright eyes rose to the starlit sky. "It flew over at just the right time on that night—when the devil was rising. To you, it happened a year ago. But up here—well, who really knows? So I come up here today, and I saw the pieces of that plane raining down, and I looked out in that forest, and I saw you in those woods before you even got in your car to leave. So I knew. I knew I had to bring you to the devil."

Watching Motherfucker's silhouette, Foard realized he'd slid the shotgun back into the crook of his arm.

"Why are you doing this?" Natalie called.

The man's eyes glared like lanterns in the darkness. "Because I am the keeper of the Spheres. And I've gotta stay the keeper."

Foard's head reeled faster and faster. His hand slipped on the wall, and when he reached to grab it again, his fingers closed on a hunk of rock.

A loose hunk of rock.

As deftly as he could, he tugged the rock free, and then leaned with his back against the wall, clutching the rock close at his side.

Did he see me grab it? It's so dark.

Eubanks unleashed a vile laugh. "Feeling pretty dizzy, ain't you?"

Foard exhaled in relief.

No. He hadn't seen.

"Don't worry," Eubanks went on. "It won't last much longer. For you, nothing's gonna last much longer. Well, except pain. Time's fucked up, remember? You're gonna suffer a long time. Maybe forever."

However fucked up time might be, theirs was short. Years ago, Foard could pitch a fair baseball. But his head was swimming, and the darkness lay deep. In the faint starlight, he could see that Eubanks still held the gun in a relaxed grip.

Now or never.

Taking one step forward, he wound up to pitch. By the time Eubanks realized what was happening, the rock was flying through space. An instant later, a dull, fleshy thump assured Foard his aim was true.

Eubanks cried out and staggered backward. The shotgun's barrel dropped, but he somehow kept a grip on the handle.

"Natalie! Spray!"

She was already leaping forward, canister clutched in her outstretched hand. A second later, a scream of agony drowned the raucous music, and Eubanks toppled to the ground. Foard heard the gun clatter away—and for a moment, he almost stormed forward to make sure Eubanks was down for the count. But a terrific crash of harsh, ringing sound from the nearby darkness changed his mind.

"Natalie," he called. "Let's get the hell out of here."

"I'm good," she breathed. "I'm good."

He grabbed her hand and half-scrambled, half-felt his way toward the beckoning gap in the boulders. At last, he stood at the top of the broken-rock stairs. But it was twenty feet or more down, and now he couldn't even see the stone beneath his feet. His phone light would help only a little—but he kept a 1,000-lumen flashlight in his backpack. Could he get to it and still escape from whatever was emerging from Eubanks's Spheres Beyond Sound?

He had to get to it, or they'd never make it down without falling. Foard released Natalie's hand and maneuvered to stand with his back to her. "Quick. In my pack. Flashlight. Top pocket."

She immediately dug into the pack—and moments later reached forward to slide the cold metal cylinder into his hand. But he thought better of this and handed it back to her. "You navigate, I'll help hold you steady. If we slip now, we've had it." He took a firm hold of her bicep.

The brilliant white flashlight beam fired into the darkness ahead.

"It doesn't matter what's back there," she said, her voice quavering. "We've still gotta go slow."

"Slow and steady."

Down and down they crept. Twice, Foard nearly lost his footing, but both times he managed to recover and maintain his grip on Natalie's arm. At last, they reached the narrow but level ring of earth at the base of the stone wall, where they inched their way back in the direction Eubanks had brought them. From above, the screams rose unabated, weaving a weird harmony with the pounding, screeching music.

Foard knew it was no longer the pepper spray that was responsible for Eubanks's agony.

They reached the gap in the trees through which they had entered and slipped into the near-pitch darkness beneath the trees. The flashlight beam cut a narrow path ahead.

It was a long, long way back to the car.

Beneath their feet, the ground vibrated. A series of thunderous booms shook the woods. They picked up their pace as best they could, tripping and stumbling, desperate to put as much distance as possible between them and whatever horror had emerged from its lair on Dragon's Roost.

Foard drew his phone from his pocket and took note of the markers he'd dropped on the map for both his SUV and the site of the airplane wreckage.

"Almost four miles to the car," he breathed. "Can you make it?"

"I'll make it," she said, her voice still strong. "You?"

"We will make it."

On and on they went, yet the screams—and the wild music—from behind them refused to fade. At last, they drew near the site of the wreckage they'd first discovered. In his flashlight beam, Foard saw a yawning chasm of darkness ahead.

They slowed their pace, and he stepped to the edge of the ravine. Natalie aimed the flashlight beam into its depths.

Nothing.

Nothing but old branches, leaves, roots, and rocks.

"Gone," Natalie whispered. "As if it never existed."

"Did it?"

Her eyes turned to his. "I don't know."

Now, for the first time, they looked back. They peered into the darkness through which they had retreated, back toward Dragon's Roost. Natalie snapped off the flashlight.

Far, far up that long, dark incline, beyond the silhouetted branches and boughs of autumn leaves, they could see the black contours of Dragon's Roost blocking out a portion of the starry sky.

John Gray Eubanks's screams continued on, as loud and shrill as if they still issued from just above their heads.

Something was rising from that rocky lair.

Something massive.

A winged black shadow that rose higher and higher.

Higher than a skyscraper.

From that perch on high, a pair of brilliant, molten gold eyes peered out over its dark domain.

As if performed by a macabre orchestra, mindless screams and insane music filled the endless darkness. If what Eubanks had told them was true, those screams—which had almost been theirs—would go on for a long, long time.

Maybe forever.

At last, they started walking again, back toward his car. The screams finally began to diminish with distance.

But not the music. Not for him.

"Do you still hear it?" he asked after a time.

She shook her head. "No. Not anymore."

But I do.

This he understood.

That devil, that demon, whatever it was, no longer had a keeper.

It was looking for a new one.

Someone to lure the prey it desired.

Someone who could hear the music of the Spheres Beyond Sound.

After a time, she asked, "Do you still hear it?"

He nodded. Then he stopped and turned to gaze back the way they had come. He felt his heart begin to pound like a piston.

Natalie's eyes gleamed with concern. "What? What is it?"

His hand closed around hers and became an iron vise. He started walking back toward Dragon's Roost.

He didn't feel her struggling to break his grip or hear her sharp cries of protest.

All he heard now was the music.

The beautiful, beautiful music of the Spheres.

NORTHERN VA

THE WOODS BEHIND MY HOUSE

Sonora Taylor

I tried to write a story of the Balls Bluff Woods,
Named for a civil war battle.
A national park in the town of Leesburg,
Whose streets are named for generals of wars revolutionary and civil,
Where brick-lined paths and preserved buildings
Hold ghosts of the past and haunted hatred in the present.

I tried to write a story of the woods
Behind my house,
The battlefield of days of yore
Where bodies torn by bullets
Found by metal detectors and marked by faded graves
Sat adjacent to a neighborhood with children, pools,
Pets and bikes
And cars pulling in to the gravel parking lot
That sat at the mouth of hiking paths
That wound us to our fates.

I tried to write of trails flanked by mulberry bushes
Fat and ripe in summer that burst with purple juices
Bruising the ground beneath them when they fell,
Falling upon the dead both past and present,
For surely such woods held more bodies than those of long-forgotten soldiers?

The woods wouldn't tell me so,
But something did.

It's why I tried to write of the woods
I walked in every day with my parents,
My dog,
My brother with whom I caught minnows from creeks
Slicing through the paths where soldiers trod
And bled
And died
And yet those minnows thrived inside our tank,
Free of the ghosts that bathed their feet in the cool waters of the Balls Bluff Woods.

It's why I tried to write of the woods where
I walked along a stone wall with perfect balance,
Walking round and round a cluster of graves of Civil War soldiers
Forgotten to all but the trees that keep them buried.
I circled death with hands outstretched
And even smiled when I saw a black snake slither under
Leaves decayed and brown as all the corpses left behind
To fade from us and feed the woods.

It's why I tried to write of the woods where
The steepest path led to the river
Now polluted to the point where dogs can't swim and people can't fish,
And as a warning to those who wouldn't listen,
The muddy banks clasped my grandmother's ankles and tried to drag her in.
My father saved her, but her shoes remained behind.
Forever on the banks of the woods
To sink and swim with bones and flesh
That make the forest flourish when the weather warms.

I tried to write a story about the Balls Bluff Woods,
One that added ghosts and darkness I created,
But alas, I couldn't do it—
Because that darkness was already there.

THE WRONG TIME

Ivy Grimes

Kay was cutting vegetables at the counter when she noticed a peeper, but she was more excited than scared. Since moving into her new apartment, she hadn't met many people in the neighborhood.

Unwilling to cover up the floor-to-ceiling windows so intrinsic to the character of the place, her only option was to live on display, like a model woman in a model home. She wore her best silk pajamas whenever she went into the main room, and she only watched documentaries. When the neighbors saw her life she wanted them to know she belonged in this sophisticated neighborhood.

The community in Reston, Virginia, was supposed to be artistic, designed in the 60s as affordable housing for commuters. The prices of the apartments had skyrocketed since then. To save up, Kay had had to live with her parents in the sticks where she had to commute more than an hour each way to DC, where she worked as a paralegal for the DEA. But it was all worth it to be where she was. Now her life would finally begin.

Kay hoped the peeper was a nosy neighbor who would introduce her to the gossip in the neighborhood. She strolled over to the window as if she just wanted to admire the garden and saw a face below almost swallowed by the night, illuminated only by the glow of Kay's lamplight. It was the face of a young woman with long hair and a peasant-style green dress. Maybe she was a 60s enthusiast like Kay, who had always felt she'd been born in the wrong time. At least Kay had felt that way since she'd learned about

60s counterculture from a documentary in middle school. Since then, she'd memorized every Janis Joplin and Jimi Hendrix song. It felt like her rural hometown was still stuck in some black-and-white 50s fever dream, despite being within an hour of DC. Everyone in her hometown hated DC, but no one had been surprised when she'd decided to live and work in the city. She'd never quite belonged at home since she didn't like watching sports or pinching children's cheeks.

When Kay locked eyes with the woman in the retro green dress, she felt a thrill like what she'd felt after meeting her high school best friend or her college boyfriend.

The woman held up a glass of red wine as if to toast her, and Kay couldn't contain herself any longer. She motioned for the woman to come up and join her. The woman only laughed, so Kay went outside to try to find her and invite her up for dinner.

When she went into the garden, the woman was gone and Kay felt like a fool. Had she been pranked, lured into the garden and then ditched? It was like something a kid would do to another kid (something that kids had done to her once), but it wasn't supposed to happen to adults.

She reassured herself that the woman was probably running late for something, or maybe she was called in to dinner by her husband. The raised glass had seemed like such a friendly gesture, though. It couldn't have been for nothing.

With a heavy heart, she returned to her apartment to answer work emails until her soup was ready. All anyone ever did in her new neighborhood was work, and she had almost found a friend who was interested in some other kind of life.

That night she fell into a bad dream, something innocent that quickly became ominous. She was cleaning up wine someone had spilled on her kitchen floor, but as she soaked it up with paper towels, she realized it was blood. The stain kept spreading, impossible to wipe away.

A loud knock at her bedroom door startled her from the nightmare and she hurriedly opened it, forgetting where she was. Dazed, she turned on the living room lights and saw the woman in the green dress.

"It's me," the woman said, as if she and Kay had already been introduced.

Kay stumbled backwards, ready to run for the pepper spray on her bedside table.

"I don't know you."

"I'm Lydia. You invited me in. I belong here." The woman reached out with a friendly hand.

It was true, she had invited her. Instinctively, she touched Lydia's hand and a static shock moved through her body.

"Sorry!" Lydia said, laughing off the electricity. "I forgot that I'm not supposed to touch you. I have a weird energy now."

A deeper shock coursed through Kay's body—contact with another world. A ghost. Or a demon? Or an angel? She had wanted new experiences, but not to meet a spirit. Her heart was beating so fast, she gasped for air, and it felt like blood was filling her lungs.

"What do you want?" she said, rasping at Lydia as if she were the ghost.

Lydia gave her a calm, inviting smile. "Would you like to come to a party?"

There was nothing dangerous about this woman, even if she was a ghost. She was just lonely, most likely. She was looking for a way to cope with her own death.

"A party? Where is it?" Along with the shock and fear Kay felt, she also felt so... *invited*. So accepted. She hadn't felt that in a long time.

Kay blinked, and suddenly her living room was filled with dancers and loud music. Their raucous laughter filled her apartment and chased away the holy silence of the place.

Young people. Most of the people in the neighborhood were older, but these were kids who were full of life. They smiled at her as she passed them. A smoky haze filled the air, and several people wanted to offer her a puff of whatever they were smoking.

How could she ever get in touch with the 60s unless she met a few ghosts? It was the only way to time travel. And these ghosts seemed safe. They were from the right time, and they were her people. She reassured herself it was perfectly fine to join a party of ghosts.

With trembling fingers, she tried to take a pipe from a guy with long, wavy hair, but when it touched her fingertips, it felt like an ice cube. The cold stung her, so she dropped it on the floor. The man shrugged and gave her an "it's cool" smirk. He picked it up and took a puff.

"Come over here!" Lydia said, motioning for her to sit on the couch too.

Kay sat on the closest edge and noticed her reflection in the window, which showed herself and no one else. When she looked at her apartment, it was filled with people, but when she looked into the glass, she was alone.

"I feel dizzy," she said.

"I get that way all the time at the end of a party. I take whatever people give me. It pays to be open like that, right?" Lydia's eyes took on a watery look, and she turned very pale, but it only lasted a second.

"Why are you here?" Kay said.

Lydia picked up a glass of wine from the coffee table (the same one she'd held when she'd stood in the garden earlier that night) and took a sip.

"I guess you know what I am."

"A ghost?"

A trickle of wine dripped from the left corner of Lydia's mouth and she wiped it away with her flowy green sleeve. She turned her face away from Kay.

"You can tell me," Kay said.

When Lydia turned back, her face was bloated and her eyes were wide as silver coins. She put down her wine glass and rose, as if to lunge at Kay. Or to embrace her.

Kay jumped up and backed away. It wasn't real! This dead woman was just a dream, an illusion. She forced herself to turn around and stare at her solitary reflection in the window. She was losing her mind. She'd heard of people who had taken too many psychedelics and were left with a permanent loss of their sense of reality, but she'd never taken anything. She'd always been afraid of getting in trouble, making a mark on her record. People in her hometown who got in trouble never left. They hung around trying to score pills.

And now she was seeing things, like she was strung-out. When she'd always been so careful.

"It isn't real. It isn't real," she told herself. "I'm alone in my apartment."

She was comforted by seeing herself alone in her reflection. But when she turned around, Lydia was still there. She was back to normal, her face full of life and feeling. But the party was gone.

"I'm sorry for intruding. See, I need somewhere to crash. This was my place once. It was where I threw the best parties of my life. I lived here with my husband until he left," Lydia said. "But he came back one day."

With a bang, the door flung open, and a man with auburn hair ran into the room.

"No!" Lydia screamed. And the room went dark.

Kay fumbled towards her lamp and managed to flick the knob with trembling hands. The light showed a mess of red blood spreading all over her kitchen floor. She'd never get it out. Visitors would smell it. She could never sell the place. There was rot and sickness everywhere, infecting every joist and nail. She screamed, but her voice was hoarse and powerless. She walked over to see where the blood was coming from, and then she saw the auburn-haired man and Lydia lying together in a heap on the floor, a knife on the floor beside them.

"He survived," a voice said behind her. When Kay turned around, she saw Lydia looking healthy and whole again. "Is there any justice? He said he didn't like my lifestyle."

"Why did you show me that?"

Kay looked back and the kitchen was clean again, the hardwood floor refinished and sparkling.

"I didn't mean to. I just wanted to have a party. Like old times."

The music started up again, and the people returned. Dancing, smoking, laughing—they had more life in them than any other people Kay had seen in the neighborhood.

"I have work tomorrow," Kay said, suddenly afraid she'd never go to work again. How could someone meet a ghost—a whole roomful of ghosts—and go back to work as if nothing had happened? And yet, she had no choice.

"I'm so sorry," Lydia said, looking at the floor. "We'll clear out of here. You go on to sleep."

With that, Lydia was really gone. The blood was gone, the smoke was gone, the music was gone. Kay felt like the only person at the center of an infinite cosmos.

She couldn't lose her mind. She couldn't. She had a mortgage to pay.

Rather than stay up and shiver at what she'd seen or record it in her diary or call a friend, she took a sleeping pill, and then another pill, and she slept like the dead.

When she woke up, there was no trace of the odd visions of the night before. She wondered if it was a dream. Since she didn't have any meetings, she decided to work from home. If she was losing touch with reality, she didn't want to do it while driving. Also, in spite of the shock she'd felt at meeting a ghost, she sort of hoped Lydia would return. There was something so beautiful about Lydia, some kind of fire inside of her. Kay had never met anyone like her.

It was like she was waiting all day for a guy to text her back. But nothing happened. She did her work, and when evening came, she closed her laptop and made dinner for herself. She ate while staring at the blank TV, piecing together what had happened the night before. Lydia was a ghost who had lived in her apartment. She'd died there.

Kay looked over at her clean kitchen floor and remembered the blood spreading everywhere. No matter how well it had been cleaned, some specks of her blood must have remained in some cracks in the floorboards. Some real part of her must have been left behind.

She started to take a sleeping pill when night came on, but she decided to wait to see if the party started up again. In the darkness, she sat on her couch.

"Lydia? Where are you?" she said, her voice squeaking a little. It was the first time she'd spoken that day.

The party didn't return, but Lydia did. She sat on the couch beside her, holding her glass of red wine.

"Most people who live here don't let me in. You're so friendly, though."

The compliment warmed her. She wished she could share Lydia's drink, but she didn't want another shock.

Kay's fear of her visitor was outweighed by a strange sense of rightness. Lydia belonged in the apartment, and so did Kay. No one else seemed to understand Kay, but maybe Lydia would. They had both been held back for so long by people who didn't like their lifestyles.

"It's weird here," Kay said. "I thought I'd like living in this place. I thought it would be like going back in time. But until you showed up, everything was so…"

She faltered.

So what?

"It was like that when I lived here, too," Lydia said. "We're so close to DC. All the power and everything. My husband got high on that. He got a little too high."

Even in the darkness, Kay could see Lydia grow paler.

"Maybe you shouldn't think about that. You don't want to remember it all over again, do you?" Kay said. She was sure that she didn't want to see blood on her floor again.

"Of course, of course. Better to remember it when I'm in his presence. You see, I have business with him during the day, settling old scores," Lydia said, taking a sip of wine. "But it frightens me to be with him at night. Do you think I could come here to stay the nights?"

It felt like Kay was lying in a pool of blood, warmth flowing all around her. She wanted Lydia to stay, but she didn't like to think of what she really was. Was there a way to have Lydia stay with her but not as a ghost?

"I'd like that. I really would. But I have to sleep at night to get to work on time."

"I wish you could quit and do something you love," Lydia said. How did she know that Kay didn't love her job? "But people like us can never really be satisfied. We were born at the wrong time. That was how I always felt about myself."

The words felt like a stab in the heart. Lydia had been alive at the very time Kay wanted to have lived. If Lydia wasn't born at the right time, then who was?

"You should party with me," Lydia said. "That is, when you can. Otherwise, you can stay in bed. You won't hear the noise unless you open the bedroom door and join us."

Lydia was pale again, giving her a weird smile, a too-wide and frozen smile. Maybe she was remembering her husband again, seeing the blood in the kitchen. Kay didn't turn around to confirm. She thought about how nice it would be to have a friend who was always there, with a party whenever she felt like it. It was like she and Lydia had always known each other, like they'd danced in fields and braided each other's hair sometime long ago. Maybe she had known her in a past life.

"What's it like to be dead?"

"There was a funny feeling, like static electricity, and then I found myself traveling. And I found other travelers. And now I'm here."

"Getting drunk in the afterlife," Kay said, gesturing at her friend's ever-full glass of wine.

Lydia laughed. "I bet I have more fun dead than you've ever had alive."

Kay laughed, too. It felt good to be teased, to be known that well. She knew what her neighbors would have thought if they'd walked by and peeped at her inner life. They would have seen her sitting all alone in the darkness, and they might have heard her laughter. What kind of person laughs at nothing, all alone, but someone born at the wrong time?

ROOM 1968

Nicole Willson

The window in Heidi's office had a clear view of the Washington, D.C. skyline, with the U.S. Capitol Building looming over the Potomac River. That sight always made Dustin feel so close to the important action, and yet so far away here in Crystal City.

Heidi greeted him with folded arms and an unsmiling face. "Ready for today?"

"Definitely. Everything I sent you sounded okay, right?"

"It did. Excellent, even." She leaned over the papers scattered across her glass-topped desk and fixed her dark eyes on his. "But that won't do you a damn bit of good if you're not on time. The Overlords can't stand lateness."

"I know. You said that. A few times."

The Overlords. That was what Heidi called the heads of their parent company; Dustin chalked the nickname up to her weird sense of humor. The Overlords had arrived in town earlier in the week, and Heidi's department had to give them a presentation on what they'd accomplished this year, what their goals for the next fiscal year would be, and how they were planning to meet them.

For reasons Dustin still didn't quite get, Heidi had chosen him to give the presentation today. By himself, no less. He'd been racking up hours of overtime to get it just right. As soon as the meeting was over, Dustin was taking the rest of the day off and going home to sleep. His eyes felt like sandpaper from staring at his laptop screen day in and day out. Colorful pie charts danced in the darkness behind his eyelids whenever he closed them.

"So where's this meeting?"

Heidi stabbed a gnawed fingernail downward. "In the Underground. Room 1968."

"*Where* down there, though?" Dustin had walked the corridors under Crystal City several times. 1968 didn't sound familiar.

"It's between the shopping centers at 1750 and 2100. And it's a little tricky to find, so I'd leave here a bit early if I were you. You have *got* to be there on time, Dustin."

Dustin glanced down at the framed photos of Heidi's pink-cheeked children. One blond boy and one brunette girl, giving him gap-toothed grins.

"Is there any way to get there above ground? That's usually faster." This wasn't always true. But the crowds of business-suited people staring at their phones and bumping into him at crosswalks sounded more appealing than the narrow escalators or piss-reeking elevators that led to the infamous "underground city."

"No, there isn't."

She leaned so close he could practically taste the floral perfume she wore. "And I'm not fucking around. Don't stop for coffee. Don't decide you need a donut break."

His ears burned. He wasn't *that* bad about being late. Not usually. "I won't."

"You get a call from your dear sainted mother? Send her straight to voicemail."

Dustin stiffened. "My mom's dead, Heidi. Both my parents are. Remember?"

A lock of blonde hair fell out of her bun as she shook her head. "Sorry, I forgot. You're so young. But my point stands. If you're late to this meeting, make sure your resume is up to date. You get me?"

"I get you."

The meeting was at 10:00. At 9:30, Heidi buzzed over to Dustin's desk and shooed him out of the office. He adjusted his suit jacket, ran a shaky hand over his blond hair, and headed out into the sauna-like summer humidity. He hoped he'd get a chance to cool off before the meeting, as he didn't want to show up all shiny-faced.

A discarded scooter lay on the sidewalk by his office building, and he had a quick mental image of riding it all the way through the Underground. Would that get him to the meeting fast enough to suit Heidi? It would certainly show initiative. He grinned.

Crystal City. He'd always thought that name sounded neat. It made him picture some futuristic place full of tall glassy towers sparkling in the sunlight.

But the actual place where he worked every day? Squat, dingy, ugly buildings. Boring and overpriced chain restaurants. Rosie over in Copywriting said the city's name came from a crystal chandelier in the lobby of a nearby apartment building, a story Dustin figured was just ridiculous enough to be true. Rumor had it the area was going to get a major makeover now that Amazon was in town, but he doubted even Jeff Bezos's fortune could make this place somewhere he'd want to be after business hours.

He crossed the street, brushed off a couple of people waving clipboards at him for some cause or another, and headed down the escalator into 1750 Crystal Drive. The Crystal City Underground was another thing that sounded way more interesting than it really was. The network of belowground corridors connecting the local buildings, businesses, and the subway station was dingy and full of shops that were mostly either boarded up or selling fast food or overpriced touristy crap Dustin couldn't imagine anyone wanting. Did people really come here looking for prints of all the Republican presidents playing poker together?

The rumble of trains in the Metro station and the smells of greasy fast food faded as Dustin turned into the first corridor. Someone had lined the white walls with huge, brightly-colored floral prints, but they didn't do much to make the place more appealing.

1968, was it? The overhead directional signs gave no indication there was such a room. The speckled beige tile floor sloped upward. Dustin climbed a small set of steps and turned left into the corridor heading towards 2100 and now he was alone, away from all the office workers streaming between the subway and the shops.

The empty parts of the tunnels, broken up only by random barbershops, doctor's offices, and a few planters, always creeped him out a little. He tried not to come down here unless he had to, and he rarely had to. The soles of his brown Oxfords squeaked on the tile floor as he searched for any signs pointing to 1968. That sound reminded him of the noise his shoes had made as he walked the hospital corridors towards his mother's—

No. Dustin couldn't think about that now. He was already tense enough without getting emotional. He thought about The Overlords instead. Who were they, and what were they like? He'd seen a picture of them once on the company intranet, but they'd looked so normal he'd forgotten all about them as soon as he closed the browser window.

Well. He'd be meeting them soon enough now.

And then the entrance to the shops at 2100 came into view, and Dustin's stomach tensed until he could taste the bacon and egg sandwich he'd had for breakfast. He'd overshot Room 1968. How?

He cursed under his breath and headed back into the corridor. He scanned the walls as he walked, trying to move slowly enough to see everything and yet fast enough not to lose too much time, looking for any sign he could have possibly missed. But before long, the sounds of trains and recorded subway announcements greeted him as he turned back into the busy walkway that led to the shops at 1750.

"Shit," he said out loud. His pulse pounded in his ears. It wasn't that he particularly loved his job, but he couldn't afford to lose it.

On his third pass through the corridor, he spotted a white door with a metal push bar set into the wall. Those doors usually led to underground parking garages, and so Dustin hadn't paid any attention to them. But this one was about halfway between 1750 and 2100, right where Heidi had said Room 1968 was.

The door squealed as Dustin opened it onto another empty stretch of bare walls and glossy gray tile. He pulled out his phone and glanced at the time. 9:50 already?

He was pretty sure he'd never seen this stretch of the Underground. The walls were a listless pale yellow, and the main hallway branched off into different corridors. One of the overhead lights flickered on and off. A section of the ceiling appeared to be crumbling, and creepy brown stains oozed from the dilapidated tiles and down the yellow wall. Dustin's forehead began to sweat as he walked down the sloping floor, searching for any sign of Room 1968. Would The Overlords really be stuck back here?

And then footsteps sounded in the hallway, coming from around a corner. Maybe this person knew where Room 1968 was.

A woman came into view, and Dustin sighed in relief as he recognized the halo of frizzy dark hair and the slight limp.

"Rosie!"

Maybe he and some of his coworkers called Rosie from Copywriting a crazy cat lady behind her back, but she was always decent to him, always willing to tweak some marketing text when he asked. And right now he was thrilled to see anyone he knew.

"Rosie, do you know where the hell this Room 1968 is? Uh, pardon my language."

Rosie stared at him, and Dustin thought she didn't look so good. Her face was as sickly yellow as the walls. Her eyes didn't have their normal warmth or friendliness. In fact, they looked blank. As if she didn't recognize him.

"I'm going to be late," she said.

"Me too. Probably." He looked at his phone. 9:54. *Damn.*

"They don't like it when people are late." Rosie wrung the hem of her black sweater and shook her head.

"Wait. Are you going to the meeting too?" Not to be mean about it, but he couldn't imagine why anyone would choose Rosie to represent their department. Her purple skirt and black sweater bore her trademark smudges of cat hair.

"I'm going to be late." Her voice quivered.

"No, you're cool. Meeting doesn't start until ten. That's what Heidi said. We'll find it."

He took a deep breath and started down the dingy corridor again. He turned left into the first side hallway. But the only room down here was an open janitor's closet cluttered with mops, rusty metal pails, and stacks of bright yellow "CAUTION/*CUIDADO*" signs. He spun around, gnawing his lower lip. Rosie trailed behind him.

"They don't like it when people are late," she said.

God, would she stop saying that? "How are you, Rosie? It's been a while."

"I'm going to be late."

He sighed. "We got time, OK? Don't freak."

Now that he thought about it, it really had been a while since he'd seen Rosie. Had she been sick? Could that be why she was acting so weird now?

"Hey, Rosie?"

When he turned towards her she walked away from him, down the hall towards the janitor's closet.

"I'm going to be late." She talked over her shoulder. "They don't like it when people are late."

"There's nothing back there, Rosie." His stomach clenched again. Was she having some kind of stress episode?

More footsteps sounded nearby and a tall dark-haired man rounded a corner, shaking his head and muttering. He looked familiar. Dustin had seen this guy in Sales, he was pretty sure.

"Hey, man. You know where Room 1968 is?"

Something about the man's blank eyes, as if the house was all lit up with nobody inside, made Dustin's skin crawl.

"I have to be on time," the guy said.

"They don't like it when people are late," Rosie chimed in from down the hall.

O-kayyyy. Dustin swallowed hard and looked at his phone.

9:58. Shit. He still had no idea where he was going, and now he had less than two minutes to get there.

He ran around the corner the dark-haired man had just emerged from. He definitely hadn't been this way before; a dusty pipe crossed the ceiling, and a dripping noise sounded nearby.

More people paced the halls now, and a warm wave of relief surged in Dustin's chest when he recognized some of their faces. Wasn't that Deb from Editorial? He thought she'd left the company a while ago, but there she was with her trademark flamingo-pink hair. And there was that redheaded guy who always stunk up the fifth-floor bathroom. With all these people from his company here, he had to be in the right place.

"I'm going to be late," Deb said as he blew by her, his heart pounding.

9:59. *Come on.*

He stopped at a white metal door with a shining golden placard.

1968.

He fought the urge to cry with relief. He reached for the knob just as the door swung open.

The man standing in the doorway made Dustin's legs freeze.

His skin looked like old, yellowed paper. His slicked-back dark hair gleamed in the ceiling lights. The man's pale gray eyes made Dustin think of falling into an icy, bottomless chasm. Something dark stained his gray pinstripe suit. His thin lips parted in a wide, unfriendly grin.

"Mr. Dustin Templeton?" The man's voice was foghorn-low and scratchy, like he'd just woken up.

"Yes sir," Dustin managed to get out.

"I am Mr. Bartholomew."

Dustin automatically reached out for a handshake, but Bartholomew seized Dustin's forearm with dry, cold fingers. Hard. And then even harder. His grip felt like a blood pressure cuff that wouldn't stop inflating.

Dustin shrieked in pain and tried to yank his arm away, but Bartholomew's grasp felt like steel.

"You're right on time, Mr. Templeton. Don't ruin things. We're on a very tight schedule." The man's grin spread across his face until it was much wider than a normal human mouth could get. He pulled Dustin into the room. Behind him, a group of men with similarly pale eyes and stained clothing stood around a long wooden table. The ceiling lights flickered and a metallic, rank odor hung in the air.

Dustin wrenched his arm downward and broke Bartholomew's grip. He whirled around and flew out of Room 1968, up the sloping floor towards the door that would take him back to—

There was no door, or any sign there had ever been a door. The wall was solid yellowish tile. He stopped in confusion, and cold hands gripped his arms and his ankles and yanked him off his feet.

"Where's the fucking door?" he screamed. The dark-haired guy from Sales clutched his legs. Deb from Editorial had one arm. Rosie held his other arm. He thrashed and kicked, but none of them so much as stumbled as they carried him back to Room 1968.

"Well done, everyone," Bartholomew said. "Put him right there, please."

They dropped him on the wooden table and continued to hold him down as Mr. Bartholomew leaned over his body, closer and closer until Dustin could see nothing but his old papery face, smell nothing but his mossy breath.

The man pressed an icy fingertip to Dustin's right temple and pushed harder and harder until pain exploded in his head and stars danced in his field of vision. The fingertip moved *through* his temple. Something warm and wet trickled down the side of Dustin's head as the finger probed behind his eyes. He tried to hit Bartholomew. But he couldn't lift an arm.

"Just a bit more, my boy. It's easier if you don't fight it." Bartholomew's voice was far away.

No. Mommy. Help me.

"Ah, yes. There we go."

One last endless second of burning pain, as if something inside his skull was ripping apart, and then Dustin didn't hurt anymore. He drifted above the table, wondering if he'd always been able to fly. And for a moment, he could see everything. He was on the table, looking up at The Overlords with their gaping shark grins as they gathered around him. But he was also watching them probe his head from up above. And yet he also stood in the doorway, and that Dustin's eyes were as empty as Rosie's had been.

"I'm going to be late," the blank-eyed Dustin in the doorway said, and then the world disappeared.

Heidi's desk phone rang at 10:30. The caller ID read PRIVATE NUMBER.

She swallowed a mouthful of bitter coffee and lifted the receiver.

"Heidi Garrett," she said.

"Good morning, Ms. Garrett. Your tribute was right on time. The company will have another very successful year."

That *voice*. It made her think of bones clattering over an ancient stone floor. Heidi shuddered.

"I'm glad to hear that. But look…"

"Is there a problem?"

"You might have to think of some other way to do this. The authorities are starting to wonder why our employees keep disappearing. We try to pick people who won't be missed, but everyone's got neighbors and creditors, right?"

There was icy silence on the other end of the line for a moment.

"We do not recognize your authorities, Ms. Garrett. We're sure you can think of a way to handle things. You were in Northern Virginia Magazine's *40 Under 40* edition for your innovative work approaches, yes?"

"Yes..."

"Well, then. Innovate. See you next year."

Click.

Heidi rose from her desk. She stared out her office window as a plane descended into the nearby Reagan National Airport. The Potomac shimmered in the sun, separating Crystal City from Capitol Hill. Two places so close, and yet worlds apart. Maybe someday she'd get out of this place and make it to the other side of the river.

That poor kid. She pictured Dustin's dumb, trusting face for a second before banishing him from her mind and turning back to her desk. When her hands stopped shaking, she opened up a new document on her MacBook and began drafting a job advertisement.

THE FLOODED MAN

Michael Rook

When they saw the ghost tour huddled outside Gadsby's Tavern, Xavier knew Brianna was going to tell them about the drowned guy. He got lowkey nervous, first eyeing her, then the dozen or so tourists under umbrellas by the Revolutionary-War-era Tavern. Most were high schoolers like them, except for a couple of chaperones and a Colonial-costumed guide pointing to the Tavern's second floor. They were also the only people out on a drizzling August night. Visitors had stopped clogging Alexandria months ago, early in 2020. It'd left the city weirdly quiet, but good for COVID-lockdown walks like he and Bri had been taking all summer, talking about Nineties movies and urban legends they found online. Like the ones repeated on a ghost tour…

Bri sped up and Xavier's anxiety freaked; she was definitely headed towards the tour. Which could have been fine, good even. One of the things that kept them close was their internet investigating, knowledge dropping, myth busting. And ghost stories of the 19th Century were just the conspiracy theories of today, right? The same viral bullshit, people happy to turn off their brains. And look where crazy fables were getting everyone now… Xavier's COVID mask was itchy in the humidity.

Still, the *way* Bri was going to bring these people some truth. Even if he was mostly done with the church, something about Bri's brutal approach when she woke people up… sometimes it felt like a sin, or, if sin and church were ridiculous, at least a bit *mean*.

The rain ensured she would do her work by telling the poor out-of-town kids about the drowned guy. A light storm had been squatting over Alexandria for two nights. The restored 18th and 19th century buildings of the Old Town neighborhood, Gadsby's included; the brick sidewalks; even the gaslit lanterns fronting the restaurants and boutiques that made the riverfront city as Instagrammable as Charleston or Savannah—it was all wet. It was also the perfect setting to one-up an old horror story with a new one, making the point about how silly they all were.

Hearing about the drowned man, however, might fuck some of these tourists into nightmares beyond any story the guide could share.

Real bodies did float up in the Potomac River near Alexandria, after all.

Even Xavier had had a nightmare about it once, though he hadn't told Bri.

Speaking of, she'd be pissed if he didn't help her truth-bomb the ghost tour. And with them headed to different colleges in a month—if COVID allowed that—any failing made it more likely that she'd dump him, as she'd already been getting distant. Would he land another girlfriend like her? Not likely. And the idea of losing her was a worse hell than any belted about on those old Sundays.

They'd nearly closed on the group, near enough that they could hear the guide:

"If you tour Gadsby's, they'll be happy to tell you about how often George Washington danced there, but they won't say anything about the Female Stranger. No, they're too refined for that. But she *died* right up there, in room eight. Legend says—"

Bri jabbed a big step forward and Xavier almost grabbed her, to steer them away.

But it was too late.

"You want a *real* horror story?" Bri bellowed, cupping her hands. "Something scary AF?"

The group twisted. Their eyes ran over Xavier and Bri, from their COVID masks to his Public Enemy tee to her vintage Aaliyah crop top. A few dudes' gazes stuck on Bri, including a male chaperone in a *Land of The Free* shirt. That was also Bri—gorgeous.

"Tell 'em about the drownings," she said, ignoring the looks and still advancing. "Tell 'em about the bodies that float up when the river floods." She pointed to where the Potomac, a couple of blocks away, already lapped nastily into low-lying Union Street. "Tell 'em about the coal plant."

The guide's ironic beard and Colonial specs screamed history teacher in training. He pulled up like a mongoose but steadied and returned to his group. "Legend says the Female Stranger arrived from the West Indies deathly ill. But her husband didn't want to give their names—"

"*Trash*," Bri cracked.

Xavier got a better look at the group. They wore shirts from some school in Wyoming. They also didn't wear masks, despite Alexandria's rule about wearing them inside and out. And they couldn't say they didn't know about the mandate: their guide wore one. Xavier keyed on *Wyoming*. The kind of place where people said *plandemic* with a straight face? It pissed him off. Maybe they needed—*deserved*—a scare. Suddenly not feeling uneasy, he pulled out his Pixel and framed Bri. These COVID-deniers would get to see themselves on #urbanlegends freaking out over the story Bri was about to throw their way.

"C'mon," the guide said. "Don't."

"Ghost tour?" Bri said.

"Yes. And you need tickets, so—"

"*So*, tell them a true story. Tell them about the Flooded Man."

The group got chatty. The guide's face hardened, but some of the teens meandered Bri's way.

Expertly positioning herself below a streetlamp, Bri jabbed a finger past Gadsby's. There, the Washington Monument and parts of D.C. could be seen over Old Town's shallow skyline. It was also where, blocks away, eighteen industrial acres sat on the riverfront, abandoned.

"We used to have a working coal plant right here in Alexandria," Bri said. "But people kept finding ash on their windows and worried about getting sick. People got it shut down, in…"

She seemed to be reaching for the detail.

"2012," Xavier said.

Bri lit up, eyes and all, at his playing along. "2012, *yeah*," she continued, "but the city left it there. Until…"

Now she paused intentionally.

"*Somebody* else decided to use it. Secretly."

"Who?" a kid asked.

"Nobody" the guide said and tried to motion them down the block. "This way."

But Xavier trained his camera on the guide. Old-timey Spectacles shrank. Some guilt nipped at Xavier. What had the guide done? Though while he'd worn his mask, followed the rules, he'd let his group skate. Probably for a shitty tip.

"The CIA," Bri said.

A couple kids scoffed.

"*The greatest trick the Devil ever pulled,*" Bri said.

Xavier got the movie reference, but none of group seemed to.

Bri sighed. "Langley is thirty minutes that way." She pointed east. "*CIA* HQ. They were looking for spies in D.C. Like, *terrorists*. They caught a guy who worked for one of the embassies and took him to the old coal plant— which they'd been using as a black site. And if you don't believe me, it's online."

It was. They'd found the first mentions on Reddit, then gone deeper and deeper on the web, looking for cracks.

"And you know how the CIA gets its answers, right?"

Bri pulled up her mask, tipped her head, and lifted her hands.

She mocked dumping something on herself.

And started choking.

The sounds were so harsh that some of the kids cringed.

Bri thrashed wildly, faking ugly coughs.

"Stop!" someone shrieked.

Bri eased. "Did you know they waterboarded the 9/11 planners like a hundred times? And the guy they took to the coal plant was big. Like, *Thanos* big. But he wouldn't say anything. They waterboarded him *two* hundred times."

The group gasped like a choir. Xavier filmed. He also tried to ignore the tickle in the back of his neck. It was only a story. And they wanted a scare, right? Isn't why you took a ghost tour?

"Did he talk?" someone asked. "Finally?"

Bri shook her head.

"What did they do?" someone added.

"By itself, waterboarding is supposed to be the worst torture," Xavier jumped in, the want to do it coming over him. And when Bri nodded hungrily, he went on. "But that dirty water is called coal ash. It's toxic. Cancer toxic."

Someone whispered the start of a prayer—one Xavier had said himself for years.

Bri cut in. "The CIA was totally pissed. The guy hadn't told them anything." She raised her hands over her head. "Some say he was still choking on the ash when they dumped him in the river, right over there."

"No way," the creepy chaperone blurted, shaking a finger at the dense townhouses and shops. "The CIA ain't *sloppy*."

Xavier shoved the camera his way. "How do you know?"

Like Old-timey Specs, *Land of The Free* backed off.

"Then what happened?" a girl asked.

Bri lowered her hands. "Bodies started floating up. And they have for years now, especially when it floods. Which it does all the freaking time." She looked at Xavier. "We had a floater earlier this summer, didn't we? And the cops *still* don't know why they drowned."

"So what?" a boy said, maybe as tall as Xavier. "The Smiley Face Killers have been drowning people for years. It could be them, not the CIA. We have TikTok too."

Bri grinned. "The Flooded Man doesn't paint a stupid face when he gets you. And you can't *call* the Smiley Face Killers."

The tall kid ducked his chin into his throat. The others went silent and still too.

"You *can* call the Flooded Man," Bri said. "If you stand in the floodwaters and say the right words, he'll come. And if you make it to the city limits before he gets you, he'll go after the people you *hate*. And he'll keep going—killing them—until the next flood. Imagine that."

Tsch the tall kid huffed. "What if you don't make it?"

Bri gave him a bitchy head tilt. "He kills you."

The tour guide, who'd drifted away, pressed his phone to his ear with an expression that screamed he'd called the cops. Xavier stiffened. Even if he couldn't name what commandment they were breaking, what law, the sense of *wrong* lit up his nerves. He tugged at Bri and they jogged across the street, leaving the group.

The tall kid yelled after them.

"Oh, *yeah?* How do you call him?"

On the far sidewalk, Bri spun. She rolled her wrist at Xavier. *Film.* He hesitated but did.

"What'd you say?" she hollered, almost singing.

"The Flooded Man! What are the words?"

Bri made another megaphone around her lips. "You've got TikTok, right?"

She took off towards the waterfront parks. Xavier filmed for another second, catching the group's stricken faces and the guide apologizing, but then he ran off too.

No cops had come, so they sat on a bench under some trees in Oronoco Bay Park. Already, their post had racked up hundreds of views and comments. While Bri thirst-scrolled, Xavier didn't, the ill feeling having only grown along with the soft rain. Instead, he surveyed the river-facing park. It featured a rainbow-shaped break wall made up of big rocks, dotted at either end by wooden decks where you could feed the geese. It was dark and empty, including the high school rowing club's boathouse on one end and an abandoned warehouse on the other. Waves lapped over the rocks and flooded near the redevelopment site. Floodwater also gathered in the grass all around. Xavier wondered what it would take to fix the city's ancient combined rainwater and sewer system—a main reason for the constant flooding in town, as well as for the faint odor of shit in the park, made possible by the raw sewage being funneled into the river. But Bri was tapping him and shoving her iPhone in front of his eyes.

"They're calling us out! Daring us!"

Xavier lingered on Bri's face, mask dangling under her pretty chin. They could have beautiful kids, and they could settle down, even wild Bri. Not that she ever wanted to talk about that stuff, the far future. Like now, shaking her phone.

She was right, though. TikTok-land was calling them out. Amongst the terrified emoji faces and creepy music, the taunts were best boiled down to two words:

DO IT!

"They always want someone else to try," Xavier said, shaking his head. "So many people just want to watch."

But Bri's gaze said she wasn't listening. She was intensely focused on him, like when they fucked. But she wasn't thinking of walking the ten minutes to his Camry where they'd left it at a marina north of the city limits. He could tell.

"*Who*," she said, teasing out the words, "do you *hate*?"

He couldn't hold her gaze. "C'mon, we're already trending like crazy. You know it never gets better if you do the dare."

Bri pouted. Not sexy. Disappointed.

It tore at Xavier's guts. Maybe too quickly, desperately, he replied. "Who do *you* hate?"

"Those Wyoming fuckers, for one. The fucking anti-maskers. We wouldn't have to live like this." She turned away. "Did you know that UVA might be remote when I get there next month? We wouldn't have to shut down if people did what they were fucking supposed to do. What did they say about VA Tech? In-person? Remote?"

Xavier exhaled. "Same." He didn't want to think about the fall.

"Fucking cowards," Bri said. She hopped off the bench. "Speaking of."

Xavier leaned forward. "No," he said, not liking the eagerness of her tone, or what it might lead to. "C'mon, let's—"

"What? You said yourself all anybody does is watch. Let's be the ones who do it. Nothing's going to happen. We can bust this one too. And maybe those Wyoming fuckers will see it," She affected a bro voice: "*Uh, we've got Tik Tok too.*" She returned to her own tone. "*Ass.* But if they see it, they won't be so freaked out. And you know they're in their hotel right now searching 'Flooded Man.' Won't that make it better? I know it bothered you."

Xavier stood up, straightening his lacrosse shorts. "And what if it doesn't? What if we're just adding to the shit out there? You know how easily people get hyped on stupid stuff. *Especially* stupid stuff. What if we're making it worse? Ever think that?"

Bri gave him a head tilt. "*The greatest trick the devil ever pulled...*"

"*Was convincing the world he didn't exist.* I get it. Bad shit happens if you don't put it in the light. That's why we do this. Yeah, yeah, yeah."

Bri shot him her adoring look, the genuine one he'd die for. He shouldn't do this, they shouldn't…but it was myth-busting, right? And it was a *story*. What did it matter, really?

He looked around but found nothing other than shadows and puddles rippled by rain and breeze.

When he started to raise his Pixel, Bri smiled wide and finger-gun pointed at his camera.

He hit record.

"Hey losers," Bri said. "Starting the Flooded Man Challenge here. The FM Challenge. Ha." She tugged up her mask "We're all going to die anyway, so why the F not?"

She strode to a massive puddle in the park's grass, near a rainwater grate. She kicked off one sandal, the other, and stepped into the waters.

"Flooded Man," Bri said, and raised her hands in a summoning gesture.

Xavier's back tingled, the Potomac and its churning waters right behind him. Again, he thought to stop her, felt it more deeply this time, but again he let the moment slide by.

"Bring us the deep and the dark," Bri continued, almost chanting. "Flooded Man, I want to sink. Flooded Man, sink us all."

A wave crashed. Xavier jumped, twisting as the water nearly licked his heels.

"Shit!' Bri yelled. "Did you get that? That's perfect!"

Xavier tried to find his breath as she bound up to him, chest pressing his arm. They watched the video a few times, clipped it, added the instrumental of NIN's "Dead Souls," and posted it with the same hashtags as before: #urbanlegends #scary #stories #creepy #fyp

The likes and comments came like a hurricane.

Bri pushed down his phone. "Thanks."

Xavier meant to meet her gaze, but something moved under the trees in the park. His skin suddenly as jumpy as a cheap touch screen, he peered over her shoulder.

But nothing moved in the park. Only branches in the increasing rain.

"The devil," Xavier said, the word, the idea, leaking out.

"Eww," Bri said, squeezing his hand. "Honestly, Spacey is skeevie.

We're done quoting him."

Xavier grit his teeth. Her saying the words, doing the calling, and him...not stopping it. *Wrong*. He was suddenly furious at himself. And a little scared.

The devil.

"What?" Bri asked.

"The Flooded Man's story—it's a devil's bargain, right? The CIA doing bad shit in the name of making things 'safe.' Hurting other people to help yourself—it's a devil's bargain. Like the Flooded Man's 'deal.' But people don't think about that now, do they? They do whatever's good for them. And we just did the same thing, didn't we? For some likes?"

"Are you serious?" Bri said, stepping back and grabbing her hips. "It's not *real*. What the fuck is wrong with you?"

"But what if it was?" He kicked a puddle. "Maybe not the Flooded Man, but people do drown out there and pop up nameless."

He recalled the pictures of drowning victims they'd looked up after reading about the Flooded Man. About what happened to the body. The bloating, sure, they'd known about that. But "sloughing" hands? Where the skin slid off like boiled meat? It made him sick to his stomach.

"We're using that for likes, right?" he continued. "And what if someone did get murdered like that? Being waterboarded by...the CIA, the FBI... whoever. That shit has happened. Can you imagine if you were that guy, choking on coal ash? On the receiving end of someone else's devil's bargain? Can you imagine your last thoughts?"

"I'd want..." Bri said quietly, seeming to get that he was serious, that he was hurt. She turned towards the coal plant—and quoted another Nineties movie:

"*And I*," she said, "*will strike down upon thee with great vengeance.*"

"Yeah," Xavier said. "Fucking *great* vengeance.*" His heart ran at a speed that would have made sense if he'd been sprinting.

But was *vengeance* the right word? *Justice*?

No.

A devil's bargain.

A deal with Hell.

He eyed the dark coal plant—where *surely* nothing had happened. He was being silly, tripping. Not a good look with a girl you were desperately trying to keep.

"I'm sorry," he said and tapped at his chest, then his head. "I'm just being fucked up…"

Bri smirked. "C'mon," She tugged at him, steering him towards the marina, which lay past the coal plant and further down the Mt. Vernon Trail. It ran along the river, alternating from blacktop to boardwalks when it had to cross marshes, creeks, and outflows. "I want to go down on you. And I want you to do it to me. How does that sound?"

Blood surged under Xavier's shorts. They locked arms and trekked far enough that the coal plant loomed over them and the brick-and-glass riverfront office buildings. Water lapped onto places they avoided. Kayaks, which must have broken free of the high school's rowing house, smacked against the shore. The storm seemed to be getting more powerful, maybe the worst of it now aimed straight for Alexandria.

Then the power went out.

Bri had already turned quietly miserable—and it wasn't only the growing fatness of the rain. They'd gotten bunches of likes for the new post, but fewer than for the original. And though once or twice they'd thought someone was behind them, possibly cops, they hadn't seen anyone. It was almost as if Bri had *wanted* him to come, the Flooded Man, as if her wisecrack about everyone dying from COVID was real. She had a fatalistic streak. But didn't he? Didn't they all now? Everything was so fucked.

Bri whipped out her phone. "I'm getting an Uber. This shit—" She waved her hand at the increasing rain. "Isn't romantic."

But she huffed. "No service. That's not funny. Not even in a LOL way. Shit."

As she ambled away, Xavier's stomach flipped from one kind of anxiety to the other. Losing Bri. What they'd done. Had he sometimes agreed to sketchy stuff for her? Maybe. Did that make him a simp? *Maybe.* But also, when you had something great, you didn't let it go. For sure not now.

He wrapped Bri in a hug.

"Stand under me," he said, "I'll be your umbrella."

She frowned cutely. "You're corny AF. And you're not that tall."

She kissed him, but gently pulled away. Her gaze cast upwards as she drifted down the trail. The coal plant, thanks to a break in the trees, had come into full view.

Xavier peered up.

The plant looked like something out of a Tim Burton movie. It was all rusted towers and metal walkways and tall light poles, which had probably let it run all night. Even with the power outage on their side of the river, there was enough light pollution from D.C. to see fine. It let them make out the murals painted on the wooden walls erected all around the abandoned plant. The city, or someone, had drawn scenes of renewable energy and picnics and even colorful fish along the path, as if the site was some happy carnival—though a few of the fish had red eyes. Further down, where the walking trail wormed between the wall and the river, a wooden access door had been cut into the wall before the path snaked into a dark turn. There, like many places, water glistened on the blacktop, though it kind of looked like flooding from inside the plant.

"Fuck this," Bri said, then slunk another few steps onward, arms crossed and head dropped. Xavier meant to say something. Was Bri thinking the same thing as he was? Feeling the same concern? Not only that, but maybe a little fear too? Impossible to avoid if you dwelled on devils too long.

But when she reached the wooden door, she twirled around to face him.

"Get me, will you?" she said, leaning against the moss-covered mural. "With the plant?" She gave a sharp laugh and stretched her shirt hem, making Aaliyah pop. "Outfit of the Day. Ha. Whenever we get online again. If we get online again…"

She was scared. Maybe that was his fault.

"Hey," Xavier said. "Baby, are you good? If I scared you or whatever, I—"

But she popped out her tongue—which she did when she was anxious and didn't want to think about it. Or talk about it. "Get the picture, okay? I want to go home."

Would she ever want to talk about it? Talk about *anything*? Or was she actually just like everyone else?

Was he?

No, Xavier thought. *No. She's thinking about it. She will talk about it. All of it.* He lifted his phone, toggling the filter to make Bri stand out from the weird mural. *No more of us telling fables when we know the truth. Especially not to each other. It'll be—*

But the wooden door opened.

Bri's eyes went wide.

"Bri!" Xavier shouted.

From out of the darkness came a form so big it had to duck its head. With it came the smells of oil, sweat, mucus, chemicals, and blood. And it moved fast, wrapping a heavy, dripping forearm around Bri's throat.

"No!" Xavier screamed.

The Flooded Man was bloated like the drowned victims they'd seen online. His veins too had "marbled" blue against his grayish skin—that was, where his hand flesh hadn't torn away with the sloughing.

But the worst thing, by far, was the *adipocere*: brownish, waxy stuff that grew across his face like a husk. It left shadowy indents for his eyes, nose, and mouth, like a rotted scarecrow.

Then something happened.

Great cracks split in the Flooded Man's skin. At his eyes, nostrils, and lips. Along his huge scalp. Down the forearm crushing Bri's throat. Even the other forearm—which he raised above her head.

Xavier gaped at the arm-hammer ready to crush Bri's skull.

But the Flooded Man clenched his fist.

All his seams gushed fluids into Bri's screaming mouth as if she was under a waterfall. She gagged, like she'd pretended to do before, but with none of the pretend now.

Xavier dove, grabbing at the Flooded Man, but slipped in the ooze. An arm roared at him in a blow fiercer than a brutal lacrosse check. He crumpled to the wet wooden planks and pawed at his crushed face.

When he managed to open his eyes, Bri's gaze had gone dull, *dead*, her jaw slack and drooling as the Flooded Man's liquids drenched her chest, a mess of ugly reds and browns and dark charcoal. Then the dead man dropped her lifeless body down the riverbank.

"No, no, *no*," Xavier spit through broken teeth. He lunged towards Bri's ragged form, but one of the Flooded Man's massive legs crashed into the space between them. Xavier managed to scramble backwards, towards the tree-covered parts of the trail. He wheezed and wept, *Bri, Bri, Bri* running through his head.

It was darker under the trees. Xavier's eyes swelled and he could barely see the puddles and floodwaters glinting in the grass. But he also thought he could see *streetlights* to the south. Maybe downtown still had power? The rain was heavier, things were slippery, but if he could get to downtown, maybe he could find someone, a cop...

Bri, Bri, Bri.

And he could scream until they got him beyond the city limits.

He wiped at his face, arm coming away slick, but halted, falling to a knee in a bit of cool water.

Up ahead, between him and the streetlights, stood the Flooded Man.

"*Fuck you!*" Xavier screamed.

And though the rain and blood and shadows and pain made it hard to be sure, the Flooded Man pointed *down*. Not to the flooding and the earth, but to something *deeper*. Something more powerful. A thing beyond the Flooded Man.

The devil...

A *thud* of fiberglass on wood sounded from the river and Xavier jolted, even pissing a little. But in a moment, two things occurred to him. One, he remembered the kayaks floating by the shore. Second, he realized that the city limits were far away to the south, the north, the west—everywhere inland. *But* the line between Alexandria and D.C. was just yards out into the Potomac.

He thrashed through the brush before the Flooded Man could move. He fell down the rocks, driftwood, and sharp metal of the riverbank. There it was, as if sent by some guardian god: an Alexandria Titans kayak, paddle rattling around inside.

Shuddering, he shoved the boat into the water. As he paddled against the whipped-up waves, something replaced the broken mantra of *Bri, Bri, Bri.*

Rowing as hard as he could, he recalled the dark form pointing downwards. He imagined being caught in a water-logged and lightless cave, forever stuck in the moment of near drowning. Rolling free onto a sandy beach from an undertow, only for a typhoon to sweep him away. Being sealed in the engine room of a sinking submarine, creaking its way to the depths. It all came together in a few words:

Hell is flooding.

That's what he'd been thinking about when Bri had said *vengeance.* Even when he'd thought *justice* but had known that wasn't right either. It was something that tied to *devil,* to *hell.*

Punishment.

He'd said the Flooded Man's deal was a *devil's bargain,* hadn't he? *A deal with Hell.* What if it was real? What if what had been done to the Flooded Man and the conspiracy around it, at a time of so many conspiracies and so little truth, had created an instrument for devils that found all the world's selfishness and bullshit-sharing *delicious,* a prime time to tempt foolish souls like never before?

And punish them.

You didn't have to believe in COVID for it to kill you, did you?

What if the same was true of Hell?

Xavier paddled with fury, almost whimpering aloud that he didn't hate anyone, didn't want to see anyone punished.

But it would have been such simple a thing to save Bri, wouldn't it? Even at the end? To stop her?

But he hadn't.

Instead, he'd helped put a new devil into the world.

The D.C. coastline was all lights in the storm, from the treatment plant to the Navy lab to the Wharf's shops. And he didn't need to go that far. He only had to paddle into the river's heart, beyond the boundary between cities. And if God granted him that, he swore he'd never come back. He'd do so many good things.

But on the next turn, his paddle caught. Something pulled on it like he'd snagged a hundred-pound catfish. The handle slammed to the fiberglass, catching his hand, sparking agony. Something grabbed the paddle's opposite fin, the one out of the water.

He had time to catch a rotted arm and another decayed *adipocere* face break the waves, this one smaller—a girl's. But more wet and slick arms wrapped around his thighs and chest, even his throat, lashing him into the kayak's body, then over its side.

Alexandriatitaness_2024: They found two more bodies in the river by ALEXANDRIA today! And it's so much worse. They were in LOVE, but they didn't get away. Can anyone???

#FMChallenge

THE BUNNYMAN OF CLIFTON

Brýn Grover

If old enough, you might recall
The stories we were told
Of how he could come for us all
This killer who was bold
They said he wore a bunny suit
And carried 'round an axe
He'd stalk young children like a brute
Committing horrid acts
They said he was the Bunnyman
As thusly we were warned
In tones that seemed a bit deadpan
It made us feel forlorn
He stalked the woods and streets at night
But many also thought
There was in fact a bridge that might
Be where he could be caught
Colchester Road they said was where
This horrid monster dwelt
And had you balls to venture there
A death blow could be dealt
But none of us dared ever go
Beneath that bridge's span
To try and face the fears below
And fight the Bunnyman

PIEDMONT

THE SONG BETWEEN THE SONGS

J.T. Glover

We'd heard about the Tripwire show in Church Hill that morning, and we were both giddy as we opened the rusty gate and started down the worn flagstones. The aging house leaned, one window boarded up and a tarp bricked to the roof, and the rest of the block looked about the same. As we headed down the unlit stairs to the basement, Robert's bald spot bobbed ahead of me like a ghost, and I wondered just how much lead and asbestos we'd be breathing tonight.

Inside, lights bloomed from oscilloscopes, theremins, and other instruments I didn't recognize. Grime and cobwebs coated the cement walls, and the air was heavy with that scent that you get near the peak of summer in Richmond, when everyone's pores switch over and start pumping out sweat thick as motor oil. We'd heard the band made some seriously weird music, but the scene was just a few people standing around, not even a hint of weed in the air. One kid wearing a pink backpack was kind of bouncing on the balls of his feet, swigging from a forty and muttering to himself. The place felt chill—maybe too chill. I looked at my part-time boyfriend and raised an eyebrow.

"You want to go?" Robert said.

"Not really," I said, shrugging. "They sound cool, if they ever show up. Wait and see?"

We'd loaded up with Svedka minis in advance, so I tossed back a Citron, trying not to grimace. During my first year away from home I hadn't gotten to *like* drinking, but I'd learned it was what you did in college and definitely during summer break, when you had too much time alone with your own thoughts. I pulled out another mini, Robert did likewise, and we clicked plastic before downing them.

My shoulders loosened as the alcohol took hold, and I started to see the crowd. There were old white guys wearing checkered suits, a few black kids in super-clean clothes who looked like they'd just come in from the corner, a group of women who looked like they worked downtown, and a random sprinkling of others. The flier that had appeared without warning in Robert's mailbox said that Tripwire played "sacred noise," so I hadn't expected the mustache and ukulele crowd, but this didn't look like *any* kind of crowd. It was just people in a room.

Two guys came in the door and headed straight for the instruments, an Asian kid wearing board shorts and a tank top and an aging white guy in a priest outfit. That gave me a pang—I'd stopped going to church when I moved here, easy as taking off a coat. This was the closest I'd been in a while to anything religious. It felt like nothing at all, and I thought guiltily of my mom, crying the day before I left, making me promise to pray every night.

The musicians started fiddling with the electronics, and an unsteady stream of beeps and crackles filled the basement. The crowd began to draw together, and then a low-powered spotlight flicked on at the far end of the basement, past stacked crates and moldering boxes. A dreadlocked girl, the pale child of Björk and Bob Marley, had been standing in the shadows next to a table covered in exotic brass. She ran one hand over an instrument that looked like a trombone, but with all sorts of extra valves and keys and twists in the pipes where they usually weren't. She lifted it up, made a few adjustments, and then blew.

The sound wasn't like what an instrument is supposed to make. Like wailing, maybe, which I know people sometimes *call* the sound of a horns, but this was... One time I was hiking in Florida with my cousin Rhonda and we came across a wild pig shoulder-deep in quicksand, black eyes rolling like dice and letting out these shrieky gasps. This was like that.

The wailing didn't blend with the hum and the static, not the way that most music is supposed to come together—somehow, some way. It wasn't Ryan Harris, but it wasn't the Sex Pistols, either.

The wailing died off. I looked around, and the audience had gotten tight up on the duo with the electronics. I didn't know how long had passed, but it was hotter, and I'd unbuttoned my shirt partway. Robert was nodding, a puzzled expression on his face.

"Welcome," the woman said, her voice high and reedy. "We've been saving up all week, just for this."

Laughter, and a kid in a Bulls jersey screamed, "Fucking Tripwire!"

Nodding and clapping. One of the yuppies looked like someone had just pinched her ass, eyes bulging, but her friends were whistling. The room felt like wind chimes jangling before a storm.

The woman put down the fucked-up trombone and hefted the world's biggest set of panpipes, built for a twenty-foot satyr. She squatted, hiking up her skirt and letting the dreadlocks cover her face. Her pose resonated in my head, faint echoes of the Mycenean lecture I'd dozed through in Art History 109 last fall.

A ripple went through the crowd.

When she started to blow, I got that what we'd heard already was preamble, and this was the real deal. The sounds the trio was making now were not coherent, a fractured chorus that hurt my ears, but another part of me was listening to something that I hadn't known I needed to hear—it drove out the lost feeling, the wondering if this was all there was to life. A snagging sensation hit my guts, and I couldn't tell whether it was the right thing or a fishhook or a promise of diarrhea from the cart we'd eaten at earlier. Before I could decide anything, the confusion exploded into colorful sweetness, and everything faded away.

Late the next morning found me groggy and pounding on Robert's door.

"Come on, answer the fucking door!" I yelled.

Nothing. I scowled, trying to think through the throbbing headache. I'd woken up alone in my bed an hour ago, memory a blank after the show got going. That hadn't happened since my first weekend away from home, and I guessed it must have been the heat and excitement adding to the booze. The place had been so quiet, with my summer roommate sunning herself down on Ocracoke for the week and Robert not responding to my texts.

His apartment was in a newish building over in Carver that was almost all college students, everything carpeted in a battleship gray that didn't stain too much from puke or party fouls. Nobody had come out into the hall to investigate my pounding and hollering, but at some point someone was going to complain. I scrawled a note on a scrap of paper ("What the fuck, dude. Call me.") and slipped it under the door. Then I headed outside into thick heat that bounced off the concrete and cracked bricks all around. My meandering walk to the apartment took me past The Village, a onetime hippy hangout that had aged into a diner that felt almost like home, so I checked my wallet and slipped inside. A bored-looking server wandered over with coffee, and I ordered breakfast, then took another look at my phone:

Robert, at 11:21 p.m. Hey, where you at?

Robert, at 11:33 p.m: Hellooo...? People are leaving. Are you still inside?

Robert, at 11:58 p.m.: OK, dumbass, I'm headed back in to see if you got lost. If you come back, wait for me on the sidewalk.

Mom, at 8:40 a.m.: Casey, you still coming home this weekend?

I felt uneasy, wondering where I'd been. Mom and dad were downright liberal for country Baptists, but waking up after a blackout was one thing on their Top Ten Do-Not List that I actually avoided. I ran a hand through my hair, thinking that it was going to be time to henna it again soon, then wondering if I should be concerned with my hair after a night like that.

"I'm just saying to watch out." A woman's voice, from the booth behind me. "He's not everything you think he is."

"I'll be fine," a man's voice, trying for brave.

I opened my eyes and looked down at my plate

I'll be fine.

My breakfast lay there, the remains of a meal put together by a cook who liked beauty and order, things that made sense. There was a flower on one side of the plate, a garnish of parsley to the other. The syrup had been drizzled in something that wasn't supposed to be a pattern, but had been—

"Bred from order, bread for order," I said, loudly.

The noise dropped in the booths on either side of me, then picked up again.

Get you home, girlfriend. Someone needs a nap. If you aren't going hunting for Robert again right now, don't just stare at your scrambled eggs talking nonsense.

I rubbed my eyes, and it felt like sandpaper on sandpaper. Out the window, across Harrison Street I saw a woman in a camisole and a ragged peasant skirt limping north, talking to herself. She looked familiar, with her pale skin and dreadlocks, but she'd passed out of sight before I got that it was the singer from the show. I threw a handful of crumpled bills down on the check and bolted, not stopping to ask myself why I was in such a hurry.

Outside, the heat was a wall. Cars were coming and going, but the sidewalk was empty for a block in either direction. Even the crazies were staying out of the sun.

The next day I went by The Full Rack. Flipping through the LPs, I zipped past Tegan and Sara, They Might Be Giants, then Tricky. I got to Tropic of Night...but no Tripwire. Hadn't really expected to find anything, not after fruitless googling, but it had been worth a shot. The A/C in there was heaven on a boiling hot afternoon, though, and thumbing methodically through the records had been an antidote to the sick feeling I was getting about Robert.

Thirty-six hours since I'd lost track of him, and nada. Too early to be worrying about an adult, and he'd dropped out of contact before, but... Deep down I liked him because he was square. He should have been in touch by now, at least tagged me on social. During the semester we might not see each other for a week, but we texted every day, and we always checked in after a wild night. And my patchy-to-absent memories said that show had been kind of wild.

I let the LPs lean back in the bin and wandered around, the mossy green walls lending the place a welcome gloom. Today there was just too much sun, the kind of glaring, brick-oven heat that I'd been told to get used to if I was going to stay in Richmond. That idea itself felt unnatural, having to decide where I—

"Help you find anything?" one of the clerks stocking nearby asked.

"I don't know," I said, shrugging and smiling.

She nodded, tucking a stray lock of aqua hair behind one ear.

"Yeah, this heat, right?" She rolled her eyes. "By the time I get home from a shift, I'm half-blind and just lie in front of the fan."

"It's bad," I replied automatically, wondering at myself.

Why say something so bland? It didn't make sense, but maybe that was okay.

Okay, go play, sound logic.

She was a rail-thin alt-Adele, could have been a dozen girls I'd seen around town at shows or on First Friday or wherever. Record store employee, though, so...

"You know a band called Tripwire?"

"What do they play?"

"It's kind of hard... Ambient jazz? Weird industrial? Something like that."

"Doesn't ring any bells." She frowned, then turned and hollered toward the front. "Hey, Ben, you ever heard of Tripwire?"

At the counter, a balding middle-aged dude in a too-heavy-for-July corduroy sport coat looked up from his laptop.

"Look like crust punks, kinda?" he said in a committed smoker's rasp.

"Maybe," I said. "They didn't seem all that punk, though. I heard they were into 'sacred noise,' when I saw them the other night."

"Sacred noise, huh?"

He looked at his screen again, fingers flying over the keyboard.

"Ben's good," the girl said in a low voice. "I mean, he won't know—probably—the band that your friends formed last week that barely even has a name yet, but he can find anything. Used to be a librarian."

She wiggled her eyebrows, and I didn't know what to say. Where's the bun? He doesn't *look* like an It Girl? The clerk's lips twitched like she was going to say more, and then she turned back to the records.

"Yeah," Ben said, "I thought that's who you meant. They look right?"

He spun the computer around and I saw a dim, grainy picture of the trio from the basement sitting in a forest clearing, circled around a pile of...rocks and bones? It looked like their eyes had rolled back into their heads.

"That's them," I said, eyes flicking to the URL, which was just a string of numbers. "How'd you find this?"

He gave me a sardonic look and said, "I know a guy who knows a guy. This isn't a publicly available website."

"Then how the fuck do I find out about their next show?"

"Gotta be in the know, cutie. But just because you're sooo sweet, it's tomorrow night in an old warehouse down in Manchester. Let me get you the address."

I put a lid on the anger and waited while he wrote. Staring at the pen, it seemed like the world was blurring, the parallel lines writhing on his tablet.

More sleep. You need more sleep.

I took the slip of paper he tore off and walked out the door. The heat swarmed over me like a living thing, but hopefully it wouldn't find me while I slept.

Robert must have been on the other side of the door when I knocked this time. His face was slack like bread dough, and his eyes had gone completely white. The lights were on inside the apartment, but somehow he was still shadowed.

"Come in, come in," he said. "It's about to start."

"Okay."

He turned and trotted back toward the living room, so I stepped in and closed the door. The security bolt caught on the jamb, and I yanked harder. It finally slid across the gap with a screech.

Girlfriend, his door doesn't have *a bolt. Wait...*

"Am I dreaming?"

I looked around at the walls of the entry. The world shimmered, and then it settled down again. The Goya print, the vintage *Empire Strikes Back* poster, and a mask—which was a cool, dead white, and could have been Robert himself, if he'd died young. Maybe a class project from childhood.

I walked into the living room, which was a clearing in front of a cave. Dank, stinking of rotten flesh. Mist covered the ground, and through the thick wall of pines behind me came a thick, chuffing call I'd never heard before. The woods were alive with a terrible vitality that was nothing like the spare and comforting forest rhythms I'd grown up with, and I didn't think...

There isn't any place like this on Earth, not today.

Robert stood facing into the cave, and I saw that his back was covered with sores, some of which were beginning to break open and weep, even as

I watched.

"This isn't real," I said. "I'm dreaming."

"Maybe," Robert replied, "but can you afford to behave as if it's *only* a dream? Everything feels so alive here, don't you think?"

I stared at the ground, which was covered with spongy, yellowish moss. Squatting, I rasped my fingers over it and the ground beside it, marveling at how the tiny rocks and roots snagged at rough spots on the edges of my nails.

Pretty real.

With a start, I came to and realized I'd been in a daze, crouching for a long time. My back hurt and my spine popped like firecrackers as I stood up. I shivered. I'd never noticed such a thing before while asleep, and I was no stranger to waking up in my dreams.

"Where is this?" I said.

"It doesn't matter. We're here now. What matters is what you choose."

In the dim light, it appeared that Robert's sores had begun to blister? They were pulsing as if something solid was going to erupt from them— tentacles? Spines?

"Then I choose a double with fries."

At this, Robert turned around, smiling, and I wished that he hadn't. His sagging face had gone a scabrous, pale gray. His eyes looked...soft, and they were no longer quite spherical.

"Choose," he said, holding out both hands, which opened to reveal what looked like ordinary house keys.

"What's the difference?"

"Look and see."

I stepped closer, edging around a puddle that had welled up among the moss, covered with a nasty, oily scrim. The keys, on closer examination, were brass, each with different ridges and no label. They could have opened any door.

"Take one or both, enter the cave, and choose a door."

"What's behind the doors?" I asked, looking over his shoulder toward the darkness.

"One thing leads to another," he said, "or it doesn't. That was the hardest thing to learn."

I looked up then and stared into his eyes. They were cold and lifeless, the ghosts of eyes, and I could not imagine what they saw.

"Robert, what are you?"

At that his lips quirked, and I knew Robert was still in there, somewhere.

"What I always have been. I've just been away, Casey, for so many years. Time moves different there."

I reached for his left hand, and then the right, hesitating, unable to choose. Then I grabbed both, wrapped my hands around them. When I looked up, the cave was gone, along with the forest and Robert. So was I.

The apartment unspooled from my bed as I awoke, spreading out like a roll of reality. My eyes ached, dry as withered apples. The clock said I'd slept the whole day away. The purple fake-velvet curtains prickled with light-holes, like a ruddy night sky.

Fuck. After a dream like that, why aren't *you over at his place? Or talking to the fucking cops?*

None of that sounded wrong, but it didn't sound right, either. I looked around my room, fallen into disorder that was slovenly even by my I-hate-cleaning standards. In the half-dark, I could hear scuttling sounds that meant I wasn't alone, and my stomach clenched. What was I going to do?

Far away, bells were ringing.

"Gotta go," I said. "See the show, watch to know."

Not thinking, I jumped out of bed and started throwing on clothes, grabbing blindly in the closet. Something inside fell over with a crash as I slammed the apartment door. I should have jumped out of my skin, but instead I headed for the bus stop. The sky was red gold, shadows blooming under the cars. I thought I saw something moving there and blinked hard.

My eyes opened and there was no sound at all, just a crowd seething in a hopping, jerky dance. The ceiling was high, the floor filthy, even in the shadows that were broken only by blue and purple spotlights. I spun around—

Robert, where are you? I saw you—you were in a cave—

At the other end of the room was the band: gyrating, hammering at

drums—enormous copper pipes—

The singer saw me. She grinned and crooked her finger in a beckoning gesture. I started to walk toward her, threading through the crowd, hot pounding inside my skull. This wasn't the basement from the other night. I could smell oil, chemicals. The rounded shapes off to one side could have been barrels. I could just remember the man from the record shop saying something about a warehouse...

A person wearing Robert's face was swaying with his back to a wall not ten feet away.

I felt a rush of relief at first, but then I saw the sores and cuts on his neck, noticed the clothes I'd never seen.

"Robert!" I called

He might have started to turn toward me, but then I felt a pull, as if invisible hands were wrenching my head toward the stage. The singer had donned a mask of hammered bronze and she beckoned again, winking this time. Robert dwindled in my mind—a minor concern, a memory, gone. Logic flickered like a dying light bulb.

That mask. How can a mask wink? I don't—

The sound came back, and it was a dark ocean.

This time I came to on a bench, in a park I didn't recognize. My mouth was open, as if I'd just been speaking. I was soaked with sweat. The clothes I was wearing looked like I'd been crawling around in an auto body shop. They smelled of gasoline.

"The gods don't care who you are," the pale woman was saying, her eyes like bottomless voids as she ran a hand through her dreads. "If they care about anything, I've never figured it out. That's the reward for what we do: not to have to care about anything other than their will."

Smoke was rising in great billows several streets away and screams were audible even from here. I knew with a sick certainty that—but, no, was it sick? Was I certain?

No wind at all, not in a summer heat wave strangling an old part of an old city in an ancient land, heavy with bricks and strangler vines and killing on killing. The sound of sirens came chugging through the air more slowly than it would have elsewhere, and I was glad. Looking around us, I marveled at the great gaps, shimmering holes that made no sensible picture.

What am I here? I am a sculptor. I taste a god in the air. I am Casey Tribbett. I kissed Luke Hawkins' cheek under the magnolia tree in third grade. I belong here, in this world.

The humming of cicadas rose, meshing not at all with the sirens, nor the commotion from the other street.

"Someone died," I said, feeling that the words had nothing to do with me. "I can hear a child screaming."

"There's always a child screaming," she said, squeezing my hand even as her face flickered. "We make sure of that, or not, but we do what we can to make sure that it doesn't matter. To make sure that chaos waits, whichever path you take."

My stomach clenched, like I was ready to vomit, and my head...the pain had eased. The world had fallen to a low, irregular burring sound. My past and all my choices were flowing away from me, like rivulets of ink-stained water.

"Your eyes," she said, smiling. "You're going to the black throne, where the whirlwind reigns. We'll be here if you return."

The pale woman spoke and I could feel the soft wetness of my eyes spreading, the way the body—my body, once—came to seem less and less substantial. Those thoughts circled and swirled like black smoke against a black sky. They were the last things in my mind for a long time.

Where I went and what I saw are release itself, and They took away the pains and doubts of having to choose anything at all. I returned purified, and now I'm part of the band, too. Helping to spread the word, helping to unravel that which should never have been woven. What I learned out there—in lightless rooms where it is always midnight—is for the initiated, but our number is unfixed. There is a song that we have heard between the songs, something that has no love for ordered streets or upright walls. You can hear it, too, if you only listen.

Perhaps in time you too may learn to sing.

A MISCHIEF IN GORDONSVILLE

Valerie B. Williams

The small grey creature balanced on its hind legs, stretching toward the morsel of stale bread just above its head. It reached with tiny pink forefeet, extending the toes like small human hands. Finally, it leaned back on its haunches and leapt straight up, snatching the prize from the fingers of Sergeant Beau Amberson.

"Well done," he chuckled, watching the rat stuff the bread past its long yellow incisors.

A door opened behind him, releasing a babble of noise from the crowded hospital ward. Amberson's heart accelerated and he spun toward the doorway, blocking the view of the rat's hairless tail as it disappeared through a small opening in the wall.

"Oh. Sergeant Amberson. You gave me quite a start!" The matron of the Gordonsville Receiving Hospital stood in the narrow doorway of the storage room, hand to her chest.

"Just getting fresh bandages, Mrs. Millett." He gestured at the shelves piled with linen.

"With the door closed?"

He shrugged. "Must've swung shut."

Abigail Millett frowned. "Sergeant, I do appreciate your assistance, but remember that you must work with the staff. Next time, ask someone to retrieve supplies for you."

"But they were all busy. And Corporal Winston's wound has soaked through." He dropped his gaze. "I was only trying to help."

She patted his shoulder. "I know, my boy. We are all doing our best." Picking up a handful of clean rags, she led him out of the room, but not before hesitating in the doorway and sniffing the air.

Amberson exhaled slowly as he shut the door to the storage room. The stench of urine was becoming stronger. He'd need to find another location within the hospital to meet with his friend.

Sergeant Amberson had fought valiantly at Chancellorsville under General Stonewall Jackson for three days before the general was wounded. Along with most men in his company, Amberson was fiercely loyal to General Jackson and the injury of his commander had shaken him.

Two days after Jackson was wounded, Amberson took a musket ball in his left forearm, just missing the elbow. However, he continued to fight one-armed until a cannonball landed nearby, knocking him unconscious. He remembered little of the transport from battlefield to hospital. When he awoke from surgery to remove the ball from his arm, the doctor told him how lucky he was. He could have lost the limb, as did his beloved commander. Two weeks after his surgery, Amberson heard that General Jackson had succumbed to his injuries. The dreadful news released the guilt he'd been holding at bay, overwhelming him and sending him into a deep depression.

The Gordonsville Receiving Hospital, like many near the front lines of the war, was severely understaffed. With consent from the doctors, Mrs. Millett recruited soldiers who were on the road to recovery to help care for those more seriously wounded. Amberson believed that keeping busy would help him escape the jaws of the black dog of depression, so he agreed to help. With little training and sketchy supervision, Amberson joined the ranks of soldier/orderly three months after his arrival.

Amberson's new role allowed him to roam the hospital at will. Situated next to the railroad tracks, the building had been The Exchange Hotel before the war. Its faded elegance still shone through, even when the bedrooms, parlors, and both large outside porches were filled with wounded men. He took advantage of his newfound freedom and explored all three stories of the great building.

He'd been poking around the storage room off the second-floor ward late one evening, familiarizing himself with its contents, when a scratching, scuttling noise came from the corner. He glanced over to see a large rat sitting on its haunches with front paws folded over its belly, like a man after a particularly satisfying meal. The creature regarded him with strange, pale blue eyes.

Rats, a constant presence in the hospital, ate anything they could, including poultices still applied to a soldier's body. Mrs. Millett was in a perpetual state of war with the pests. Amberson, however, had kept a pet rat when he was a boy and found them highly intelligent.

Intrigued by this unusual specimen, he crouched and held out his hand. The rat dropped to all fours, whiskers twitching, and maintained eye contact. Amberson chirruped and the rat squeaked in reply but kept its distance. Slowly, Amberson reached into his pocket and pulled out a small piece of hardtack. He held it off to the side and the rat followed the food with its eyes. Amberson tossed the scrap toward the rat, which grabbed it and disappeared through a hole at the base of the wall.

Amberson returned to the storage room the following night. Finding it empty, he was about to leave when he heard the familiar scuttling and turned to see the rat once again perched on its haunches watching him with a cool blue gaze that seemed oddly familiar. This time, Amberson waited until the rat had taken a couple of steps toward him before delivering the treat. The rat ran off with its bounty, but not before uttering a series of squeaks, as if it were saying thank you.

Over the next few weeks, Amberson and the rat became companions. He volunteered to set Mrs. Millett's traps in the areas his friend frequented, but then neglected to bait them. The animal appeared grateful for the intervention and even brought some of its brethren to visit on occasion.

Since his arrival at the hospital Amberson had been plagued by insomnia and, when he did sleep, was haunted by vivid nightmares of battle. Particularly of Chancellorsville. One night, he bolted upright in his cot drenched in sweat. The rat had the same light blue eyes as the great Stonewall Jackson! It was highly intelligent, more so than any other rat he'd ever encountered, and its posture at times was almost human. Could it be? Was it possible?

He slipped out of bed and crept from closet to closet before finding the rat in the pantry. The rat paused its scavenging and looked up, its blue eyes reflecting the dim light of the moon streaming through the single high window.

"General?" Amberson felt both foolish and hopeful.

The rat bobbed its head and squeezed through a hole in the wall.

A shaken Amberson returned to his cot, memories of the General spinning through his mind. Had the rat nodded in the affirmative? Or had he imagined it? Was he going mad?

The following week saw an influx of patients, so he had little time to pursue his theory. But after a lighter-than-usual day, he slipped from his cot and silently searched for the rat. Finding it once again in the pantry, he crouched and whispered, "General Jackson?"

The rat approached him, sat back on its haunches, and raised its left foreleg high in the air.

Overcome by sudden dizziness, Amberson clutched a shelf for balance. General Jackson had once had a habit of making just such a motion! In fact, he had been injured in the left hand at the First Battle of Bull Run while holding his arm high. Amberson crouched and cupped his hands. The rat stepped into them. He lifted the creature until they were eye to eye. Tears blurred Amberson's vision.

As a member of the 18th North Carolina Infantry, Sergeant Amberson was one of the sentries who'd been ordered to fire upon Jackson and his party as they returned to camp; a horrible case of mistaken identity. He had no way of knowing whether his bullet had led to the general's death.

The rat ground its teeth rapidly, a sign of contentment. Could this also be a gesture of forgiveness?

Amberson placed the creature back on the ground. It raised itself on its haunches, gave a final one-legged salute, and scuttled into the wall. The man dropped his face into his hands and sobbed.

Convinced that the rat was indeed his beloved general reborn, Amberson did everything he could to make up for possibly killing the man. First and foremost, he ensured the rat didn't want for food, setting aside bits of his own rations to feed the creature. When he came upon a rare slice of lemon, whatever niggling doubt may have remained as to the nature of his new friend was erased. Lemons had been a favorite of Jackson the man. Jackson the rat gobbled the lemon, then begged for more.

Once Amberson realized who he was dealing with, he no longer required Jackson to perform silly tricks and was embarrassed that he'd ever asked the great soul to do so. Jackson brought more and more rats with him on his visits, seemingly building his own personal mischief.

The soldier felt a responsibility to ensure that Jackson and his friends were well-fed. Acquiring that much "spare" food in a time of scarcity was challenging, but Amberson sought opportunities to glean more food.

He'd been successful until the day a large sack of dried hominy was left unattended in the kitchen. Glancing around, he set down the meal trays he'd been about to deliver and scooped a double handful of grain from the sack, filling both pockets. He then quickly sliced a slab of pork from the chopping block. He was about to pocket that as well when Mrs. Millett swept into the room.

"Pork is not on the menu until dinner, Sergeant. Are we not feeding you well enough?" She stood with her hands on her hips, blocking the doorway.

"Umm, it's for Private Sullivan, Ma'am." Amberson shuffled his feet, holding the pork in front of his body. "He had a very bad night and was begging for meat. I should have asked permission first, but he reminds me so of my brother." He gave her his best pleading look.

Unmoved, she shook her head. "Put it back. We must preserve our rations, and Private Sullivan will receive his meat tonight, along with the others. There can be no special treatment. Do you understand?"

Amberson returned the pork to the block, continuing to face the matron to better conceal the bulge of purloined grain in his pockets.

"I'm very disappointed in you, Sergeant. You should know better. Now, deliver those trays."

"I'm sorry, Ma'am. It won't happen again."

Amberson made sure it didn't. The matron never again caught him with stolen food. But his past success at feeding the mischief led to another problem. The hospital staff noticed the increased rat population, as did Mrs. Millett, who intensified her campaign against the pests.

After noting that the traps set by Amberson never caught any rats, she took the responsibility away from him and gave it to another orderly. The matron personally inspected all traps once they were set and had poison added to the bait in the event a rat managed to carry it away. She went on a cleaning binge, assigning orderlies to move shelves and scrub everything in sight to eliminate places where the vermin could hide. Holes in walls and floors were flushed with water, then sealed off. Two weeks after she started her campaign, over two dozen rats had been trapped, poisoned, or clubbed to death.

It became harder for Amberson to meet with his friend as their rendezvous points were cleared of clutter and rat passageways through the building closed. He didn't see Jackson for the next three weeks, but neither (thankfully) had he found him among the casualties. The rat's skill at evading traps, unlike his followers, reinforced Amberson's belief in the animal's true nature.

One night after the latest losses to the colony, a doe and two pups, he felt a sharp pain on his ankle and threw back the blanket to see Jackson crouched at the foot of his cot. Blood trickled down Amberson's instep and smeared the rat's front teeth. The creature's blue eyes blazed, and he nodded his head vigorously but remained silent, as if aware of the danger of waking anyone else.

Amberson's emotions see-sawed—relief at seeing Jackson, shock at being bitten, and finally fear of being discovered. He scanned the dormitory in panic. The other orderlies were still asleep. He slipped on boots, scooped the rat into his blanket, and carried him outside to the gardening shed. By the light of the moon, he released Jackson onto the ground. The general glared and stamped his front feet.

"I'm sorry," Amberson whispered. "She's on a tear. I'm doing everything I can."

Jackson's noticeable weight loss showed the effect of Mrs. Millett's efforts. A skinny rat scurried out from the shed and stood beside him. Then another and another, a seething carpet of grey bodies. The rats were silent, beady eyes fixed on their general.

Amberson's jaw dropped. There must be nearly two hundred rats! He hadn't realized how large the mischief had grown.

Jackson stood on his haunches and raised his left front leg. After a rapid series of squeaks ending in a scream, he dropped to all fours and led his army past the vegetable garden toward the edge of the surrounding woods. Amberson followed at a distance. When the mass of rats made a sharp right turn, he realized where they were going and broke into a run.

He didn't catch up until they halted in front of two graves dug just that morning. Jackson perched on a mound of freshly turned earth and squeaked once more. The army of rats began digging. In no time they had uncovered the body of Private Massie, a boy of just seventeen, mortally wounded in his first engagement. The eyes were the first to go, then lips were nibbled and forced open to yield the tender tongue. A trio of rats joined forces to claw and chew through the belly, opening it for others to bury their pointed noses in bloody bowels.

Amberson stood frozen, sickened but afraid to sound the alarm. If he did, he would betray his general. He'd been given a second chance to serve the great soul. But the rats were desecrating a soldier's body! This boy didn't deserve such a fate after his heroic death. Overcoming his indecision, he jogged back to the gardening shed and returned with a shovel. He swung it toward the cluster of rats, scattering them. The shovel missed the rats but embedded itself in the chest of the corpse. Amberson let go of the handle and backed away, horrified. The shovel stood upright as if it had sprouted from the dead boy.

Amberson's legs gave out and he crumpled to the ground with a cold sweat trickling down his back. He clambered to his hands and knees and vomited, then crawled to a large oak, propped his back against it and closed his eyes. Exhausted, he didn't know how long he rested—he may even have slept.

A soft squeak and the abrasive crunch of grinding teeth roused him. Jackson sat at his feet, belly round and distended, fur cleansed of blood and shining. His army was nowhere in sight.

"General," Amberson rasped through his scalded throat. "This could have been one of your men." He flailed his arm toward the pitiful remains. "You always looked out for your soldiers."

The rat nodded, lifted his left front leg, waddled away, then looked back over his shoulder before continuing. Amberson wearily pushed himself to his feet and followed. Jackson led him to a clearing just beyond the cemetery. The clearing was filled with a pile of rats, bellies full and sound asleep. Jackson captured Amberson in his blue gaze, as if willing him to understand.

"*These* are your soldiers now," said Amberson, realization dawning. "But you cannot do this again." He crouched and cupped his hands. "I promise you'll have enough food. All of you."

Jackson crawled into the sergeant's cupped hands. Amberson lifted the creature to eye level, and a wordless understanding passed between them. The man placed the general gently on the pile, where he curled up to sleep with his soldiers.

Amberson returned to Massie's grave to rebury what was left of the private. He pried the shovel from the boy's chest and had no sooner filled his first shovelful of dirt when he heard a gasp. He whirled to see a horrified Mrs. Millett, clutching her dressing gown and pulling it close in the cold night air.

"What are you doing?" she cried.

"I... I can explain." Amberson stopped. How could he *possibly* explain? Surely he looked like some sort of ghoul or a grave robber. He tried again. "I couldn't sleep so I came to the pump for some water. I heard noises from the graveyard and came to investigate."

"Noises? What sort of noises?"

Amberson stepped toward the matron. She pulled a small pistol from her pocket and aimed it at his face. He halted, hands up in appeasement.

"Squeaking noises, Ma'am. It sounded like rats." Amberson silently pleaded for Jackson's understanding.

"Look!" Amberson shuddered and swept his arm toward the remains, still exposed in the night air. The ravages of the feeding frenzy were obvious. "It *was* rats, more rats than I'd ever seen before. I beat at them with the shovel to drive them away."

Mrs. Millett lowered the pistol, stepped closer, and peered at Private Massie. The color drained from her face. She made the sign of the cross, mumbled a few words, and then glared at Amberson. Her voice shook with rage, horror, or both. "Why were you burying him, hiding the evidence of this, this violation?" she demanded, pointing the pistol once more. "You didn't think to report the incident?"

"I was only thinking of Private Massie, Ma'am. It would be un-Christian to leave him like this." He looked down and scuffed his toe into the dirt, afraid to meet her eyes. "And a lady shouldn't have to see such a sight."

"Do you really believe me that delicate?" Mrs. Millett stepped toward him and shook a finger in his face. "After running this hospital for two years I can assure you I have an iron constitution." She paced, waving the pistol in the air as she spoke. "Desecrating a grave is a serious offense."

"I know where the rats went!" Amberson said. He needed to remain free to serve his general. The mischief was expendable. "I saw them run that way." He pointed to the west, toward the clearing. "Please. You must believe me."

"No, Sergeant, I do not believe you. You've become quite a problem over the past weeks. Now I discover..." She gestured toward the disturbed earth and sighed. "I must be able to depend on my orderlies. I believe it's time for you to return to your unit."

Amberson's pulse pounded in his ears. He'd hoped to serve out the war at the hospital. He'd be unable to protect Jackson from the front.

"Mrs. Millett, please. If the rats are where I think they are, we can kill many of them at once. They will likely be too sated to move quickly. Let me show you." He shouldered the shovel and backed toward the woods, never taking his eyes off her.

Mrs. Millett frowned and rubbed her temples. "Very well. But only because you showed such early promise. If what you say is true and we can finally rid the hospital of these pests, perhaps you may stay on." She dropped the pistol to her side and followed his lead.

Amberson's heart sang with hope. He wouldn't have to leave after all! He pushed aside low-hanging branches and led the way into the clearing. The empty clearing. Empty but for the glint of a pair of small blue eyes in the bushes to the left.

"This is where they went, I swear!" He avoided looking toward Jackson.

Mrs. Millett stepped into the center of the clearing and turned a slow circle. "The grass is trampled," she said. "Something was here. But there is no evidence of rats." She shook her head. "I'm sorry Sergeant Amberson, but it seems my first instinct was correct. The incident at the grave must be fully investigated. Please return with me." She raised the pistol once more, using it to gesture toward the hospital.

Suddenly, Jackson sprinted out of the bushes directly toward Mrs. Millett. She screamed and pointed the gun at the rat.

"Stop!" shouted Amberson. In two long steps, he tackled Mrs. Millett, pushing her to the ground and wresting the pistol away. Jackson stood mere inches from the woman's face, back arched and hissing.

"Lie still! He won't hurt you," Amberson promised.

She opened her mouth to scream, but before Amberson could slap his hand over her mouth to silence her, the rat squirmed between her lips and clamped onto her tongue. Her scream was reduced to a gurgle. As if that were the signal, the rest of the mischief boiled out of the surrounding woods, dozens upon dozens of rats clambering over both people.

"No!" shouted Amberson, struggling to his feet. The rats fell off as he rose, none of them attempting to bite or cling to him. Mrs. Millett was not so fortunate, as the grey bodies quickly became streaked with red. The poor woman! Her muffled moans of pain were nearly drowned out by the wet sounds and squeaks.

Amberson aimed the pistol at a cluster of rats running toward her and pulled the trigger, only to have it misfire. Remembering the shovel, he retrieved it and swatted away as many furry bodies as he could reach. The rat army finally stopped when Jackson let out a high-pitched series of squeaks, raised his left front leg, and led them back into the woods.

Amberson stood panting, leaning on the shovel and looking down at the motionless woman. He knelt and felt a weak pulse in her neck. Relieved, he drew back his hand and wiped her blood on his trousers. Mercifully, she had lost consciousness. In addition to her tongue, the rats had taken the matron's eyes, all the fingers on her right hand, and the thumb and forefinger of her left hand. But Jackson had remained honorable and did not allow his followers to kill her.

Amberson picked up the matron and carried her back to the hospital, with a quick stop to rebury Private Massie. He then "found" her on the lower back porch and called for help. Of course, he knew nothing about what had happened to the unfortunate woman.

After three days in the hospital, Mrs. Millett's sister arrived from

Georgia and whisked her away to recover from her injuries, so she was never able to tell of the night's events.

Despite the removal of Mrs. Millett, Amberson was indeed redeployed. One week after the matron was injured, the doctors declared Sergeant Amberson well enough to return to the field. The reluctant soldier was rounded up, along with a half-dozen other men, to join General Johnson's Stonewall Division in Orange County.

On the morning of his redeployment, Sergeant Amberson made certain he was the last soldier to board the northbound transport train, flicking his eyes left and right as he mounted the step. A whiskery face with striking blue eyes poked out of his rucksack, chittered loudly, then ducked back inside the warm nest. As the doors of the railcar slid slowly closed, several small shadows darted aboard.

LOST SOUL

a blackout poem of Ligeia by Edgar Allan Poe

María Badillo

My soul, perhaps, cannot *now* be my beloved.

The thrills of the unknown decay near ancient doubt,
deaden mine eyes, my own passionate devotion.

I have utterly forgotten the spirit
emaciated in vain to portray the incomprehensible slumbering souls
we have been falsely taught to worship.

Without some *strangeness,*
how cold, indeed, the regions above the temples.
The free spirit, the triumph, the magnificent ray of holy light,
scrutinized, possessed, forgotten.
We find ourselves *upon the very verge* of remembrance,
without being able, in the end, to remember.

Once, the universe passed into my spirit.
I felt aroused. I felt the falling. I felt the magnitude.
I have been filled with it by passages from books,
a great will pervading all things.

Man, that violent vulture of passion and of words
forced itself upon my attention.

The chaotic marriage of all that is ethereal
slows before me
gorgeous, untrodden, a wisdom too precious to be forbidden.
How poignant the grief.
I—wanting the radiant luster of letters golden upon the pages—grew ill,
became the waxen hue of the grave, grim and stern.
Resistance wrestled with the Shadow
amid the most convulsive writhings of spirit, of mortal aspirations.

I doubted my passionate devotion, I,
cursed with the removal of my beloved.

ODDITORIUM

Sidney Williams

A few days into the trip, Christian has stayed true to the pact—set phones to "Avoid Highways" and "Avoid Tolls" and see where that takes them. Alana lobbied for this path beyond Love's truck stops, reasoning it would get them more hearts on Insta. Until he caved, Christian was initially more interested in museums and shopping in Nashville.

Along the way, they've posted pictures with lots of hashtags, becoming part of the #*vanlife* kindred. Hey, it's a sense of community. And it's no frills with Christian's brother's Pössl letting them put problems in the rearview.

For the moment, Alana is happy not to deal with her parents' reminders she isn't the image they conjured at birth of the perfect daughter. She took little interest in Barbies and turned to books instead of baking.

Lately, their carping has focused on student loans and majors. She's at a decision point. If she holds fast on the track she's drawn to instead of the business focus they hoped for, they have suggested she might need to assume all re-payment responsibilities.

She's been told over and over she needs to commit to something. But she's tired of the business curriculum and the whole 'Dores universe. She's had enough of trying to fit in at a sorority with all the Panhellenic bullshit from The Three Bitch Sisters, Madison, Kayla, and Brooke.

At least it's all something she can think about later. This trip puts everything on pause.

Hikes outside Asheville instead of the more obvious tour of the Biltmore or botanical gardens offer the first real sense of escape, and in late afternoon, wispy veils drift across the Blue Ridge Mountains for postcard scenes as their path winds northward.

They slip into Virginia via Danville, finding an artsy—if quiet and a little dusty—downtown that's fun in spite of ubiquitous Confederate flags on the periphery. Danville, Christian discovers in googling, was the final capital of Confederate states. Explains it all, but it's still unsettling to a pair of people who track as "a little different."

"The city council voted a good while back not to display them on public property, but a lot of people and businesses don't want to let go of their old ways," a sandwich shop waitress tells them.

A few miles later, while Christian is at the wheel, maybe in defiance of their anxieties, they decide to give an old man a lift.

"He could be interesting," Christian says.

"Or he could be a Klansman who hates androgynous and or artsy people."

"He wouldn't even know the word androgynous," Christian says.

He pulls onto the shoulder, sticking one skinny arm out to wave the old man their way.

The guy trots up to the bumper, pushing back a Panama hat and hesitating only a moment when he takes in Christian's black eyeliner and death metal tee. He offers a second look Alana's way as if he expects—gypsy skirt and piercings aside—that an ethereal girl-next-door passenger with wavy blond hair might blink a distress signal. Alana just offers a smile.

"Could use a lift," he says, coughing a bit. "Trying to get up close to Lynchburg."

He looks safe enough, a tangle of gray hair beneath the hat. His loose-fitting shirt has a vintage bowling-league cut exposing faded blue tat sleeves on his forearms.

In a few seconds, the old guy is in a swivel seat at Christian's back.

"Name's Robert."

He extends a hand, which Alana accepts, and makes their introductions. "What's in Lynchburg?"

She recalls a Falwell university or something there, but she wonders what he'll say.

"Lots, but I'm looking for my brother. Lost touch with him a couple of years back. We're gettin' on in years, so I thought it would be good to catch up."

"He lives there?"

"Well, really nearby, last anyone heard. My cousin said a little place called Evington."

"That's just a few miles," Alana says, checking her phone.

"Don't want you to go out of your way."

"Looks like a straight shot."

Maybe they can at least reunite someone else with family and belonging. Her family has been dysfunctional as long as she can remember. Her brother packed his bags when she was still a kid. He'd never looked back, fed up with the family's devotion to appearances and pragmatism.

She's always admired his move, but she also always reminds herself the family way is the easy path, even as the focus of all perfection desires as the one left behind.

She glances Christian's way and ticks up and eyebrow in inquiry. Should they help the old guy? He nods.

"Plugging in the coordinates. Shouldn't take more than an hour."

"Is this a town or what?" Christian asks, picking up a bit of speed as the GPS spits instructions.

"Little community. Biggest claim to fame's the circus train wreck, I guess."

"Circus train wreck?"

The old man takes on an enthusiastic tone Alana dubs his Boy Howdy. "Ringling Brothers back in the '50s. They say a bunch of gorillas escaped and lived in the wilds nearby."

"Looks like that's considered an urban legend," Alana says after a web search.

"I've always heard it for true." He gives a nod, emphasized by the snap of his hat brim, and his eyes grow bright. "It's said once upon a time you'd see a gorilla on a housetop now and again. Though I've also heard it's a little further westerly, near an old town called Rehoboth, just a bump in the road, and there's a lot of woods there. Lotta woods in Virginia period, so it'd make sense they could live there. That's the land the Iroquois and other tribes hunted, though not many settled for some reason."

"I can't imagine apes would like Virginia winters," Christian says.

The guy shrugs. "Unless they were mountain gorillas or just able to adapt. Me, I like the summers here better than the Deep South. Ever been to Alabama in July?"

"A selfie with one of the gorillas would get us some Instagram likes," Christian says, half-joking, but maybe buying into the true off-the-beaten path call at last.

Alana throws up her hands. "I guess it's decided."

～✦～

They let the old man off at a red-brick post office in a road fork then pick a tine and drive onward, peering into woods as they cruise. No sign of hairy primates. At least this lark should bring a few laughs. After a while, Alana shoots a YouTube video of the passing trees and the shadows between, narrating with a Jane Goodall accent. A fun selfie from the hood of the van later is good for an Instagram post announcing their quest.

Rehoboth isn't in any mapping system. Alana pieces directions together and determines it once sat in the midst of a lot of green, rolling forest land at a little higher elevation, an area not as well-known as the Shenandoah National Forest or the Blue Ridge Parkway. She checks the detail against old railroad routes and finds some correlation, and it seems reasonable. They veer off their current path, where a construction crew is at work, and head up a road less traveled.

"Well, this road's had nary a lick," Christian says.

Alana gives him a puzzled look.

"Beaten path. A lick, a hit? Ah, if you gotta explain 'em... Not sure this route is gonna pay off in the likes department."

The stretch is indeed a narrow asphalt ribbon with neglected potholes and jagged shoulders.

"Look, if you're getting tired of this, we can pack it in," she says.

Christian is steering with one wrist draped over the steering wheel. He glances at Alana from the corner of his eye.

"You're not the one getting cold feet now are you? I can go a while longer at least until we get to Rio Linda or wherever."

"Rehoboth."

"Re-ho we go."

He seems a little jazzed at last.

The more isolated they become, the more a sense of trepidation sets in for Alana. She peers into dense roadside shadows, wondering if they'll spot any sign of life, and if they do, what form it will be?

The town looks as neglected as the road, which becomes a main street of cracked pavement separating parallel rows of empty shops with streaked windows. The first sign of life's a legless old man on crutches who sways up a side street before they get near him.

That at least points them to a diner at the end of the main drag where everyone left in town heads for lunch. They draw the usual circumspect looks from baseball-cap- and straw-hat locals and wedge themselves onto seats at a counter.

There they listen to a waitress shouting above other conversations to convince a woman with tangled dishwater curls and pencil-thin arms that the lunch portion now includes just three pieces of fried chicken. The woman really looks like she could use a fourth's calories. She's a skeleton with flesh.

"So, is this the area where the circus train wrecked?" Alana asks after they've placed their order.-

"Way before my time," the waitress says with a tick of her head. "Mrs. Sprague's one who might remember something like that."

The gesture's toward the skinny woman.

"Oh yes," her quivering voice answers when they join her and Alana manages to make herself heard. "It was earlier than '52. My grandfather used to talk about it. There was a big circus train wreck in Pennsylvania in the 1800s and some of the details get crossed, I think."

"Did your grandfather ever actually see a gorilla?" Christian asks, leaning past Alana to within an inch of the woman's ear.

"Can't recall," she says after eyeing Christian for a moment of assessment. "Just heard the stories like everyone else. If they're anywhere anymore, it'd be up near the lake, I reckon."

"We could kind of pick a strategic spot, walk around. Camp, even."

"Google showing any KOAs?" Christian asks.

"Nothing that luxurious. Maybe you were right. Maybe a city and some museums would be more fun. Even back to Nashville. That's quite a mall there."

He throws up his hands. "Oh, come on. We can manage a night or two in the van without hookups and shower facilities. It's for the sake of the quest. We've come this far. Gotta suffer for likes, right?"

He lifts his eyebrows and cocks his head, his best accusatory look.

"Gotta suffer for likes."

Alana just stares back. "Don't you have the zeal of the converted all of a sudden? All right. A few more lengths. Then we'll splurge on a nice hotel."

"Sure," Christian says. "That'll be glorious."

They settle on a spot with a rusty red-white-and-blue trashcan on a post near decaying picnic tables. Sometime or other this must have been a semi-official rest stop. Maybe it's park land neglected by one branch of government or another.

"You think you'll remember this trip?" Christian asks, munching trail mix beside their little campfire. "Sometime down the road when we've drifted in different directions?"

"Think that will happen?"

One of his sullen moods seems to be settling over him. "I know it will. People like you, you're kinda wannabes. You're terrified of being average, so you're tourists in the odditorium. You want to feel better about yourselves than your snob friends, so you find a pal flying a freak-flag to show the world you're different too. Oh and tolerant. You're not as bad about virtue signaling as some, but we both know any diversion from the norm for you is a dalliance. You're not going to pursue the arts or anything too far outside the lines. Take the ring out of your nose and let the piercings grow over, and you can fit right back in with your sorority friends, marry an accountant. Get that little tat on your arm and the snake-skin tat on your hip sand-blasted, you can wear high-cut one-pieces at the country club pool once the kids are born. Bingo, you're 'normal' again. Maybe, MAYBE, you'll head the arts council for the Junior League or something, but that's the highest peak."

She fingers the little gold ring that fits tightly against her left nostril. So he hasn't missed details or subtext.

"I don't have any choice about being what I am," he says. "I could get a regulation haircut, drop the eyeliner, but my voice, my manner, attitude all the defining things, they're always going to be what they are. I didn't affect those traits. They're just me. Ditto where my interests point me. There's no junior Citibank position for me in the cards."

She dwells on his point and its sting as they fold seats down and make the bed, the sky roof uncovered so they can stare at the stars. Dozing after all this takes her a while. She's not sure when sleep comes.

She only realizes her brain is fuzzy when her eyes sag open later. Some creak of metal? Or some other sound?

The face peering down is out of focus with no direct light striking the features. Then it's gone.

Gone so quickly it is an impression rather than a sighting.

She really just takes in an odd shape, a head not quite the familiar form of a person's. She thinks she'll scream, but her throat seizes so only a whimper rolls over trembling lips. Repeating that sound to stir Christian takes effort. As he mumbles through half-sleep, she regains power over her limbs and shakes him.

"Something, looking in."

"Something?"

The sky roof now offers a blank field of stars. Christian stares for a moment then checks to see if she's serious. Finally, he rolls over, folding his arms on his pillow to look out a side window for himself.

"There's a bit of mist, but I'm not spotting any gorillas. A silverback would rattle a van pretty good, wouldn't it? You think it could have been a raccoon?"

"It... It wasn't a fucking raccoon."

"You sure?" He encircles his eyes with his fingers. "Would have been wearing a mask."

"Cut that out. It wasn't anything…ordinary."

"We must be in the right spot then."

She balls a fist and slams his shoulder. It connects with more force than she intended, and he winces.

"Sorry, but I'm serious here."

"All right. I'll have a look."

He crawls to the side door and pops it open to look out, right, left, forward.

"Careful."

Mist slithers amid shadows, illuminated by a bit of moonlight seeping through the network of branches, chasing murk away while not really mitigating the gloom.

"Looks like he got *clean* away," Christian says, affecting a local accent.

He takes a few paces toward the wood's edge.

"Be careful," Alana repeats.

"It's fine. Do you really think there's a pride of gorillas living out here that hasn't turned up on Google Earth or some other satellite?"

"Maybe there's still enough foliage cover. But a group of gorillas is a troop. Pride is lions."

"Really and whatever. No troops in sight, right?"

Alana nods then turns and moves inside, muscles stiffening with her aggravation. If she were closing the door, she'd slam it.

After Christian has eased it shut, she doubles back. If he's not going to take it seriously, she at least needs to make sure the latch clicks into place, just in case *anything* out there possesses opposable thumbs.

They decide to seek fresh provisions and someone else's coffee around nine the next morning, and Alana adds a little extra black eyeliner in answer to Christian's earlier accusations. She doesn't want him to be right even if he is.

"How long do you want to keep up the pursuit?" Christian asks as they trace a curvy road that takes them to even a little higher elevation where they have a view of rolling hills covered in green forest.

She doesn't want to be the one to cave either. "We're seeing some pretty country aren't we?"

They take turns posing for selfies in front of the general store they happen upon. It was spruced up at some point with blue trim and a coat of white paint, but grime and patches of green mold have mounted a new challenge.

Inside, Pinterest-worthy displays of candy sticks and preserves in jars decorated with blue plaid cloth collect dust. The teenage clerk is reading a *People* from months back and has heard no tales of gorillas nor wrecked circus trains but suggests someone around might.

Alana's thinking it's time to call it even if it has to be her decision when they spot the bald guy in black. He loiters near the van when they emerge, not particularly tall, his skull pronounced above the forehead with a straight brow ridge that almost shades his eyes. He's looking for a ride.

"You wouldn't get far with us," Christian says. "We're practically going in circles looking for a lost tribe, sorry troop, of what I'm thinking must be mountain gorillas."

"Aw, yeah, you heard da rumors." Speech is slow with words ill-formed. "You prolly heard Ringling Brothers, but it wadden no big circus like dat." An exaggerated laugh of the ha-ha-ha variety bursts skyward as his head tilts back.

"It was further back than the '50s, one of those rag-tag travelin' shows, one of the last of the creepy old sideshows dat were banned. They tried-ah ban 'em anyway, but they'd slip from town to town and do their thing until they got run off. Some of 'em were people with real conditions and deformities. Those were the big stars, the sideshow royalty. A lot of 'em just pretended, though."

"Pretended what?" Christian asks.

"To be half man, half woman, say. Somebody'd just build up one side, tone muscles, keep the other side feminine and soft then wear a split outfit. Or they'd sit in a fake spider body or some other rig, or anything like that they could come up with, file their teeth, anything. Tough times, you know. Maybe they needed or wanted to be part of somethin', da community it offered 'em. Though I don't think after the train wreck the show ever turned up again. I guess they said the hell with it. Decided not to go back to shitty treatment by the shitty management and dispersed."

"Were there really animals on the train?"

"Dere may have been a few gorillas and other animals like's talked about. Prolly long dead."

"Unless they reproduced," Alana says. "It was in this area?"

"They could have settled nearby, I s'pose. The area north of the lake's not as popular for camping anymore."

"Well thank you for your time," Christian says, nudging Alana toward the van.

"Having some fun with the tourists," he says when they reach the passenger door.

"He made all that up?"

"How the hell would he know? Maybe he was the guy you saw looking in the window. Could have stuck with us by doing the Robert De Niro thing from that old movie *Cape Fear.* You know, clinging to the drive shaft. Do you want to give this up?"

That's tempting, and he'd be the one caving, but they've come this far. Plus, the payout in likes will be astronomical. Likes and discovery—that's what this trip's supposed to be about. It has led to a little personal discovery.

"Let's give it just a little more time," Alana says. "See it through, see where it all takes us."

She'll just be checking under the van from now on. That's for damned sure.

They head back to their campsite and, still getting about one bar on one phone, they take another look at a map, noting the position of the lake. It will be easy enough for a hike winding north even though the land becomes a little hilly there.

The trail they happen upon after a while stretches in that general direction, through a grove of oaks with thick, almost primordial-looking trunks and tangles of tentacle roots.

"Nobody's touched this for a while. We look around here, and we call it a quest then head up toward Charlottesville," Christian says. "Agreed?"

Alana plucks a water bottle from her shoulder pack and sips.

"Agreed. Just a littler longer. At least lets us get to higher ground and get some scenic shots."

"Remember likes aren't really affirmation," Christian says.

"Maybe not to you."

After a few tries, they find a break in the thickest clustering of trunks and move forward when the trail becomes a narrow dirt path, stretching past what might be rabbit runs in the underbrush.

"There's some life out here anyway," Christian says.

A little further along they spot exposed dirt with bigger openings carved into the earth.

Christian shakes his head. "Big enough for gorillas?"

He kneels and looks into one, and when he sees only shadow, he turns on his phone's flashlight and shines it into the opening. Just a short distance in, the little tunnel seems to curve.

"Rabbits again?"

"Some burrowing critter," Christian says.

The intertwining vegetation almost becomes a buttress, adding shadow to ground beneath the trees. At least it's cooler, and Alana feels a little rush. They might have confirmation on territory that could be shielded from basic satellite photos. They really could be close to proving the legend true. Okay, elation is tempered by a touch of the willies. What will wild apes be like?

The rustle in underbrush to their right startles them, but when they look in that direction, they see nothing. Christian decides it's time for an about-face. He doesn't offer an opportunity for debate.

Though Alana has had no sense they were being followed, she sees movement on the trail when they spin. Not just movement. Slithering. A thick speckled and scaly form slides across the path. *Thicker than a python. What the hell?*

It thrashes into brush, then on into deeper vines and clutches of thin, young trees beside the trail. Then the underbrush wiggles as it circles back.

Alana freezes as trail-side weeds are pushed aside by furry arms.

The face that emerges is a dark purple, and a hiss escapes drawn-back lips, exposing rows of sharp fang-like teeth. Filed-teeth? This is not a chimp, and it's way worse than anything she saw through the van skylight, but something else troubles her about it.

Christian grips Alana's arm and they spin, hoping for another direction, an escape, but they're suddenly facing a woman's body. A headless body, but it's walking. Moving toward them.

Alana's afraid her heart is seizing. This is impossible, but there's a headless thing in front of her.

Wait!

It's a stick with cascades of faded cloth, not errant wires, stretching from the neck.

Is it some kind of weird headdress that creates a headless look?

Has to be.

For a moment, Alana lets fear subside, allows her herself the notion they've stumbled into some weird LARP gathering.

But she senses this is different. More serious than cosplay.

Other forms converge then, people in deerskin, adorned with twigs, faces stained with berry juice or caked-mud masks.

Alana spots what looks like a taller rabbit run, not tall enough for them to pass upright, but enough to allow human passage.

She grabs Christian's arm. "Come on."

They stoop, push past the headless figure into the opening, fighting twigs, vines and switches walling the passage. Those slash thin gashes on forearms as shouts follow. Then footfalls. They forge onward, cheeks and arms slashed by outcropping pine branches. Clothing's ripped.

The path feeds into an archway formed by massive, twisting roots and branches. Beyond, they burst not into an escape route but to a cracked, decaying staircase with cairns of stone framing the bottom step.

They follow the jagged steps up and emerge amid small buildings beneath a virtual canyon of trees, roofed by still more sinuous vines and gnarled branches.

The figures in this shadowy space inspire more awe than the surroundings—more people adorned like the ones who forced them here. Skins, stained faces, long hair, piercings, makeshift tattoos, and other affectations.

Cries in something like a language rise, and after a few gestures among the ranks, the people converge. Grimy fingers close on forearms. Handfuls of hair are grabbed, and they are ushered onward.

Alana tries pulling back, but grips hold fast. A finger taps and toys at the ring in her nostril for a moment then leaves it to trace the arm tat. Her brain races, trying to connect dots, attempting to assemble some understanding of who has gathered in this lost colony.

Chants and clapping mingle, indicating some kind of consensus has been reached.

In moments they're pushed into what must be a massive old lodge or hotel. Walls in the great room are draped with tattered and weathered banners depicting a line-up of figures, bearded ladies, boys with "lobster" hands, rail-thin people, obese people, a woman with flesh completely tattooed. *The World's Strangest Family. Alive!* one text bubble proclaims.

"What the fuck have we stepped into?" Alana asks.

"It's like a hall of ancestral portraits," Christian says.

Figures here go about various tasks, figures covered in hair. Figures with twisted, webbed appendages, figures without limbs of any kind. Alana can identify traits suggesting albinism, possibly microcephaly…and other conditions.

One woman sits in a faded camp chair on a little dais. Her legs are massive, twisted with feet looking so swollen they might have been grafted on from a giant.

"She seems kind of revered," Christian says. "The ones outside are the poseurs. In here it's the real deal."

A few animals rest near the woman's feet in what might be honored positions. Big cats that look to be from a variety of species. Spots, stripes, black fur, long tails, short ones, rounded ears, tufted ears. A single bonobo reclines, one lanky arm resting across dozing eyes.

"There's the answer to the urban legend," Alana says. "No time for selfies now. We need to find a way out of here."

Christian's a bit transfixed. "Gonna be hard. These are their woods."

***

Eventually, one of the tall men confers with the revered woman, periodically looking back at Christian and Alana. He makes a sound at the conclusion of their exchange, something like a call. In response, a pair of very small people emerge from a chamber far in the back of the building, a man and a woman in robes dyed with decorative patterns. They're maybe three feet tall.

Certainly no taller. The small man lifts a hand to silence the chanting and utters a loud, guttural command.

"Who are they?" Alana whispers.

"There are always legends of little people in secluded forests," Christian says. "The side-show folk found them. Must've j-j-joined them."

After staring at Alana and Christian for what seem like minutes, the small people offer expressions of approval. All of the others clap, and a wild dance begins as Alana feels a drape of beads placed on her head. It's a heavy wig made of moss, wood chips and small stones. Christian's getting similar treatment but has a laurel of twigs positioned on his head. Has he been given a crown?

They bring out a bowl of berry juice for Alana.

"Looks like we've scored enough likes to stay," Christian says. "You know, gooble gobble? The old flick we saw in film studies?"

Alana eyes a slender bone needle that a woman with short hands but long, dexterous fingers has produced. She realizes the juice is not to drink and fails to pull away from those holding her.

Christian scans the crowd, then focuses on one of the tattered posters.

"The Illustrated Woman," he says in a whisper as the first poke of a needle stings Alana's flesh. "They must have an opening in their roster."

Alana shivers, tries again to pull away but finally laughs, and laughs more until her laughter becomes a cackle. "Guess you won't be able to call me a tourist anymore."

THIS IS HOW YOUR GARDEN GROWS

Joseph Maddrey

S amantha McGee could feel the cold morning air in her bones. The skin between life and death was as thin as tissue paper.

From the back porch of the little white house on Maple Street, she surveyed her garden. It wasn't much. A few years ago, she'd had tomato plants, string beans, some squash. Now it was mostly weeds. The previous winter had been tough on her and she knew she wouldn't live through another one.

When arthritis forced her to retire as the organist of the local Methodist church, she'd told Pastor Bob—the inquisitive country preacher who'd become like a son to her—that she was ready to die. She said she was ready to meet her maker and face His judgment. Whatever her sins, she'd atoned for them and then some. Like her neighbors, she saw herself as a pilgrim in a pagan world and she knew she'd done her best. The only thing that bothered her was the garden.

She didn't miss playing the organ half as much as she missed the garden and the feel of the loamy soil between her fingers. She hated the thought of abandoning it to the elements and the weeds. She knew that if she got down on her knees in the yard, she wouldn't be able to stand up again. Still, she wanted to plant seeds one more time; she wanted to leave something that would outlast her, something new. She wanted to rebuke death.

As she passed through the living room, she glanced at the life-size oil portrait of her dead husband Joe, blew him a kiss, and exited her little house.

Joe waited silently for her return.

The central Virginia town of Leeds hadn't changed much since Joe died. Twenty-seven years ago, he'd been delivering mail on his usual route when a heart attack took him. In the final moments of life, he failed to apply sufficient pressure to the brakes and his mail truck careened into an old juniper tree. He was dead when J.B. Compton found him there. The tree continued to grow, at an unnatural angle.

Pastor Bob had arrived in Leeds on the same day at around the same time, but no one said anything about that until much later.

A handful of newcomers had arrived since then but the town still remained mostly isolated from the outside world. None of the locals had any interest in the extravagant lifestyles of the suburbanites to the north or the exurbanites to the southeast. Employees of the timber company routinely ventured into the mountains of Greene County, where some old hill-dwelling families lived, but they always came back. The train rolled through the town center every other day, carrying only cargo. It seemed no one ever left. People settled here and died here.

Standing in the gardening aisle of the general store, Sam tried to remember the last time she'd heard about a child being born in Leeds. She drew a blank and that worried her. More than worried her, because she knew her failure to remember wasn't a symptom of old age. Her body was feeble; her mind was not.

She kept thinking about the juniper tree, which reminded her of a fairy tale her mother read to her when she was little, a brutal tale about an ungodly stepmother. Sam never had a stepmother but she'd had an ungodly father, and she now thought that's why her mother had told the tale, as a kind of warning. Sam heeded the warning and left home early. After the war, she met Joe. They married immediately, moved to Leeds, and never once talked about having children. "Children wouldn't be happy here," Joe had said. She'd agreed and didn't think any more about it. Until now.

"Are you okay, Sam?" a voice asked.

She turned and saw Claude Aylor, the cherubic man who owned the general store. He was a Baptist but she liked him anyway.

"I'm fine," she said quickly, embarrassedly. Her legs ached and she wondered how long she'd been standing there, staring off into space. *He must think I'm dotty.* She glanced at the nearest shelf, which was full of seed packets. "My eyes aren't what they used to be," she explained.

"Can I help you find something?" His voice was kind and gentle, which made her even more uneasy.

Impulsively, she reached out for a random seed packet. She didn't bother to read the label, simply closed her bony fingers around it and smiled warmly at Claude to reassure him that all was well and all would continue to be well.

Standing at the checkout counter a few minutes later, she wondered why she had felt embarrassed. She'd known Claude for years and she had nothing to hide from him, yet she'd felt guilty. About what?

She skimmed the covers of the sleazy tabloid magazines on display nearby. One had a big, bold headline about UFO sightings in Nevada. Sam had never been to Nevada and she knew she would never go there. Which was fine. If the tabloids were any indication, people out west were a bunch of yahoos—always looking for answers in the wrong places. The other magazine covers flaunted headlines about scandalous celebrity affairs, a time traveling psychic, and the release of a flesh-eating virus from an experimental government lab. Suddenly, Sam was glad she'd lived most of her life in Leeds, away from the madness of the world. She thought of an old hymn, one she'd played a hundred times in church.

This world is not my home,
I'm only passing through.
My treasures are laid up
Somewhere beyond the blue.

She paid for her seeds and left.

Standing in her kitchen an hour later, Sam finally noticed what kind of seeds she had bought. The front of the packet featured a photo of a tiny white flower that looked a bit like a snowdrop. Below the photo was a single word, printed in bold letters: **MOLY**. Sam read it as "Molly." Molly had been her mother's nickname, which seemed fortuitous.

Her arthritic hands were suddenly burning and she felt very tired, so she sat down at the kitchen table, opened the packet and poured the seeds into her open palm. Then she sat there staring at them, contemplating her next act.

She sensed her strength fading, her life slipping away. She'd always imagined that when the time came, she would surrender willingly, peacefully. But now an old hymn was haunting her.

The angels beckon me
From heaven's open door
And I can't feel at home
In this world anymore.

It made her angry, the sudden feeling of helplessness and homelessness. She looked away from the seeds and saw a shaft of sunlight on the dirty linoleum floor, light streaming in from the window above the sink. Behind the nearly-closed curtains, beyond the glass, she saw the sunlight, dispersed by trees, separated and channeled into thin, irregular lines, like crooked arms reaching for her. For a moment, she couldn't breathe.

She assured herself she had enough energy left for one final act. She wanted it to matter. She needed it to be life-affirming. Eagerly, she rose to her feet and walked toward the back door, then out into the green world.

In the garden, she dropped down to the earth and started clawing at the dirt like a dog.

By the time she had buried the seeds, her skin was cracked and bleeding. She shifted her weight to one side and fell over, exhausted. Lying still on the earth's red clay wound, she found herself face to face with a tiny milkweed bug. She waited for it to speak to her, like a creature in a fairy tale, but the bug said nothing. She watched it crawl away, then realized her work was done and fell asleep.

That night, Sam dreamed that her house was perched on a giant hill—taller than any existing hill in the town of Leeds. She went out to her garden and started digging again, more frantic than before. She desperately wanted to find the seeds, to take back what she had done.

The first layer of dirt was pulpy and black, like licorice. Beneath that was a layer of mauve skin; Sam thought it looked like a bruise. She continued digging until the fleshy matter broke into flaky bits. Beneath the bruise was a thin white material with tiny veins running through it in every direction. The mass gave off a distinct smell; a sour, pungent odor. When Sam caught a whiff, her eyes began to water. Suddenly she understood what was buried beneath her home. She was sitting on a giant, rotting onion.

In the morning, Sam woke up feeling incredibly parched. She struggled to her feet and stumbled toward the kitchen to get some water. As she passed through the living room, she became increasingly unsteady and almost fell when she heard the sound of a deep male voice.

"Are you ready to go?" the voice asked.

She recognized it immediately, turned her head and saw Joe standing beside her, young and handsome. At first, she wasn't alarmed by the sight of him. The oil painting of Joe on the wall beside the piano was blank and that seemed to explain the situation; Joe had simply stepped out of the picture.

He added, in a sing-songy voice, "There was an old woman, and what do you think? She went to the kitchen to get a drink. To get a drink and maybe some bread. Only to find that her husband's not dead."

Sam didn't laugh because she knew the man standing in front of her couldn't *really* be Joe. He might look like Joe, might sound like Joe, but it couldn't be him. Joe didn't sing. He was too dead.

"I know you're not really here," she said. "I must be dreaming. But it's okay. It's a good dream."

Joe reached out and took her left hand and Sam felt a mild electric current pass through her body. Now she was certain she wasn't dreaming. But she wasn't afraid either.

"Follow me," Joe said.

He led her through the kitchen to the back porch. When she stepped outside, she knew she had entered another world. Her garden was gone, replaced by an all-consuming copse of white flowers. The edge of the porch was gone too, because the flowers were sprouting out of the wood. They were also growing up the side of the house, out of the bricks and glass and shingles.

Sam looked at Joe, but his face was hard and solemn.

He said, "All will be well."

Sam's eyes welled up with tears. She was remembering the day Joe had died, how Doc Veazie explained what happened to him, how she'd wanted to believe that he had not suffered, and how she instinctively knew better.

She had so many questions she wanted to ask, but before she could say anything Joe reminded her that her time was up.

"Leave it to God," he said. "And come with me."

Sam could not help but surrender. She collapsed in a lawn chair bursting with flowers.

Joe smiled affectionately as new blossoms sprouted from her arms and legs. Sam felt some pain but it was not any kind of pain she had ever experienced before. Within a few moments, it had expanded into an alien warmth that covered her body like a thick blanket. She opened her mouth to give thanks and a perfect white flower emerged instead.

It was, she thought, too beautiful for words.

In the dim light of morning, Pastor Bob looked out the kitchen window toward Sam's backyard and saw his wife Rita standing outside in her bathrobe, staring vacantly at the neighbor's property. His heart sank.

The previous year, Rita had been diagnosed with dementia, although she was only 68 years old. Since then, she'd grown increasingly paranoid, constantly insisting that everyone in town was involved in some sort of conspiracy, suppressing some dark truth that only she knew. "I don't believe in coincidences," she snapped at her husband. Bob knew it was simply a matter of time before she completely lost touch with reality. He'd seen this sort of thing before.

He followed Rita's gaze toward the thicket of white flowers in Sam's yard, where the garden should have been. He couldn't remember ever having seen so many flowers in one place—and he was certain that these flowers hadn't been there the day before. But he knew Sam had a green thumb, and she'd always said that the soil in Leeds was exceptionally fertile.

He stepped out into the cool fall air and spoke gently to Rita, remembering his mother's warning that it was dangerous to awaken a sleepwalker. His wife allowed him to guide her inside without protest. Then he phoned Doc Veazie.

He didn't think about the flowers again until late that night, when the sound of cawing crows drew him to his neighbor's back porch. He found Sam dead, engulfed in the strange growth, and wept, wondering why God would claim her in such an unnatural way—and what it would mean for the town.

Like his wife, Bob didn't believe in coincidences; he was always looking for patterns and explanations. Over the past few years, Sam McGee had become like a mother to him, a late-in-life replacement for the mother he never knew. Now he was lost again, overwhelmed by a despair he hadn't felt since he was a child.

A few days later, at Sam's funeral, he rambled incoherently about the blossoming of Aaron's rod, one of the Bible's most incomprehensible metaphors. He wanted to make sense out of a world where anything was possible, to reassure his parishioners that no branch bore fruit without God's blessing. But then he was mixing metaphors, tying his own branches in knots. The mourners looked pained.

He tried again. "We know that the town of Leeds is God's special place, a closed system made specifically for us, His Chosen People. When one soul leaves, another soul arrives and confronts us with new mysteries. With the passing of Samantha McGee, we prepare ourselves for a new arrival and a new challenge. It is natural to be afraid, because we can never understand God's miracles in their fullness, but we must remember that everything in life is His work and part of His divine purpose. He has a plan for us and so we surrender to His will and wait, mindful that fear is the beginning of wisdom."

Pastor Bob closed his eyes, willing himself to accept these answers.

"Let us pray."

BY A THREAD

Querus Abuttu

"These are amazing!" Sari pushed away wild wisps of hair from her mouth—dark brown tendrils that refused to be confined to her ponytail. Gerad watched as she stuffed another handful of berries past her lips, then drank from her water bottle. Nearby, the mighty James River let out her constant rushing song.

July days were long enough to explore along the old canals—canals that at one time were home to flat-bottomed boats called batteaus. These boats once brought supplies up and down the river before and during the Civil War. Until the railroad made them obsolete.

Gerad nodded, admiring Sari's sculpted physique. He plucked some blackberries from a thorny bush and sampled them. A few chews rewarded him with a sweet and tangy explosion of flavor. It was so good to step out into nature and find food. Somehow, wild food just tasted better.

Better than anything you'd buy from a store.

The taste mixed well with the scents of earth, honeysuckle, and wild grasses warmed by the sun—untamed fragrances that seemed to dance all around his senses. It was all so intoxicating. But intoxicating or not, they needed to move on. He was determined to find the lost town today and motioned to Sari to come his way.

Gerad swallowed his berries and drank some water. "Ready?"

Sari bounded up, wiped her lips, and smiled. "Let's get going!"

Gerad checked his iWatch. 15:42. Not a ton of time. But enough. Enough for both he and Sari to find the place he'd finally spotted on Google Maps. The place where the abandoned town of Passage might be. His mother had told him about it once. How she'd hiked there with her own mother, his grandmother—Memy—and how they'd done tombstone rubbings in the graveyard using paper and charcoal.

"You never want to be there at night," his mother warned. "Something very bad happened in that town. It was completely abandoned in one day. No one knows why. So strange. Everything is still there too. Clothes, plates, shoes. Just as they left it. And anyone who goes there should never take anything away. The evil that took that place just might follow them home."

Gerad didn't believe the bullshit about evil. He believed in science. Nothing dead, or supposedly evil, had ever followed him home from biology or chemistry class. Except for his friend Jason. That dude was a special case.

No, if science hadn't been able to prove the existence of ghosts, demons, and the like, then it made no sense to fear them. He did, however, want to find this town. If it was perfectly preserved, like his mother said, then both he and Sari had a crack at some real anthropology work. But first, they had to verify the town was there, lock in the location, and then talk to the landowner.

Fifteen more minutes into the hike, Gerad pulled up the map on his phone and married it to their location.

"Here," he said. He felt his heart beating harder in his chest. "See that stream? We follow it up that way, and we should find the town."

"Okay," Sari's gaze followed the direction he was pointing with his finger.

Gerad read the dubious look that crossed her face. It was understandable. The stream disappeared into a thick network of trees so dense the sunlight barely poked through the canopy. There didn't seem to be an easy way to get over the old canal and up the steep bank. They'd just have to go for it, leap and push through the brush. Hopefully, it would get easier. In their favor, it hadn't rained in nearly three weeks so the water level in the canal was low. It would be easy to climb down the bank and hop over the water. The challenge would be climbing up the far side without falling back down. But he and Sari were used to exploring. Used to steep climbing.

"I'll go down first." Gerad skittered down the bank. He hopped over the algae-thickened water and scrabbled up the far side toward the forest. Sari followed him. Gerad turned to watch her when he got to the top. In seconds, felt his heart nearly jackknife through his chest.

"Sari," he called out, trying not to sound panicked, "shift three feet to your left before you drop down."

"I've got it fine," she said.

"No! Stop!" He let out a breath as she just missed planting her foot in a danger zone. He kept his voice calm. "There's a snake, maybe two, right below where you were going to put your foot. Move to the side."

Gerad saw Sari's tanned legs quiver.

"It'll be okay," he reassured her, "just keep moving left—"

Sari slipped as a rock shifted beneath her foot. It tumbled onto the snakes and then to Gerad's horror Sari started tumbling in after them. She let out a yell, and Gerad slid back down the bank after her as she hit the water. It wasn't deep. His concern was about the snakes. The venom of a Moccasin bite could cause some serious damage.

"Where are they, Gerad?" Sari was smart. She kept moving toward him and reached the other bank. Gerad scanned the water and all around. The creatures weren't anywhere to be seen.

"Guess we scared 'em off." Gerad reached a hand over to Sari. She grabbed it and he pulled her to him. Together they worked their way up the bank and to the tree line.

"Ugh." Sari wrinkled her nose in disgust, looking down. "This is nasty."

Gerad paused to survey both of their slimy bodies, wet and green-brown with algae and mud.

"Yep. You should take the lead. You're sure to scare away anything in our path." He laughed, and Sari playfully shoved him.

"You're bigger! More stink and grossness! You first." Sari bowed and gestured her hand forward, smiling. They both laughed, then Gerad looked at his iWatch. 16:20.

"C'mon. Let's get going," he said. He was starting to get worried that they wouldn't have time to find the place and it might be days before they could both come back together.

They set off along the edge of the creek and the forest engulfed them.

The terrain did get easier to follow. At first, all they had was a little stream of water that dribbled lazily along a crooked path. Finally, they hit a sign of civilization. A square section of stones along the creek edge was testimony to some kind of manmade cistern or reservoir. They were built like this in the late 1800s to capture water in greater quantities for use. They both bent down and studied the structure. Definitely Civil War era.

"We should be near the place now." Gerad stood up, stretched, and stared at his phone.

Grah! No reception.

No bars at all. He'd have to climb a hill, maybe, to pick up a signal. He held up his phone, showing Sari. "You? Anything?"

Sari pulled her phone out. She frowned, her forehead wrinkling slightly.

"Nope. Nada." She put her phone in her back pocket and smoothed her red hiking shirt. She'd told him the color was "tomato."

Yeah. Red.

A mosquito buzzed around his ears, and as he brushed it away and turned to examine the area something caught his eye. Some kind of post. Manmade.

"Sari, over here!"

They both ran to look. It was a rotted piece of wood, but hand-hewn and jutting out of the ground.

"Over there!" Sari pointed.

Three feet away there was another one. Rotten and crumbling with green moss and shelf mushrooms growing along the side.

"Hitching post, maybe?" she suggested.

Gerad nodded. It was possible. His gaze darted from the place they stood, into the depths of the forest. He could almost make out what once might have been a road.

Steady, boy. Don't get too excited. Not yet.

He looked over at Sari. She'd seen it too. Without speaking, they moved into the depths of the forest. It was 17:20.

No more than five minutes had passed when they caught sight of a building. It was two stories tall and very wide. Old white paint peeked through the vines covering it, and trees pressed against it as if trying to become one with the boards. Two windows were boarded up. The other windows—four more on the bottom and all six at the top—were open, glass broken in all of them as if a gang of schoolchildren had come here seeking vengeance on the place. Darkness filled the openings like an impenetrable barrier. Gerad caught an odd scent in the air. Salty. Strange, but still—

Sweet Hawking! It's a real thing. We're here!

Sari laughed, delighted. "We gotta get pics!"

They pulled out their iPhones and started taking pictures, circling the building. Gerad let his gaze sweep further along their chosen path. And yes, there were remnants of decayed clapboard houses, and in other places, he could see layers of brick and stone. A couple more hard structures had survived the weather of time. The slate roof probably preserved this place. It was covered with moss and lichens, but he could see it was slate underneath.

"Wanna go in, or explore outside some more?"

Gerad already knew what Sari would say. This was a helluva find, and now that they knew where to look, nothing was going to stop them from exploring more later. They'd found their site. Their Ph.D. work was in the bag. But still—how could they not just take a peek before they left?

Sari grinned, and in answer, headed for the front door.

The double doors hung crookedly in the entrance. If there had been any porch or accompanying overhang to protect a visitor from weather or to provide any shade on a sunny day, that had long ago disintegrated and was probably under their feet.

Gerad moved one of the doors to the side. As he did, the entire door fell off its frame.

"Whoa!"

It thunked to the ground and Gerad gently stepped around it. He checked his iWatch.

What the hell? It was still 17:20. He looked at his phone. It gave the same time. He also noticed the battery power on his phone was forty percent.

Sari had already stepped in and started investigating. Gerad pushed down an odd giggle that rose from his gut. This was an amazing find! Best to soak it up. Take it in.

There was nothing to be worried about. Not yet.

If it was 17:20 back at the creek, then it couldn't be any later than 18:00 now. Sunset was at 20:30. If they left in a couple of hours, they'd be good.

Gerad shook himself out of his worry. *Okay. Quit it. Investigate!*

He took a deep breath and stepped inside.

"Gerad! Over here! Oh my God, wait till you see!" Sari's voice came from a room around the corner. Gerad took note of many things in the hallway. Pictures. A small room to the left held an old National cash register. There were shelves filled with things like Magic Yeast, granite coffee boilers, and Rising Sun stove polish covered with dust and cobwebs, along with a few oak chairs at a wooden table.

He rounded the corner and stepped into a large room filled with a variety of wooden spinning-wheels. Large and small. They were lined up in two rows alongside the wall, facing each other. Next to them were additional wooden chairs, and next to the chairs were woven reed baskets filled with balls of colorful thread, or yarn, depending on the type of spinning wheel and what the worker was making that day. Gerad raised his hands and aimed his camera.

"Amazing, right?" Sari sidled up to him. She waved her arms. "It's all just sitting here. Waiting! Like the people who left are coming back any minute . . ." Her voice faded, words trickling away like water from a facet as it is slowly turned off. Then she brightened.

"Let's see what else we've got!" Her hazel eyes flared with a light of excitement he'd never seen in her before. She was so beautiful, glowing with the thrill of the find.

Across the hall were wooden looms of various sizes. Patterns of natural and indigo overshot flax were still in place, warp and weft deftly creating fabrics so often used as coverlets of the time. Completed pieces were folded neatly on nearby wooden shelves as if waiting for packaging and delivery. Sari ran her fingers over the looms.

Gerad reached out to touch the fabric, gliding his hand along a particular blooming pattern. That's when he felt *it*. He couldn't explain what the sensation was, but *it* pulled something from the center of him and his skin pimpled with gooseflesh. A chill descended on him, and the room went dark. Impending dread filled him—paralyzed him—struck fear into his heart—his chest was cold—so cold--

Someone was shaking him. Calling his name.

"Gerad? Gerad, are you okay?"

Sari. It's Sari!

He managed to turn his head toward her, taking in the concern on her face. *Sweet Sari.* He inhaled deeply. At least he was still standing. He hadn't fainted.

"What happened?" Gerad's muscles were trembling as if he'd just run a marathon.

"I went to another room to see what was there. When I came back you were, like, catatonic. You scared me, Gerad."

He gazed at her face. Then he remembered.

"You have the time, Sari? My watch died. My phone too."

Sari shook her head. "Mine isn't working either."

"How long do you think we've been here?"

"Couple of hours maybe?" she said.

A couple of hours. If that was true, it had to be somewhere between 19:30 and 20:00. They should leave now. "If we want to get back before dark, we should . . ."

"You gotta come see. Oh Gerad, this is so..." Sari shrugged, and her eyes widened. "Weird." When he didn't move right away, she tugged at his shirt. "Come. On!"

We should be going.

Another voice in his head said, *Leave. Leave now!*

Instead, he let Sari pull him along.

Just this one thing, and then we'll go, he thought. *A couple more minutes won't make a difference.*

In the distance, he heard a clamoring of birds, maybe crows.

A murder of crows.

God, he had to stop doing this to himself. He believed in science! Hard facts. Hard facts told him there was nothing to be afraid of. It would be more difficult to find their way back after dark, but they'd make it. They had flashlights on their phones.

That odd smell was in the air again. It seemed to come from where Sari was pulling him. And it was getting stronger.

At the back of the building, he walked through an archway into a room that opened up into an expansive space. But it wasn't the size of the room that caught his attention as much as it was the giant hole in the middle of the floor. It was, for lack of better explanation, a sinkhole. Right here, in the back of—inside—the house.

Gerad craned his neck over to peek in. He couldn't see the bottom, so there was no telling how deep it went. Hanging from the edges—and plunging into the blackness of the hole—were thousands and thousands of homespun threads. He eyeballed the rest of the room. There were no windows. There was nothing except some old black-and-white photographs on the walls. Some of them were cradled in ornate frames. Others were just tacked onto the wall with a nail. They were mishmash images of old and young people, and rich and poor people. Gerad's inner senses told him these were the residents of the abandoned town. A closer inspection of the photos confirmed it.

"Look at this one." Sari brought him over to a photo that was just about eye level.

It was an entire family. Two elders looked like grandparents. A bearded male in a three-piece suit sat on a wooden trunk. He held a tome open on his lap, an index finger pointing to some unknowable passage there. A woman, presumably his wife, hair drawn back into a severely tight bun, sat next to him. An angelic young girl, dressed in white, stood on the trunk between them.

Gathered around the elders were three adult women and a younger adult male, closely shaven and wearing a three-piece suit. Three other children stood at the edges of the picture. Not one of the faces in the photograph was smiling.

"This building is in the background, back when it was shiny and new!" Sari paused. "It looks as if they'd just moved here, sitting on that trunk."

Gerad nodded. "Wait." He went across the hall to the room with windows and glanced outside. "Shit!"

Sari rushed in. "What is it?"

"It's dark already."

His heart sank. It was a new moon tonight. There'd be nothing to help light their way through and out of the forest. He looked at his phone. His battery power was down to ten percent. He may, or may not, have enough energy to power the flashlight for the walk back.

Fuck.

There was a thumping sound coming from the spinning room.

Before he could stop her, Sari dashed off to see what it was. An animal maybe? The front doors were open and the windows too. He followed her, noticing the floorboards appeared polished. Had they looked that shiny a few minutes ago?

He started feeling like neither of them should be alone in this building. If he hadn't looked up when he did, he would have run right into Sari. She was standing frozen at the threshold of the spinning room.

Gerad looked over her shoulder. The spinning wheels were spinning. They moved just as if someone were sitting in the chairs treadling the wheels, but there was no wool, no linen, nothing nearby to spin. Still, the treadles moved up and down and the wheels went around. A chilling breeze blew across Gerad's neck and then he heard a clackity-clack!

Turning, he saw the looms in motion, impossibly serving their function even though no one was working them. A shuttle passed from left to right as the batten squeezed the threads together. The brake treadles moved on their own, switching up and down according to the needs of the pattern. Sari came up behind him.

"How is this happening?"

Gerad shook his head.

This isn't real. What is happening right now—it can't be real.

Still, he tried to answer. "No idea. But my mother warned me about this place."

A place is just a place. And this—

"What? What did she say?"

He heard panic rising in Sari's voice.

Taking a few steps backward, he tried again. "She said something bad happened in this town. It's why everything is still here. My guess is they got some kind of disease. Smallpox or something."

The rationale sounded hollow to his own ears—an excuse without substance. He paused and continued to watch the looms, mesmerized. Just then, something flashed, and smoke puffed into the air. They both turned.

"Ah. Good! Now we do your faces!" An elderly white man stood there with some kind of old-fashioned camera on a stand, and he was preparing to take another photo. Gerad looked down just as Sari looked up and the flash went off again with more powder. More smoke.

"Perfect!" The man held the camera, folded the legs of the stand, and started to walk away.

"Wait, wait!" Gerad called after him. This was way too surreal.

First the spinning room, then the weaving room, and now a photographer in the middle of nowhere? Maybe he'd fallen asleep. Was dreaming. That could be it.

"Yes?" The old man faced him.

"How did you get here? Do you have a car?" Gerad felt breathless trying to get his questions out. "What's your name?"

The old man shrugged. "My, my. Three questions at once. I shall try to keep up. I live here. We use the railroad if we need to go anywhere far. And my name is George. George Oscar Brown. Now if you will excuse me, I must see to my photographs."

The man left the camera stand and flash at the foot of the stairs that led to the second level, then disappeared into the next room.

"Did that just really happen?" Sari giggled. "Have we gone insane?"

Gerad noticed that whereas everything had looked old, dusty and unused when they'd walked in, now the wood was polished, the front doors were back on their hinges. Peeking back into the weaving room, he saw women sitting or standing at their looms, working diligently at their craft.

He was about to speak when he both felt and heard footsteps down the hallway. A very large, imposing woman with hair twisted into a severe bun atop her head swept through the corridor in a green bell-shaped dress, her baleful gray eyes upon them.

"You there!" She pointed at them. "What is your business here?"

A young girl, maybe twelve or thirteen, hustled up from behind her.

"They've come for the festivities, Mama. Remember?" The girl tugged at her mother's sleeve and looked up at her with an angelic face.

"Fest—? Ah!" A sudden realization dawned in her eyes. "Right, then!" She walked up to Gerad. "I'm Rose. Everyone calls me so here. This is my Little Rose," she said. The young girl curtsied. "She will get you ready— find you some—" there was a long pause here as she looked at Gerad and Sari's dried mud and algae clothing "—proper attire."

The large woman turned away and pounded up the stairway, the long walnut banister shaking with every step.

"Don't mind her," Little Rose giggled. "She's been grumpy all day. She will be better tonight. You'll see. Come. You better change."

Gerad pinched himself, and the pain of that pinch felt very real. How could this place suddenly be bustling with life?

Sari tiptoed and whispered in his ear. "Do we just go with it? I mean, maybe there will be somewhere for us to sleep for the night. We can leave when we wake up in the morning."

"*If* we wake up in the morning," Gerad muttered.

This was all so strange. But there was no foreboding feeling like he'd felt before, not that he believed in that kind of thing. And he did want to see more.

"Yeah, okay, let's go with it," he agreed. "If something seems dangerous, we'll run. We can survive a night in the woods."

Let's see where this takes us. It will help us know more when we come back to dig.

Little Rose brought them upstairs to a room with a red door that was wide open. There were three other doors. All white and shut tight.

"You can change here." Little Rose gave him a cute little grin and squeezed her shoulders toward her ears. "Take turns if you need. There should be something to fit each of you inside. Come downstairs when you're ready."

Gerad ushered Sari in, closed the door with his back, and let out a huge sigh. He looked over at a wooden wardrobe and raised an eyebrow at Sari. "You first?"

"Sure." She opened the large doors, squealed in delight, pulled a privacy screen over that was decorated with hand-stitched roses on linen panels, and changed her clothes behind it. A moment later, she came out wearing a lacy pink dress that accentuated her tiny waist but fluffed out all around her hips and feet like a cone of cotton candy. The buttons were still undone in the back.

"Can you help?" she asked. "I can't get back there. I can't imagine a woman getting dressed by herself if all the clothing came like this."

Gerad obliged and then stepped toward the wardrobe to see what it offered. Oddly, there was not a hint of women's clothing in the wardrobe when he inspected it. Had the pink dress been Sari's only option? On the other hand, on a wooden rack hung something that seemed as if it would fit him perfectly. A handsome black fabric three-piece suit that would give Armani a run for his money. A pressed white shirt hung next to it, and when he tried it on it was as if it were tailored just for him. He dressed quickly and when he emerged from behind the privacy screen, Sari pretended to swoon and together they laughed.

"I didn't know you could clean up so well, Mr. Gerad," she cooed with her best Southern belle accent.

Gerad opened the door and presented his arm. Batting her eyes, Sari took it. Together they went downstairs.

Little Rose was at the foot of the steps, waiting.

She clapped her hands in absolute joy. "Mais Oui! Perfect. So lovely!" Although she was cute, her smile held no warmth.

There was something practiced about her response, as if she'd done this kind of thing a hundred times before.

And she probably has, his logical brain reassured him. *This house hosts many guests.*

So, what had him on edge? Besides the fact that none of this should be happening in the first place. He worked to quiet that insufferable part of his worry-wart mind. There was no danger here. Nothing he'd seen had shown him there was any cause for worry. Either this was a real paranormal experience—which he didn't believe—or he'd fallen asleep and was having a hell of a dream, which was the more likely explanation. It was something like that because—

In the great room, music was playing although it was unclear where the music was coming from. Then he noticed the phonograph in the corner.

"Thomas Edison is such a love, isn't he?" Little Rose appeared, wearing a pink gown dotted with pink roses, and gestured toward the music box. "I love the waltz, don't you!"

She squeezed her hands to her chest, then grabbed their arms.

The great room was completely transformed. Where the giant hole had been, there was now a beautiful, parquet wood floor. A magnificent crystal chandelier hung from the center of the ceiling, resplendent and sparkling in the candlelight. Sconces in the corners of the room added to the ambiance.

Little Rose brought Gerad and Sari to the center of the room. Other people were already there, dancing.

Gerad tried not to shout in Little Rose's ear, but had to raise it over the din of the music, "What's the occasion? What are you celebrating?"

She smiled, shyly. "Why, of course, we are celebrating you! The both of you!"

The music stopped and so did the dancers. Each person pivoted and turned to face them. Another tune started, but then the dancers stepped forward, danced a circle around them then stopped, turned, and stepped away. The tune changed again, and everyone moved in a pattern where some dancers stepped in toward them and some stepped out. Gerad looked over toward Little Rose to ask another question, but the girl was gone.

Then—that smell again. It was overpowering now. Noxious. And he felt lightheaded.

He reached out to grab Sari's arm and she grabbed his. He looked at the portraits on the walls. Ice ran through his veins when he noticed there was a photo of him and Sari on the wall, the one the man George had taken. But instead of wearing their hiking gear, they were attired in the clothes they were wearing now.

The ghastly smell. He remembered it now. *Sulfur. Was the photographer's flash-powder supposed to smell like that?*

Sari gripped his hand hard. "Look," she hissed. "Now they are all holding threads!"

It was true. Every dancer stood in a circle surrounding them, each holding a white or blue thread. They stepped in and out in time to the music—as if weaving something around Gerad and Sari.

"We gotta get outta here!" Gerad yelled. He looked around desperately for an exit.

Nothing.

"I'm going to lift you up and then you jump over to the door, okay? I know it's dark, but when you hit the floor, just keep running. Don't look back." Gerard gazed intently into her eyes.

"But you . . ."

"Don't look back!" He got her foot in his interlaced hands, she grabbed his head, and he pushed up as she jumped. He couldn't see if she made it or not. He tumbled backward and then suddenly he was falling. Down, down, down through the floor and into the tunnel—and everything turned black.

Sari was trying to remember something. She stared at her woven basket full of translucent fiber. It was almost invisible, but once the indigo dye was applied to it, it would be a beautiful blue. She caressed the fiber, feeling it sing, struggle, and cry beneath her fingertips.

"Sari, are you okay?" The girl next to her, Gina, spun her soul-fiber so easily.

"Yes, still learning. These tendrils are so strange." Sari kept trying to remember, but the floor shook, reminding her that Rose would be coming soon to inspect her work. She pulled at the translucent fiber, humming, and singing to it.

"Don't worry, Gerad," she sang. "Soon you'll be part of a beautiful blanket. Soon you'll capture souls too." She twisted and sang, spinning the thread. Thread that could also be used in the town's next dance to feed the underground womb of life.

COASTAL VA

CHESAPEAKE BAIT AND HOOK

Sirrah Medeiros

Straight away, the chill is gone.
Powerless to focus, hard to discern.
A dense veil of frigid blackness
Weighs along mortal perceptions.
An abyss so intense that
The slightest sliver of light racing by—blinds.
Ominous echoes swirl in the pits below.
Crimson trails glide down an unseeable plane,
Persistent waves of despair.

Ultimate affirmation of life—pain...
Extends each fibrous nerve—taut and raw.
As daggers gleefully plunder
Bones rupture via metallic teeth.
Breath escapes into obscurity
As anguish creeps deeper within.
No use in fighting the drag.
Would prayer sustain in this moment?
If only they would hurry the haul.

Can they revive this wretched soul?
Pluck the hooks from the marrow...

Heal the gaping, dangling flesh,
Where the fish now feed?
But this is not the prize they seek.
Roe... the sea's savory jewel
Is not inside this vessel.
When hoisted up, will the decision be
That this ghastly catch is garbage?

Or will they simply throw me back
Into the bay
To bait a larger hook?

BEACH HOUSE

Bryan Nowak

Wind and rain pelted the sand like it was being punished for some perceived misdeed. It was easy to imagine nothing surviving the hurricane threatening Virginia Beach as it started to erase the sand, shops, and homes along the shoreline. That included a solitary two-story colonial home with a wraparound porch. There was little to stop the tempest outside from utterly wiping it away.

A twelve-year-old boy stood at his grandmother's curio cabinet, examining a smoke-colored stone. It had captured his imagination like nothing else on their walk that morning when they'd found it. The iridescent striations in the minerals played on his imagination. The stone appeared, like the storm raging outside, ever changing; dangerous and beautiful at the same time. It pulsed with an odd energy suggestive of the rhythm of the sea itself.

He turned toward his grandfather, who sat nearby. "Grandpa?"

"Yeah?"

"Have you ever been in a home destroyed by a hurricane?"

The grizzled old man who walked with a limp looked down at his grandson peering out the window. "Was in a house once that was destroyed by a tornado, but never a hurricane. Those damn twisters strike without warning. Suck you straight out of your bedroom and into the sky like nothing."

"Herb, you're scaring the boy." A maternal voice chastised from the kitchen.

"It's okay, Grandma. He's just teasing me." Aydin rolled the strange stone in his hands, then put it back in the cabinet, and closed the door.

The old man gave the boy a wry smile. "Nothing to worry about, Aydin. Some say storms are a world unto themselves. Creatures, cities, and whole civilizations live inside of them. There are lots of terrible stories of what happens to us humans who disrespect the storm's power. Just a bunch of nonsense, of course."

"Oh, Herbert Tillerman, you stop right this instant or I'll paddle you with my soup spoon." Grandma's voice rose again in earnest.

Grandpa laughed and Aydin, with a final glance at the cabinet, slumped on the couch next to him and laughed too. He loved his grandparents. Their beach house was the best place in the world. Summers were spent on the sand with his grandfather and nights were spent playing cards with his grandmother.

"Nah, no hurricane will ever take your Grandpa out. I'm too stubborn for that." With that, the old man boosted himself out of his chair and made his way to the door leading to the lower tier of the home. Not a true basement, it was subject to flooding during intense tropical storms. It also held a few storage rooms and another staircase leading to a carport. From the noise he made, Aydin though he was probably checking the flashlights to make sure they were all accounted for and ready for use.

The storm had been small as it made a turn toward the coast—which was uncharacteristic given the hurricane data of the last hundred years. Weather models had it turning out into the ocean, as most had. But this storm made a beeline for Virginia Beach and only seemed to strengthen upon its approach. Most residents left when the warnings came in, but by the time Aydin's grandparents could arrange to leave, it was too late. Washed out roads ensured they were trapped.

"How are we doing, Herbert?" the silver-haired woman asked from the hallway connecting the kitchen to the living room.

"As good as we could be, Love. Flashlights are all powered up and in chargers. I double checked the propane canisters, and they are ready in case we need them. Our emergency drinking water is downstairs and ready to go."

Soon, though, the internet feed and the cable cut out. Grandpa switched over to a pair of what he called rabbit ears which accessed a few local stations. No matter the station, the news of the storm was all bad. Lights began flickering as the power seemed to be going the way of the internet.

"Okay, time to go to bed, young'un." Grandpa said, pointing up at the clock on the wall.

"I really want to stay up and watch the storm."

"You need to get your sleep," Grandma interjected. "Tomorrow may be a busy day of cleaning up around here. You just git now and remember Grandma loves you."

"Yes, ma'am." Aydin stood from the couch and gave her a peck on the cheek. "Love you too. Night."

"If it makes you feel any better kiddo, there ain't that much to see out there. Just gotta wait this one out. No sense in losing shut eye over it," Grandpa said.

Sleep found him with surprising ease. The wind and the excitement of the impending storm drew energy out of him, leaving him ready for a rest.

Unsure of how long he'd slept, he was awoken by a crash so loud he wondered if a freight train had slammed into his grandparents' house and continued pushing its way through the lower level. He grappled around in the dark for the small lamp near his bed. A few clicks confirmed the power was out. He growled in frustration at not remembering to grab one of the flashlights.

He listened. The crash gave way to a maelstrom, like the storm outside was waging a war on their house with rain and wind its ammunition. A low groaning occasionally pierced the chaotic din which reminded him of an old ship creaking as it crossed wave tops.

"Grandpa? Grandma?" He heard himself sounding unintentionally terrified. Still, he repeated his plea, only to be met with the persistent storm winds.

On his first step into the dark hall, he stepped on chunks of wood, glass, and other detritus strewn across the hallway. Wind blew through the house from somewhere, unabated. With the door open, the sound was even more deafening. He had a moment of indecision, unsure if he was more concerned about the darkness of the hallway or checking on his grandparents. While dark, the ambient light in the hallway was enough to navigate by, so he turned right and pushed open his grandparents' door.

On the far side, the roof and wall had a large crack. Water gushed through the opening. The room was soaked, and the wind had thrown belongings everywhere. The storm groaned its way in, almost hollering at him, somehow, shouting that he should not be seeing these things, that he should shut the door and walk away.

Shaking, he yelled out again: "Grandpa? Grandma?"

The only answer was the deep howl of the wind.

Aydin backed away as a gust blew the door shut with such force it rattled the walls.

Then something slammed in the kitchen, grabbing his attention. It sounded like someone rifling through cabinets—which gave him both a start and a reassuring feeling that someone must be there.

Certainly, it made sense that Grandpa would grab a flashlight before coming to get him in the dark.

Picking his way downstairs, careful to avoid broken glass, wood, and family memories which once hung on the walls, Aydin reached the first landing. Movement in the family room caught his eye, but he dismissed it as his mind playing tricks on him.

He glanced through a small window on the landing to see if any of the other homes were lit. In the distance, all he could see were sheets of rain, branches, and other unidentifiable things tossing around. He headed further down.

Pushing down his urge to run into the kitchen to find his grandfather, he moved toward the hallway leading to the storerooms where the flashlights were. He would need a flashlight, if it only served to calm his growing fears.

Something brushed past him the darkness.

The force caused Aydin to lose his footing and trip over his grandma's sewing basket. He landed on the floor next to Grandpa's chair. When he opened his eyes, what he saw challenged his own deepest and darkest fears for supremacy. If he had been able to, he would have forced himself to pass out so he did not have to lay eyes on the nightmare which had come to life.

A gray figure stood in front of him.

Standing at least a foot taller than his grandfather, it lacked facial features, and had skin holding the shape and form of something solid and yet mist-like. The more the lightning struck outside, the more he could see its constantly changing form swirling and shifting. This thing, this cloud creature, had two eyes and a mouth that were nothing more than black holes. Where a neck should have been, it was just a continuous nub to the top of its head. Arms and legs served only form rather than function.

The cloud creature stared at Aydin. While it displayed no aggression, Aydin just knew it posed a very real danger.

He scrambled around the couch, trying to get to the kitchen. And to Grandpa or Grandma.

A second cloud creature stepped out from the wall and shoved him, sending him crashing into the small coffee table.

"Grandpa! Grandma!" he cried. Could anyone even hear his pleas over the deafening wind?

The cloud creatures advanced, both now seeming to intend him harm.

As he backed into the wall, his left hand fell on something hard and familiar. His aluminum baseball bat, which Grandma had repeatedly told him to put away.

The second creature was almost upon him.

Aydin stood up and moved the bat to his right shoulder.

"Alright," he growled, not knowing where he suddenly got the guts. "If we're going to do this, then let's make it count."

The first cloud creature swiped at Aydin, but he ducked as lighting flashed. And counter attacked. The aluminum went through the creature like it was fog—yet it also seemed to shake the walking nightmare's resolve for a moment. More importantly, the second creature took a step back, leaving an opening.

Aydin ran into the short hallway connecting the family room and the kitchen. Reaching toward the storeroom door, he turned to see the wraiths closing the distance. He wouldn't have enough time to grab a flashlight before the cloud creatures got him. Instead, he dashed into the kitchen to either hide or fight.

One of the creatures advanced down the hallway in measured steps. The second walked through the wall, coming out to Aydin's left, effectively surrounding him.

On the center island was a space laser toy from an old cartoon show.

It was no flashlight, but the muzzle would pulse red when the trigger was depressed. In the sparse light the storm allowed through the windows, the toy could give him enough light to make an escape.

Aiming the laser, he pressed the trigger.

A small beam of light lit up the first cloud creature—and it recoiled from the weak beam.

Aydin ran around the island for some distance between him and them.

For a few moments, both of his assailants stood watching Aydin, perhaps trying to determine the best way to attack. Or maybe they simply weren't used to something pushing back. The thought gave him some more courage.

"Get out of here, both of you!" he shouted. "Go on! Leave!"

The one who had walked through the wall made a move for Aydin. He mashed the trigger again. But nothing happened.

The toy stubbornly refused to work. Aydin glanced around wildly, looking for an escape.

Behind him, a door led to the back of the house. Although he didn't want to run, he also had no way of knowing where his grandparents were. *And where were they? Hurt?* Whatever the truth, they'd want him to seek safety and get help.

Faking a swipe with the bat, which forced the wraiths back a step, he found room to make a break for it. Plunging through the back door, he fell into the chaos of the storm raging outside.

Wind and water pummeled him as he stumbled onto the sand. He regained his feet and ran toward the street. He risked a look back. What he saw made him stop in his tracks and his heart sink.

Lightning not having let up, gave him a glimpse of the chaos: All along the sand, hundreds, if not a thousand, wraiths advanced from the surf, attacking each home along the shoreline. They ripped through houses with a ferocity that sent chills through his spine. They tore wall from wall, door from frame. Roofs collapsed. It was no storm. Or not *just* a storm.

How could this happen? In the years Aydin had come to his grandparents' house, he'd never seen anything like this. He'd even ridden out a storm or two in his time at the beach.

Looking to his left, toward the Atlantic, a legion of the cloud creatures descended from the roiling ocean, aimed at the house next door. He tried to yell, to warn anyone who may have been sheltering from the storm, but the wind and rain carried away his voice.

The cloud creatures crashed through the home. Windows shattered, walls, siding, wires, and home furnishings were thrown like they were nothing. It all came down piece by piece.

Aydin spun back to his grandparents' house. If he couldn't help anyone else, he had to help them. Time was running out.

The wraiths towered over him by a few feet and were stronger than any normal human. They frightened him, to be sure, but he had defended himself. With tears stinging his eyes, he steeled his resolve once again and ran around the house as quickly as possible.

Against the sand, it felt like he was taking two steps back for every step forward. Rounding the corner, he was suddenly sent rolling into the sand. The work of an unseen wraith skulking near the house.

He pointed the pistol at the wraith who'd hit him, silently praying it would work.

"Get away from me, whatever you are!"

As he depressed the trigger, the small beam radiated forth.

And the thing halted. Then retreated a step.

He stepped forward, toy gun lit up, driving the creature further back.

"That's right! You just back off!"

Maneuvering himself just so, he saw a clear path and sprinted toward the back door.

More of the cloud creatures rose from the ocean, joining their fellow creatures. They likewise seemed scared of the light, and kept their distance. Aydin sensed something behind him. He turned just in time to see a tremendous hand swat him off his feet, throwing him into the sand.

He skidded to a halt and rocked back. Pain radiated through his body, but he seemed otherwise fine. He couldn't take many hits like that.

Aydin lifted the gun and pulled the trigger, but nothing happened. Even after he shook the toy.

The creatures sensed the sudden change in the boy's defenses and rushed at him like one solid mass.

Not wanting to find out what happened when they reached him, Aydin rolled to his right, narrowly avoiding one. He'd lost the bat, but Grandpa's words crept into his mind.

Flashlights are all powered up.

He ran, but his own terror made him miss the two steps into the house, causing him to trip and roll through the doorway. He crashed against the couch and the remains of a door.

Aydin climbed back to his feet and looked over his shoulder to see if any of the creatures were on top of him yet. While a few had renewed their pursuit, most hadn't. It created a merciful bit of space.

The first two cloud creatures were still in the house. One was pulling apart the spice cabinets in the kitchen. Crashes from the other side of the room suggested the other one was smashing its way through the family china. It was as if they were both desperate to find something.

Aydin flung himself down the back hallway, making a racket. At the same time, cloud creatures from outside began to pour in from a massive hole in the living room wall.

Aydin yanked open the storeroom door, hustled in, and slammed the entrance closed. He fumbled for the lock but couldn't find it. The handle to the door started to jiggle. Wispy hands came through and reached for him. With his free hand, Aydin groped for the flashlights on the wall.

One of the unseen hands in the dark grabbed his shirt and threatened to pull him *through* the door. Stitches on his pajama shirt gave way, though, leaving the monster with just cloth. But the sudden rip sent Aydin rolling down the stairs. He came to rest in a foot of water at the bottom. Choking, his heart convulsed as a new a pair of hands yanked him up.

"Aydin, thank God you're alright!"

"*Grandpa?*" He wiped water from his eyes and saw the old man, Grandma behind.

"I'm so sorry!" Grandpa said. "We would have come to get you, but the basement door was wedged shut. We only prayed that you made it out and to someplace safe."

"What *are* they, Grandpa?"

"From the storm, Aydin. Those things, whatever they are, came from the sea. I think they are looking for something. We need to get out of here." His grandfather looked him over. "Are you hurt?"

Aydin smiled weakly. "No, I'm fine. I'll be better as soon as we get out of here."

"Those things, Aydin. We need to keep our voices down so they can't hear us." The fear in his grandmother's face was evident.

"Don't worry, Grandma, I figured out how to hurt them."

"Oh yeah?" Grandpa said.

"The light. Light is like hitting them with a sword or something. But we need to move. I don't want to be around when the batteries run out. We should try and make it away from the beach, toward the main road."

Back at the top of the stairs, Aydin and Grandpa swept the room while Grandma covered their rear. Once in the living room, they pushed their way past the collection of broken and upturned furniture.

"There was a ton of them in here a second ago. Where did they all go?" Aydin scanned the room for any sign of the wraiths.

"Never mind. Let's not look a gift horse in the mouth." Grandpa motioned toward the open door and the small path leading to the main street. "Let's make a run for it."

They moment the trio stepped out onto the steps, they immediately stopped in renewed terror.

A wall of wraiths closed off any path to their salvation. A quick check on either side of the house confirmed the wall of creatures completely encircled the home.

"We need a plan!" Grandpa shouted.

Aydin swept his flashlight beam across the wall of wraiths, but it had little effect, which caused him to step back in horror. "It's like since they're together, it doesn't hurt them!"

"Back to the house, barricade the door!" Grandpa hollered.

They ran back into the kitchen and blocked up the remains of the door with furniture. They did the same at front of the house.

Efforts were meaningless as the creatures passed through as if the barricades weren't there.

The flashlights managed to slow them down, at least, but they were surrounded in the living room.

Aydin swung his light in mad arcs, just trying to hit the nearest wraith before moving onto the next. He heard himself sobbing, almost moaning, but he didn't stop. His wild beam hit upon the remains of the curio cabinet and something reflected back with shimmering brilliance.

And the wall of wraiths all shrieked, as if something had stabbed them.

Aydin circled the light over the curio once again. The flashing reflection came once again. And the wraiths screamed.

"Turn off the flashlights!" Aydin suddenly commanded.

"They'll kill us!" Grandma protested.

"I know what they want!" Aydin shouted.

They all switched off their lights.

Aydin pulled the shiny gray stone from the curio cabinet, the one they'd rescued from the beach that morning.

"*This?*" he said to the wall of cloud creatures.

The mass of wraiths didn't move. But they halted their movement toward them.

Aydin thrust the stone towards the nearest one.

"Take it! Take it and leave us. Please! We didn't know."

Swirling appendages, two of them, reached out and grasped the stone.

And the world went gray.

Before Aydin passed out, he could swear he caught the briefest glimpse into another world. One filled with monsters of all shapes and sizes existing only in the most violent parts of Atlantic storms. Whole civilizations of grey beings staying mostly out of the prying eyes of the surface dwellers. They vowed to only venture forth when threatened. And in return Aydin must now be the bearer of their tempestuous message.

Never again dare to take what doesn't belong in human hands.

A HOUSE'S TALE

Brad Center

The House

The House slumbered. It lazed off the main road, tucked behind an old-growth forest deep in the Virginia countryside. It had been built four hundred years ago by men long since turned to dust. Surry County had stayed pretty much the same since its founding in the mid-1600s: rolling hills, farmland, and forests. Like an island in an ever-rising sea of modernity, it remained, for the most part, silent and tranquil.

The House came into being in 1622. It sat upon blood-soaked land where Native Americans had fought against the English settlers. The battle had been horrific, and many souls had been lost. Their pain and anguish flowed into the very soil upon which The House now stood. Each soul had deposited its own personal misery into the land, and The House absorbed all of that raw emotional energy. Down the road from The House was the famous Bacon Castle, which had been erected on the outskirts of the battlefield. It had assimilated far less of that emotional force and was, therefore, less alive than The House. The Bacon House was famously haunted, but The House was alive.

Over the years, The House had been home to many souls, each unknowingly leaving some of their psychic and emotional energy behind. Slowly, over time, the emotional energy accumulated within The House. Perhaps it was fate, bad luck, or just an accurate reflection of the human condition, but The House received vastly more negative energy with each passing generation. That energy acted as a catalyst, lighting a match to the toxic land on which The House stood. Once The House reached a critical mass, it became fully sentient. The House was a complex being, but one formed predominantly from the darker side of humanity.

Now The House stood alone, long ago deserted by human inhabitants. It did not know precisely why, but it surmised that having achieved sentience, humans could now feel its darker nature and shied away. Alone with no one to interact with for over sixty years, The House had time to consider all that it had been given, and now it was ready to give back what it had consumed.

One winter's day, it perceived something new. A car approached. Its headlights glinted off the falling snow, illuminating The House. The front door opened, and finally, after so much time, people were inside its four walls again. It sighed with anticipation.

The family stepped inside, a mother, father, and young girl. The House could immediately feel the emotional force that emanated from the new inhabitants. The energy that swirled within and between them was intense, and The House immediately felt the influence. The depths of the resentment and cruelty from the older inhabitants bombarded it, replenishing The House, slaking a thirst that stemmed from its very foundation.

The Girl

It was evening, and the sun was sliding down the sky but hadn't yet said its final goodnight. Adeline peered out the car window as they drove up the long winding road that led to their new home. The building became larger in the car window like a camera zooming in for the perfect picture. The House was dark, and it seemed to Adeline like it was sucking in the last vestiges of light from the darkening sky. *This House*, Adeline thought, *was asleep*. Like a dormant sentinel, it sat waiting. *But waiting for what?* she wondered.

A gentle snow began to fall and glinted off the car's headlights as her father brought the car to a stop about a hundred feet from The House, far enough away that you could see the entire front of the structure. It was that big. Adeline waited for her parents to give her permission to exit the car. She dared not get out before they gave consent—that would lead to a tongue-lashing or perhaps the real thing. Her father glared at her and gave her the slightest of nods. That was her father's traditional signal to proceed. In her father's opinion, that was all she deserved—just the merest of nods.

She got out of the car, her eyes never leaving The House. The front porch sagged a bit, the wooden posts seemingly unable to fully support the structure's weight. To Adeline, it looked as if The House wore a melancholy expression. She was all too familiar with that emotion, like a pair of jeans she'd worn out.

Her mother pulled on her arm. Apparently, she had been staring at The House for quite a while.

"Get moving, you insufferable child," her mother seethed. How many times had her mother uttered those despicable words? Hundreds? Thousands? Adeline had lost count. She understood that her parents thought of her as a possession. A thing to be used as they saw fit. When they weren't punishing her, they ignored her. She supposed she served as an outlet for all their negative thoughts and emotions. Perhaps they hated themselves and found it easier to vent that hatred outwardly than inward. She could only guess, and in the end, did it really matter?

As they entered The House, her father began to take note of every detail. He started a running monologue.

"This place is enormous for a home originally built in the 1600s. You know that about a mile down the road sits the Bacon Castle. Some say that house is haunted." He laughed at his own comment. "Of course, people will believe just about anything," he mused.

Adeline listened to him describe The House. He dutifully cataloged every room as they walked through the building. Adeline listened attentively because her father required it. Still, while she listened to him, she could almost hear another voice in her head. It whispered to her in images. She saw a battle, then a house—this house—and then the faces of hundreds of people flashed before her, their faces filled with anger and pain. It confused and frightened her, so she tried to ignore it as best she could. She shivered involuntarily.

And, as usual, her parents ignored her.

There were six bedrooms on the second floor. Adeline selected the one farthest away from the master suite where her parents had taken up residence. She unpacked her things meticulously, placing her toys and puzzles at seemingly random but predetermined locations. Then she took out her magic kit and her most cherished possession, a copy of *The Rohonc Codex*. Adeline had purchased a copy in a small bookstore in Old Town Alexandria, not far from where they used to live. The book was believed to contain real magic, incantations, and myriad ways to access dark powers. It was an illustrated manuscript written in some ancient language that Adeline didn't know, but the pictures captivated her. She would often take the book out and stare at the pages, entranced by a power she didn't quite understand. Her parents knew about her fascination with magic but chose to ignore it. They deemed it childish and inappropriate for a young girl of twelve. Adeline thought differently.

Adeline washed up for supper and headed down the winding staircase that seemed to spiral on and on into infinity. It was an optical illusion, but it fascinated Adeline as she made her way down to the main floor. In fact, everything about their new home fascinated her.

As Adeline sat down, her parents glared at her. For the millionth time, she wondered why her parents had even bothered to conceive a child since they seemed only to enjoy berating and beating her. It was a terrible thought, but one that refused to go away. She ate in silence. It was the easiest and smartest thing to do.

Just then, somewhere deep down in her core, she felt a comforting presence, like The House could feel her dismay and understood.

"You realize that you will be going back to school in a couple of days?" her mother said.

"Yes, Mother," she responded. She'd learned the hard way not to annoy her parents with anything less than a direct and polite reply. If she needed any reminders of what would happen if she didn't, the scars on her back and bottom served their purpose well.

Her mother looked at her reproachfully. Adeline could feel resentment in those eyes— eyes that seemed to hold no love. Eyes that dismissed and diminished her with a mere glance.

"May I be excused?" asked Adeline. Her parents said nothing and simply continued to eat their food. She froze with indecision. Should she get up? Her parents hadn't responded, but they also hadn't objected. She sat there for a minute or two, then slowly rose, hoping to slink quietly back to her room where she could relax.

"Just where the hell do you think you're going!" her father bellowed.

"Um…I asked to be excused, and well…no one said anything. So, I was just going to…" she stammered.

"You sit your ass down right now and wait until I tell you you're excused."

She sat down immediately. Fear ran through her, piercing her skin like a thousand bee stings. She lowered her head, glancing furtively at her parents.

What would her father do?

Tiny beads of sweat formed on her brow. Dread spread through her like a malevolent virus, attacking her insides, causing her stomach to lurch and her heart to pound in a dissonant and chaotic rhythm. Then her father stood, and terror replaced dread as he advanced upon her.

"Never you mind," he said. "Don't sit. Just stand your insolent ass up and learn some manners."

He removed his belt with one hand while grabbing her with the other. In one smooth, well-practiced, and deft motion, he bent her over the dining room table and thrashed her with his belt on her bottom, weakly protected only by a thin skirt. The pain cascaded through her body, lancing down her legs and up her back simultaneously. The pain came in torrents with each lash. Waves of it washed over her, like hail slashing across her flesh in a fierce wind. Each crack of the leather pierced into the marrow of her bones. As she absorbed the pain, she took a moment to look in her mother's direction, and to her horror, she saw a wry smile creep across her face—growing wider with each blow she received.

She closed her eyes—and suddenly, she could feel a spark of light deep down inside her. It was like some external force had struck a match, alighting her anger and resentment.

The beating lasted five full minutes. After it was done, Adeline staggered upstairs, holding back her tears as best she could, knowing that crying only brought her parents the perverse pleasure they seemed to desire.

As she reached the sanctuary of her room, she collapsed on her mattress, lying on her stomach to avoid further pain. She lay there for some time, giving the pain a chance to subside to a mere throb. She would be sore for days until the welts, now red and inflamed, would eventually fade. However, the memory of her mother's smile would likely never fade; it would find a nasty hiding place in her mind forever.

Adeline moved to the floor with slow, deliberate motions and took out her copy of *The Rohonc Codex*. The pictures in the book soothed her. She wished she knew what the words meant. Perhaps then she could cast a spell and find herself far away from the horrible creatures that passed for her parents. Slowly Adeline caressed the pages and began to whisper. She prayed to powers she neither saw nor understood, hoping for some kind of miracle.

The House

The House understood that while it owed part of its sentience to people and their emotional energy, it also harbored deep resentment toward them. The House now lived, but it could not move. It was stuck here in the woods. It could not wander; it could not do anything except simply exist. It would sit here alone and without purpose until the elements wore it down or men destroyed it to build something shiny and new. So, it resented the humans that had helped give it life. Yet, it was a life without purpose, without companionship—a life alone. Over time, this resentment had grown and turned to hate. Inside, a furnace of hate blazed and raged. It would need to be released.

Now that new humans inhabited it, The House considered what to do next. How should it react, especially to the sadistic parents of the young girl? It had decades of powerful and corrosive energy stored within its walls. It could unleash that power and feed off their fear and resentment until they vanished into nothingness. Yes, it could do that. That would suit The House just fine. Yet, The House hesitated. While it stood ready to destroy the adult humans, the young girl was a different matter. It had witnessed the raw abuse, pain, and sadism of the adults. There was something different about the young girl. It began to feel wisps of something other than hate, something it could barely recognize, something buried for a very long time. The House paused and considered how it felt for this young girl. Did it care for her, and if so, why?

The girl seemed to be on the verge of sensing beyond the shroud of normalcy that cloaked most human activity. In fact, she might be able to feel The House's presence, which greatly intrigued it. The House considered how it might reach the girl. To reach her, it would need to release some of the human emotions it had absorbed over the years. Carefully, it decided to release the merest quantity in the girl's direction.

The House watched as the girl lay in her bedroom as she reacted immediately to The House's contact. Goosebumps raced down her arms. She held tightly to the book in her hands, but at the same time, her eyes began to wander around the room. A tinge of excitement seemed to run across her face, like a mouse peeking out of its hole. Then it disappeared, replaced by alarm. The House considered the girl's reaction. It examined the emotional energy it had just released and noticed remnants of anger and resentment within the stream. It made some adjustments and filtered out those emotions, concentrating on only positive ones. It didn't have a great reservoir of these emotions within its stores, but there was a sufficient amount for this purpose. This time the girl responded without any hesitation.

She looked up for a second time. The House could tell it was reaching her.

"What's happening?" she said out loud.

The House could tell the girl was confused. This was hardly natural for her, even though she was no ordinary girl. The girl looked down at the book she was holding, and again she spoke out loud, "Is this some type of magic? Who is this?"

The House considered how to respond. It realized at that moment that it did not have a name. It was The House. It paused in reflection and then simply responded into the child's mind with the thought, "The House."

"The House?" Adeline replied.

"Yes, I am The House." It conveyed this to her as a series of images and concepts.

The House watched as Adeline processed this and could see the mix of curiosity and apprehension wash over her face. "Was this possible? Could this be real?" She didn't know for sure. She looked down at her book, *The Rohonc Codex*, and wondered. In the end, she didn't know what to think but decided she had to explore this further.

They shared a couple of initial images with each other. The House could see the concentration on Adeline's face as she learned to communicate with it. After a few minutes, a weary expression crossed her face, and she collapsed onto her bed. Obviously, she was exhausted from the beating and these initial communications. Quietly she drifted to sleep.

Over the next two weeks, The House continued to converse with Adeline. During the day, when Adeline went to school, The House waited patiently until her return. It watched as she did her homework, and then they spent evenings just sharing experiences. They shared concepts, thoughts, and emotions, but most of all, they shared their pain. Through those exchanges, Adeline learned about The House's past—its bloody history and its anger, loss, and resentment. But she also learned that underneath it all, there was a vast loneliness as wide as the sky and as deep as the forest around them.

And for the first time in The House's memory, it had a companion. During this period, it felt the long-neglected emotions stir. This experience was totally foreign to it. For the first time in its solitary existence, The House *cared*.

During this time, The House watched with anger and dismay as Adeline's parents punished her for imagined slights, perceived disobedience, and insults. They hit, slapped, pounded, and punched her, enjoying every ounce of pain they inflicted. They used fists, belts, high-heel shoes, and kitchen utensils. They were quite inventive in satisfying their evil appetites. However, the parents could not hide their actions from The House. It saw and felt every stinging blow and every tear that rolled down Adeline's cheek. At night The House watched as Adeline cried softly into her pillow. Between her sobs, The House tried to comfort her. It was painful for both of them. The House decided that this had to end. It devised a plan, but it could not reveal the full nature of that plan to Adeline—at least not yet.

The Girl

Adeline listened as The House spoke to her. As always, their conversation existed not in spoken words but in thoughts, images, and concepts. To Adeline's surprise, this led to more truthful and meaningful communication. Slowly she began to comprehend The House's plan.

Could she go along with what The House intended to do? Hating someone was one thing but seeing them punished was another. The House would hurt them. It would frighten them, and ultimately it would threaten them. They would no longer inflict pain on Adeline or suffer the consequences. If she was being honest with herself, that was precisely what she wanted, what she had prayed for to unknowable gods, what she had wished for on so many painful nights, and what she had to finally confess to her own heart.

The plan was was simple. When her parents came home that evening, she would tell them that the lights had gone out just before they got home. She would lead them down to the basement where the circuit breakers were and close the basement door as they descended the steps. She would quietly lock the door behind them, and then The House would reveal itself to them, and they would feel just a tiny taste of the pain they had given her. No one would hear them scream from the basement, and they would not be able to escape.

It was evening when her parents came home. Adeline and The House were waiting. The home now lay in complete darkness, every light asleep as they waited for the nightmare plan to unfold. Adeline noticed she was sweating with a mixture of fear and anticipation. Her stomach lurched up and down like a ship caught in turbulent seas.

"Adeline? Why is the blasted house completely dark? What the hell have you done now?" her father said.

"I'm here," Adeline responded in a whisper.

"Well, isn't that wonderful," he said with evident sarcasm. "Now answer my question before your mother and I trip in the darkness."

"The lights just went out a few minutes ago. I guess a circuit went out."

"So, now you're an electrician?" her mother spat into the blackness.

"Hold on just a second," her father said. He ruffled in his pocket and produced a lighter. He flicked it, and the room lit with a soft glow. He scowled in Adeline's direction. That scowl said he planned to beat the living tar out of her as soon as he fixed the lights. Adeline cringed reflexively but then remembered what awaited her parents in the basement, and she let the fear drain away from her.

Not this time, she thought. *No, not this time.*

Her father walked toward the basement door, but her mother did not follow. For a moment, Adeline panicked. What would she do if her mother didn't follow? Then inspiration arose in her like a submerged lifeboat popping out of the water.

"Father, maybe Mother should go with you and hold the lighter while you flip the circuit breaker?"

Again, he scowled at her, but Adeline could see that he was seriously thinking through her suggestion, even if he would never admit as much.

He motioned to his wife to take the lighter. Together they descended the stairs. The tiny flame cast pale shadows on the walls as they made their way down into the gloom. Adeline gave her parents one last glance, and then slowly, gently, with only the merest sound, closed and locked the door behind them.

The House

The House felt the parents enter the basement. While Adeline believed that The House's plan was merely to scare and threaten her parents, The House intended to do much more—so much more. When they reached the basement floor, The House struck them with a barrage of images that simultaneously pummeled them from everywhere and nowhere. It did not just want to end them; it wanted them to know who was doing this to them and why.

Adeline's parents froze. They turned to each other, mouths agape. They saw images of The House and all the evil things that had taken place within it. Then they saw images of the pain they inflicted on their daughter.

"Did you see that?" gasped Adeline's father.

"Yes," stammered his wife.

"Dear God, what are we seeing?" he asked.

"I don't know. It's pitch black. How are we seeing anything? Make it stop. Please just make it stop!"

Then The House struck. In a ragging deluge, it poured forth all its black and terrible energy, all of the hatred and resentment stored deep within. It hit Adeline's parents like a powerful storm, forcing them to cower in pain and fear from the onslaught. The force of the energy ripped into them. At first, they felt tremendous heat, then their skin began to peel, and their blood began to boil. They screamed in agony.

Upstairs, Adeline heard her parents wail in utter anguish. She froze for an instant. This sounded far worse than she thought it would. What was The

House doing to them down there? The screams of torment faded into an eerie silence, and Adeline started to move. She opened the door and walked cautiously down the stairs. What greeted her were two semi-liquid forms at the bottom of the stairs. She gasped. The sight was horrible; in that instant, she knew The House had tricked her. The House had always planned to kill her parents. Adeline knew that now, and while she had not planned for this gruesome end, she greeted it stoically. She looked at what was left of her parents, and try as she might, she could feel no grief or remorse.

"They don't look human anymore. But this is the way I have always seen them, how they were on the inside. They were always less than human to me, and now they look the part." She spoke these words out loud in part to confirm what she was seeing. She would need to clean up this mess and put the remains of her parents in the furnace. If she were ever asked, she would say they went for a walk that evening and never returned.

But there was no one who would ask. No one who would ever know. Only Adeline and The House.

She walked up the stairs, out of the basement, and into an unknown future. But a future without constant torment. She understood that she was now bound to The House. They would share the future together. She nodded outwardly as if to confirm this to herself. Then, slowly, the corners of Adeline's mouth turned up, and a small smile crept across her face.

NOTCHES

D. Alexander Ward

"I heard all things in the heaven and in the earth. I heard many things in hell. How, then, am I mad? Hearken! and observe how healthily—how calmly I can tell you the whole story."

—Edgar Allan Poe, "The Tell-Tale Heart"

I come awake with my jeans bunched around my ankles, slouching on the toilet in a gas station bathroom. I'm halfway through a cigarette that smoldered out a while ago but still dangles from my bottom lip and I'm apparently more than halfway through answering nature's call, so I decide to finish up both.

Lighting and dragging on my smoke, my head's clearing a little. I wonder how long I've been here like this. Hell of a bender last night, I guess. Or was it the night before? Either way, I don't reckon it's important.

I finish up, toss the smoke into the bowl, flush, and stand on shaky legs. I reckon I ought to be awarded a medal or something by the owner of the gas station, just for having the courtesy to actually use the toilet. Judging from the stank and stains that decorate the floor and walls, this particular porcelain throne don't get to see all that much use.

"Fuck the medal," I say, buttoning my jeans and cinching my belt. "Maybe a free fill-up, though."

Just then, I get to wondering about my ride. And since every memory in my brain more recent than a few minutes ago is dark and murky, there's a lot to wonder about. I go to wash up, roll up the sleeves of my flannel jacket, and reach for the handle on the spigot.

There's a nickel-plated 9mm Colt pistol in the sink. Walnut grip with half a dozen rough notches scratched into one side. Some were there when the gun came to me, some I've added since.

Not that I'm a killer, but it pays to look the part.

I check the clip and find a few rounds missing. Odd, but then again, maybe not so odd for the kind of day I'm having. I start washing up, looking down as I soap my hands, then something drops into the sink with a crisp little *plink* as it hits the porcelain. But the water's running and there ain't no stopper, so I only get a quick look before it goes slipping down the drain, a ribbon of blood trailing behind it.

A tooth.

Mine also, just like the gun. Except the tooth didn't look much like mine, which are crooked and yellow, some of them half-rotted. Mountain Dew mouth, it's called in the hill country of western Virginia, though I reckon you can find it everywhere there's poor folks. Naw, that sucker that just went for a swim had a nice shape, white and shiny. Looked more like one of my buddy Hector's teeth. Everyone calls Hector "Pearly" on account of his perfect teeth, see. He made it through three years in Powhatan Correctional—a gladiator camp, they call it—and came out not only alive but with his mouthful of pearly whites intact. A thing unheard of.

Me and Pearly have been tight ever since we were just kids growing up in Saluda, which is just a blip on the map among other blip towns that barely deserve the distinction. Like many of those towns, it was—and still is—nestled among family farms and so many creeks and rivers leading out to the Chesapeake Bay it'd make your head spin to count them all. His unpainted cinderblock house was right next to our weathered old Colonial with the leaning porch and sinking foundation. We spent the summers together on that porch, reading comics we'd lifted from the corner store, fighting over who could get the rabbit ears on the TV just right so we could watch *Miami Vice* and *Dallas* and *Hill Street Blues*. Always dreaming and scheming how we could have better lives than the hardscrabble one we'd been born into. Better lives, like the ones we saw on that TV screen.

But it was just a dream. Pearly's folks were migrant workers from Mexico or El Salvador or some place. From day one, they toiled in those fields and barns, picking tomatoes, corn, and soybeans for damn near slave wages. My old man had been a waterman all his life until long after the cost of fuel to run the boat was more than what he could catch and sell. Back then, whenever he got deep into a bottle of cheap whiskey, he'd rant about how the big companies were overfishing the bay and how the pollution was killing everything off.

But just ranting about an evil thing ain't never once fixed the thing. So, when Daddy sold the boat, quit the water, and went to work in the fields, me and Ma went with him—just trying to keep the lights on, you know—and Pearly was there, too.

Hell, me and Pearly have always been friends.

Anyway, I push all the memory lane shit to the side and look into the mirror and open wide. Sure enough, I'm missing one of those flat little numbers just to the right of my two front choppers. Red droplets ooze from the crater it left behind. I spit, rinse my hands, dry them on my jeans, and head for the door.

It's nighttime, the sky clouded and starless. Feels late, but I don't know. The sodium light burning high up on the outside wall of the building stings my eyes and my head so badly that I consider a retreat back into the shitter. But there's my ride parked over yonder in the lot. A red 1977 Lincoln Continental. A real boat of a car. Rough and faded on the outside, sure, but I keep the interior clean, and she runs just fine.

It's colder than a well-digger's ass, so I shove my hands into my jacket pockets and cross the lot, cursing the wintertime as I climb in behind the wheel. First thing I notice is the smell. It's earthy and sour. Could be piss, but I ain't sure. Second thing I notice is Brenda in the backseat, leaning against the door, eyes closed, mouth open.

I flick on the overhead light.

Brenda's a gal me and Pearly met a few years back. She runs with us every now and then, parties with us, fucks one of us every now and then. Nothing exclusive, though. Brenda runs around with whoever she wants *whenever* she wants. She's mean as a snake on a good day, but she gets real nasty sometimes when she's been in her cups or is good and high on uppers. Gets all riled and wants to fight. Used to be a trauma nurse at Norfolk General, until they caught her lifting pills from the hospital cookie jar—pills to support the habit she got because of that very same job. Pills to stay awake during her sixteen-hour shifts, then pills to fall asleep. And round and round it went. Same old story, no surprises. When she's not high, Brenda's sharp, quick, and usually more than a little twisted—just the kind of woman who'd run around with a couple low-rent motherfuckers like us.

She's not dressed for the cold, though. Acid wash jeans yellowed from the nightly fog of smoke-filled beer joints, a dingy black halter top that looks like it's choking her, and sandy yellow hair teased up to the stars with hairspray. Brenda always looks like she got lost on the way to a Whitesnake concert back in 1987 and somehow ended up here instead. She's trash, but so am I. She just wears it better.

I start the car and slide the heater to full-blast, rubbing my hands together in front of the vents on the dash. "Brenda!" I holler, adjusting the rear-view mirror to see her. "I swear to fuck, if you've OD'ed in my car, y—"

I stop not because I decide she has OD'ed—in fact, I can now see her breath fogging the cold glass of the window—but because I catch sight of myself in the mirror. My...my face. My eye. For a second I stop breathing because...shit, can that really be me looking back from that mirror?

A jagged scar, open but not bleeding, like split raw chicken skin, slashes a diagonal from my left temple to my bottom lip. The eye that it crosses over is grayed out, a white film over the iris. I press at it through the lid and find it soft and terribly fragile.

"Like a glob of Jell-O," I whisper.

"There's always roo-oom," Brenda says in a sing-song voice from the back, but for the moment I ignore her and keep staring at my poor damaged mug.

I was just in the shitter, checked my mouth when the tooth fell out, and I didn't look this. Unless I was too fucked-up to see it.

Or unless I'm just plain fucked-up and that's why I'm seeing it.

I turn around and look Brenda in the face. "What the hell'd you say?"

But she doesn't reply; just kind of lolls her head about. Eyes distant, like she's following trails, like she's tripping balls. And that makes some sense, don't it?

"Shit," I spit out, turning back around. "What the hell'd we get into?"

I try to remember, but can't. Can't put shit together. The past couple days are a puzzle and all I've got are the corner pieces. Did me and Pearly pull a job? Our usual gig is a pharmacy. B&E smash-and-grab-type shit. Whatever we can get our hands on—from Oxy and Vicodin to Valium and Adderall—and get the hell out in less than five minutes. Then we unload the pills in Richmond, or sometimes sell to the River Lords, a local motorcycle club that buys in bulk.

I glance over at the empty passenger seat. "And where the fuck is Pearly?"

From the back, Brenda giggles like a devil. "Pearly's fishing," she says. "Pearly's gone fishing."

Damn, this girl is high, but maybe not useless. Pearly has a place on a backwater creek off the Pamunkey River. It'd be a stretch to call it a house—more like a shotgun shack. Picked it up at a county auction for next to nothing, which is about what it's worth. We spend time there, lay low there sometimes after a job. Maybe that's what she means.

I slam the shifter into drive and ease out of the parking lot. Whatever's going on with me—bad drugs, bad booze, or just losing my marbles—I have to put it out of my mind.

Pearly will clear all this up. I just have to find him.

On the divided highway, I open it up and the engine growls as the Lincoln feasts on the empty roads of night, winding eastward, deeper into the river country.

An hour later, I pull up to Pearly's clapboard shack crouched at the edge of a tidal bog thick with reeds and cattails. It doesn't look like anyone's home. The place is a dark spot set against an already inky black vista, broken only by the brilliant lights of the paper mill across the river in West Point.

The mill, with its towering steel contours and skeletal crane arms blazing with light, looms in the distance like a stark and deadly temple of industry. The smoke rolling out of the stacks is elegant and pure white—fair weather clouds that belong to a blue sky, rising into the night instead and stinking of chemical rot. Breathing around here without retching is a learned skill.

Pearly's place don't have electricity or anything like that, but it has a genny which, if he was here, would be running and powering the dozens of naked bulbs strung up everywhere. Pearly ain't fond of the dark, so he won't even sleep with the lights off. I reckon that's on account of the times he spent in the hole back at the pen, but he don't like to talk about it much, so I never ask too many questions. It should look like Christmas around this place, but it doesn't.

I check the rearview and find Brenda still sacked out in the back, still sleeping off her high. My face, lit from the glow of the dashboard, is still a mess. Even worse than before. My skin has gone fishbelly white and it's slick with a sheen of sweat.

Except I'm not actually sweating; I'm freezing even with the heater running on high.

It occurs to me all of this might be more than a bad trip from some bad dope. Might be something worse. Am I having some kind of stroke? Maybe it's brain cancer or some shit? I haven't exactly lived at the foot of the cross, as they say, so anything's possible.

All the same, it does me no good to keep wondering about it.

I glance out the window at the expanse of night around me. I know I'm gonna get out and check the place over, but I don't feel like leaving the warmth of the Lincoln. From my jeans pocket, I fish out a small key that opens the glovebox. In the box, I sift through random junk—a near-empty pack of smokes, an old burner cell phone, deck of cards, a Buck knife, book of matches—until I find the key to the Lincoln's trunk, where I'm pretty sure I've got a flashlight stashed.

Pulling on the door latch, I pause because, weirdly, there's something tumbling around in my mouth, and with it is the burnt, metallic taste of blood. I know what it is before I even spit it into my hand.

And there it is. The pointy tooth next to the one I lost earlier. It's covered in a pinkish slime of blood and saliva, but it still don't look like mine. Not with its perfect cone shape and the smooth, even brightness of it. I flick it to the floor, glance in the mirror just to confirm that, somehow, I'm still tripping, and sure enough there's now a gaping space along my top row of teeth. Also, still there? My mangled features.

"Jesus," I groan, then look away.

I decide to leave the engine running because I don't intend to linger here long. I don't even bother with locking the glovebox. The frigid dark slaps me across the face when I step out, and I find myself cursing the chill again. I go around back of the car, slip the key into the lock and raise the trunk lid.

The spare tire sits right in the middle of the deep well of the trunk. My tool bag's on top of it, a hammer and the wooden grip of a handsaw poking out. There are two nice, new duffle bags on either side, too, and like so much else today, I don't recognize them or remember how they got here.

I go to satisfy the next natural question and unzip one, then step back, rake a clawed hand through my hair, and blow out a long breath of smoke.

Brown Sugar heroin. A lot of it. More than I've ever seen and certainly more than me and Pearly have ever sold. Must be about twenty bricks in this duffle, so I check the other and find the same.

Has to be a hundred thousand bucks of the stuff right before my eyes.

"Holy fuck. Where'd we get this shit?" I whisper to the night.

I zip them back up, grab the flashlight from the tool bag, and shut the lid, making sure it's good and locked. Leaning against the car a moment, I shove the trunk key into my jeans pocket and take a couple drags off my smoke. I wonder where the hell we'd ever come across that kind of haul. I could ask Brenda, but she's still in the back seat passed out hard. Anyway, who's to say she'd remember any more than I can.

Still, the question gnaws at me. Everyone we messed around with was small-time, and transactions were usually no more than a few thousand dollars at most. Who had the kind of capital and the juice for something like this?

And then, like a thought whispered into my ear, it comes to me.

The River Lords MC.

Mules, I think. *We were muling for the bikers. Picking up, then dropping off.*

That was it. I can't say the memory was clear as a bell. Everything, even things I damn well ought to know, still feel like a dream only half-remembered. Me and Pearly aren't gangsters. We're small potatoes—expendable nobodies. Using us, the River Lords don't risk getting caught with it if shit goes sideways. And if all goes well, we deliver it to them and they give us our transportation fee.

But us dumbfucks decided to keep it, so we could sell it ourselves.

Talk about bad ideas. Christ, what were we thinking?

Could have been nice and easy. Should have been.

But I reckon there's nothing like a hundred grand worth of smack in the trunk of the car to give a couple small-time crooks delusions of grandeur. I try to remember, for a moment, if it was Pearly's idea or mine…or someone else's. I try to recall, but my head is still swimmy and aches with every stretch of thought.

The cigarette pinched between my lips, I click the flashlight on and start toward the house. The front porch overhang is eaten up with rot and tilted like a smirk. A couple weathered wicker chairs flank the doorway and over to the right sits the generator, silent. My light flashes over a can of Steel Reserve beer on the railing. My preferred brand. I push open the screen door into the house.

It's grave-cold in here. Just as dark and quiet, too. The two rooms of the shack are nothing special. A couch and a couple of chairs we pulled out of dumpsters. An old TV set with rabbit ears and lots of empty bottles and cans piled up in the corner of the first room. No Pearly snoring on the couch, though, and nothing out of place.

I walk deeper into the house, and the second room—the bedroom, we call it—changes things.

There's a kerosene heater in the corner that's turned over, the fuel having soaked into the thin rug and the floorboards beneath. The sheets of the mattress shoved against the wall are mussed, which ain't nothing unusual. But there are pools and swaths of something dark, now frozen to the fabric in the chill air. It's all over the sheets. I don't have to guess what it is. Along the floor, heading out the back door, more droplets and splashes. The back window is missing a couple glass panes and the edge of the door has a round hole burrowed into it that's cracked the wood in every direction. I slide my fingers over it as I approach and know it's from a bullet. I reach under my jacket to the small of my back, draw the Colt pistol, and think for a moment of the missing rounds.

Cautious now but also eager to see where this trail is leading me, I step through the door with the gun up. There's not much to the back of the house. Just a landing and some rickety steps that lead down to the dock stretching out over the creek. I take the steps with care. There ain't many sounds this time of year, just the lap of the water as the tide ebbs out into the bay, and the cold breeze rustling the reeds. But with the adrenaline surging through me right now, those gentle sounds are loud as firecrackers.

Out in the dark, down by the water, there is a memory—a truth that's calling to me.

I walk to the end of the dock, casting about with the flashlight. I don't see anything. It's too damn cold even for the croaker and spot and other fish that might occasionally breach the surface of these waters. I creep closer to the edge, shining the light down into the murk. And that's when I see it.

The faded red and white bobber dancing in the current, and with it the corner of a familiar blue bandana caught around the frayed rope all but invisible beneath the dark water.

It's Pearly's bandana—the one he always wears to cover the stringy hair of his balding pate.

I bend down, set the gun on the dock, take the rope knotted to the pylon in my fist, and pull. I pull and pull, but whatever's down there is heavy or maybe stuck on something at the bottom of the creek. It ain't coming up without a fight. So, I drop the flashlight and it rolls across the boards into a position not at all helpful to the task. But it allows me to use both hands.

Part of me—maybe a big part—doesn't want to know what's at the other end of this rope. It's telling me to drop the whole damn thing and get the hell out of there. The other part of me is louder, like ants crawling in my brain, and demands to know.

I've never been one to debate the devil on my shoulder.

Squatting at the edge of the dock, I yank upward with the strength of both arms, but the other end of the rope still won't budge. I'm frantic now, so I keep tugging and jerking and pulling. Then I feel the release as the suction of the mud along the creek bottom is broken, and I go down onto my ass. Now, with legs kicked out like opened scissors, I keep on pulling, hand over hand. The rope that passes through my fingers is not only cold but wet, and stinks of brackish water mixed with the chemical waste from the paper mill.

It's a stench I now recognize:

It's what the Lincoln smelled like back at the gas station.

Most definitely not piss, I think.

Another heave with muscles burning from the effort and it breaks the surface of the water, flying out of it, and comes up over the edge with a metallic clatter. I go all catawampus from the sudden lack of resistance and the hand I shoot out to steady myself smacks the wide lens of the flashlight and sets it spinning. The object from the water comes to rest between my splayed legs, practically landing in my lap, and as my searching fingers catch in the web of chicken-wire, I am relieved to finally know what it is.

Just a crab pot.

A nervous laugh rattles out of me. I lean back a bit, gazing up at the cold stars and letting go a breath of relief.

Just a crab pot, nothing more.

So, I sit up to get a good look, and the chuckle at my own stupidity dies in my throat and spirals down into a low, keening sound I reckon I've not made since I was a boy. The flashlight has stopped its spinning and the beam of light shines upon the wire mesh of the pot.

Pearly's head is jammed tight into the bait basket of the pot.

And in his corpsy face, I see something of my own.

The gash that cuts a line from his temple to his chin. The same couple of teeth missing from his dead, opened mouth, frozen lips dribbling water onto the boards. The lifeless, white pallor of his skin, soaked and slick from the river.

There's a scurry of tiny, young crabs picking at that pale left eye. As I gawk, a beefy adult blue crab—I can't tell if it's a jimmy or a sook—climbs over the others and pierces that eyeball with the sword of its pincers, plucks it free of the socket, drags it away.

And just like that, my left eye goes dark.

I'm half-blind now, but I see.

I see.

Pearly's been haunting me all along. My wounds are his wounds. My ruined face isn't a bad trip, but an echo. A mask fashioned after his final likeness.

I'm scrambling, trying to make some sense of it, even if there's none to be made. Every sound is still loud as a freight train and the warble escaping my lips has joined with the banging of my heartbeat, all of it filling my ears.

That's why I don't hear what's coming.

In fact, I don't hear a thing until the point of a familiar Buck knife slips out of the shadows and presses against my throat—along with the impossibly even and sober lilt of Brenda's voice.

"You remembered anything yet, cowboy?"

I'm frozen still because it wouldn't help to move or try anything. All that time she spent as a trauma nurse, she knows just where to stick that blade. I'd be shitting my pants in seconds and done bleeding out a few minutes later.

"You still don't, do you?"

I reckon that I hoped it would all come back to me in a flashback, like on TV. Like the one on *Dallas* when, glued to the fuzzy images coming over the airwaves on that porch, Pearly and me finally found out who shot J.R. Ewing.

But I still don't remember shit.

Doesn't mean I'm not putting it all together pretty fast, though. And as I hear the low rumble of motorcycle pipes pulling up to Pearly's shack, it all clicks into place.

"Nope," I say. "But I ain't stupid either."

"Well." She leans over to snatch up the Colt pistol from the dock. "That's debatable."

Pearly and me agreed to mule the heroin for the MC. It's coming clearer now. It was our first time. Easy money. Until *someone* got us thinking how we could keep it all for ourselves. One big score to get us the fuck out of this backwater town forever. Brenda got us daydreaming about sunny Mexican beaches and endless cervezas. A devil on our shoulders whispering into our ears the whole time.

Me and Pearly just ain't that ambitious. Not on our own.

We ain't that clever.

"You weren't even high, were you?" I ask. "Back at the gas station."

She shifts her weight and saunters around from behind me. She drops the hand with the knife to her side, hooking her thumb in the pocket of her jeans next to the bulge of the burner phone from the glovebox, and brings the gun up, smirking.

"Oh, Lord knows I've had enough experience to fake it." She puffs out her cheeks and blows. "Didn't expect the little cocktail I mixed up for you and Pearly to work so well, though. Or have such..." She searches for the words. "Savage effects."

She's circling around me now, like a lioness at play. I hear other footfalls too. Heavier ones. Motorcycle boots coming down the dock toward us. There's a smell in the air of motor oil and gasoline and smoke. Flames crackle and dance behind me as the shotgun shack goes up like a torch.

"I thought you were takin' care of this," a man says, his voice sharp like snapping bones.

"I am, Baby!" she replies. "Just taking my time is all."

He snorts and spits.

The two of them get to making out. Lips and tongues smacking, all of it sloppy. Like teenagers. Like new lovers, or maybe—it now occurs to me—like old ones. Like I said, she would fuck me and Pearly now and then, but she never kissed us quite like that.

The man slaps her ass and trudges back up the dock toward the blazing shack. "Let me know when you're ready to burn him," he calls over his shoulder.

"Long as I get their fee, darlin'."

She blows him a kiss. A sweet gesture, so alien in this lethal moment.

I notice now that Brenda's bare shoulders are covered by a worn black leather jacket so big it practically swallows her. I have to admit, it's a good move for her: getting in tight with the River Lords. It's as much about status and power as it is money. But eventually, she'll be looking over that next hill. That's for damned sure.

"That biker man you were kissing on better watch his back." I snort, then my gaze drifts down to Pearly's severed head in the crab pot. She nudges it with her boot.

"You did that, you know," she grins.

I shake my head like I'm trying to get a buzzing mayfly out of my ears.

"No," I groan.

"Went plum crazy, like some animal. Some beast. All that smack sitting in the house and the two of y'all cranked up and paranoid. It was soooo damn easy."

Tears fill my eyes and the whole world goes blurry until I blink them away.

"Pearly was my *friend*," I blurt out.

The anguish drips from my lips like Spanish moss. I want to call her a liar, but because I am haunted by Pearly's face—because my murderous deed has been catching up to me all along—I know it must be true.

A memory comes; not something imagined. My eyes are as black and empty as the creek at night. I'm high on something, high on everything, probably. Pearly is face-down on the dock, the night and the water stretch out in front of us, and he is screaming. My knee digs into his back, and with the first stroke, the handsaw chews into the flesh just above his shoulder. I hold it an angle, just like Brenda tells me.

"Oh, God, what'd I do?"

It comes out like a question full of spit and tears but I know the answer already.

"Sorry, darlin'." She shrugs. "I went overboard on the amphetamine, I guess."

Brenda kicks the crab pot over the edge. It splashes into the creek and sinks from view along with all that's left of Pearly. Watching it disappear into the frigid water sends a chill through me that bites deep, like I'm going into that cold darkness with him.

"Probably too heavy on the Propofol, too." She sighs. "It was one hell of a night. I wish you remembered more of it."

She presses the muzzle of the pistol to my head, just behind the ear. "You and Pearly... I had y'all so afraid one of you was gonna fuck the other over." Brenda leans down now and whispers, her lips so close it might be mistaken for a kiss. "Y'all couldn't see that I was fuckin' you both."

I bow my head as if in prayer.

I'm scared here at the end, trembling, squeezing my eyes shut. Just instinct, I guess. Bracing for the crack of the pistol and the fraction of a second of terror before it all goes black. I don't even notice she's slit my throat open until the warm rush comes spilling down my chest, and I fall over onto my side.

She leans down, plunges her hand into the pocket of my jeans, and retrieves the key to the Lincoln's trunk. With passing interest, Brenda watches gouts of my blood spurt onto the weathered boards. She holds my Colt by the barrel and drags the reddened blade of the Buck knife across the walnut grip, scratching another notch into it.

A notch for me.

A notch all her own, earned the old way.

They'll soak me down with gasoline soon and put me to the flame. Maybe I'll be long-gone by then. Maybe not.

I cough and try to breathe, but all I can manage is a gurgle. I'd hoped death would be quick, but I reckon it's never quick enough.

Sometimes it's not the gun pointed at you, but the knife you didn't see.

That's what gets you.

Sometimes—every damn time.

THE PATH TO FREEDOM

James L. Hill

This was going to be an unusual day; Pappi woke me before the sun. I was not expecting that, being Sunday and all. I thought I had my days mixed again. I often did, not having to work the fields yet, but next year, when I turn thirteen, I'll join Pappi, Isaac, and Nate working the tobacci. My chores were feeding the chickens, goats, and pigs, and they never rose before the sun.

Pappi shook my shoulder and whispered, "Get the hickory rods and lines. We are going down to the creek and catch some fish. Be quiet. Don't wake your brothers and sister."

I peeked across the shanty, the light of the embers in the hearth painted their faces. I rolled from my straw-stuffed mat and blanket and stretched. I grabbed two long hickory poles and a roll of twine. I carefully picked up a couple of sharpened bone hooks and dropped them in a tobbaci sack. Momma was still sleeping in her bed near the door, Pappi had already gone outside.

I looked around, there was not a hint of dawn on the horizon. A strange start to the day indeed. Pappi placed a hand on my shoulder and squeezed, a sign to pay close attention to what he was about to say. He had a way, a look, or an act, that meant you need to commit what he said next to memory and never hesitate in the re-telling.

"Now, listen here, John."

This was serious. He always called me by my family name when he was serious, instead of Sonny. My eyes widened.

"No need to worry, boy. Just remember, if anyone asks, we went down to the creek to catch catfish. Everybody knows cats bite best before the dawn. And, no matter who asks, Momma, Sara, the Boys, and especially Master Stephen, we went fishing."

I nodded and followed him down the road towards the creek.

He carried a lantern but didn't light it. Not that we needed light to follow the path, but the light would scare away the black snakes. Momma always told me not to walk in the dark because one bite from a black snake could kill; even a baby snake had enough venom in its bite to kill a boy my size. But Pappi was smart, he knew that only the black snakes that lived near the creek were biters, he thumped the ground with his walking stick. Any snake would crawl from the path before we reached it. I did not know how far from the creek the really dangerous ones traveled; I thumped the ground with the fishing rods. Just to be sure.

We passed the broken tree that looked like an A. I was never allowed to call it that since I wasn't supposed to know my letters. Master Stephen had taught me some of my letters and numbers too. He said it was the only way I could properly play the game, Hide and Seek. He made me swear a death oath not to tell Master Charles or we'd both be whipped.

The path under the A tree led to the pool in the creek which was the best place for catching cats. We were a half mile past it before we went down an un-trotted embankment. Then we walked on the stony shore a bit longer. The sun was just rising when my father sat me on a thick branch over the water. He put a couple of rocks in the sack.

"If you hear or see anyone heading this way, you throw a rock into the water. If anyone asks what you are doing, remember you are catfishing. I am off in the woods that way," he pointed up the creek from where we came, "getting more worms for bait."

I nodded and he headed downstream and around the bend. I tied a hook to the twine and measured an ample length, so the hook rested on the bottom. I tied the end to the pole and waited. I was a good catfisher, but I didn't think I'd catch any with a bare hook.

The sun was peeking above the treetops when Pappi returned with a sack of four catfish. He helped me from the branch and handed me the sack. "You did good today, Sonny. Pull in four nice sized cats, right?"

"Yes, Pappi. They put up a fight, but I got them alright."

We walked the shoreline back to the path to the A tree then back up the path to our place.

We were standing in front of the big house, Sunday Service had just begun for us. Master Stephen Godwin was sitting in his father's rocker, which was now his since Charles Godwin had passed on seven years ago. Old Master, what most called him, had increased the farm to fifty acres and bought twenty field hands to work it. Peaceful Plantation stretched all the way to the creek when he was alive. The big house looked better then too, every year we all put on a fresh coat of white paint and trimmed the doors and windows in sunshine yellow.

But the creek was shrinking, and they sold bits and pieces of the Plantation to where it ended at the Deep Corner where we lived. The Deep Corner wasn't much good for planting, the ground was hard most of the time and filled with water every rain. Our quarters were built on long logs to keep them dry. During the rainy season, the water would cause the logs to shift and if you weren't careful a foot or hand would get crushed between them. Pappi would pack the logs with mud which helped hold them together.

The preacher was in the middle of his sermon when he suddenly stopped. Master Stephen rose out of his rocker like he was possessed by the spirit. It wasn't until Ol' Roy thumped his walking stick next to me that I knew why everything had become so quiet.

"Cotton." Pappi said.

"Abram," Ol' Roy replied. He winked at me and shoved his walking stick into my hand. The walking stick, which he called Albihere, was white oak, as white as his hair. There were faces carved into it, and they began their whispering. I wasn't sure why, but no one noticed the whisperings but me. And Cotton.

I worked with Ol' Roy feeding the chickens. Cotton, as he preferred to be called, said I had the gift. Every time I saw the walking stick—and I saw it every day—it had a new face. Most were the same but there was always a new one that replaced another. One day I asked him how could that be?

"Albihere shows us those who are important to us now."

"But it is you who carves the faces," I said. I must have been eight years old at the time and was watching him work on the walking stick. It was already covered from end to end and all around with faces. Yet he was still flicking little bits of wood from it.

"I only hold the blade," he said with a wide smile, "the faces come forth on their own."

The reason the congregation went silent was because Cotton never came to services. We were all made to attend, but no matter how hard the overseers looked they could never find Ol' Roy. In time they just stopped looking. The preacher started up again and Young Master Stephen slid back into his rocker.

"Abram, what did you hear from the Red Mill's folk?" Cotton asked, barely moving his lips.

"Young Master lost at auction," Pappi's head bowed as he sang his reply in tune with the hymn. "The tobacco crop was sold for less than half what he wanted. It was said he will sell half of us to make up for the loss. Mostly the women and children, I figure."

"Then you go tonight. While the moon is a sliver of itself and at your back." Cotton looked up to the sky. "No clouds, good for the hunted, bad for the hunter. Pass the word, you must all go. No one stays behind."

"There be seven families here, more than forty folks…"

"I know the count." Cotton's voice was strong but low. "It didn't matter to Moses if it was one or one hundred. Besides, anyone who stays will surely suffer the boy's wrath."

"I thought you didn't believe in their religion."

"I do not have to believe the story to understand the message told. You know the plan, bring everyone to the gathering before the moon breaches the treetops."

The families left their shoes—those who had a pair of dried and cracked deerskin moccasins—on the ground outside their cabins. No one wore their shoes inside for fear the smell of tobacco would draw snakes. Each of the cabins had a fire burning in the hearth. Three of them had stew pots sending the sweet smell of cooking pig drifting in the air.

The overseers made their rounds just after sundown, walking between the cabins and peering through the cracks in the thin planks of the walls. The four of them silently slid the iron bolts across the doors, locking them from the outside. As quiet as they were, everyone knew when they entered the Deep Corner and when they left.

I watched from the shuttered window, peeking through the spaces in the wood, as lanterns fired up one by one up on the hill. The shutters were barred just like the doors, but they could not stop me from counting the flickering lights in the big house and the overseers' cottage. When I counted ten, I jumped down from the chair. "Pappi, they are all in now."

"Are you sure?"

"Yes, sir," I said, beaming with confidence, "I used my fingers to be doubly sure of my numbers."

"All right then." Pappi lifted me back onto the chair. "Look for the faint glow of a pipe. We will wait a bit longer before we make our way."

After what seemed like half the night had passed, Pappi hoisted Isaac, my oldest brother, onto his shoulders. Isaac removed the shelf board and lifted the wall plank—its foot length—through the roof. Nate crawled through the opening in the back of the shack. He was eighteen, two years younger than Isaac and already too stocky to stand on Pappi's shoulders. This was how we escaped the shacks whenever the overseers locked us in, which wasn't all that often. Nate pulled the bar back on our door, then he and Isaac went around unlocking all the others.

I was the last to leave. I had to keep the lookout. They locked all the doors back and we left our shoes outside. If the overseer returned in the night, all would seem normal. We each wore an extra set of clothing and carried one loaf of cornbread and a hunk of meat in a handkerchief. Pappi had two handkerchiefs.

We met Cotton at the creek, past the A tree. Some of the men had torches but Cotton forbade them from lighting them. They reasoned the Peaceful was over the rise and out of sight of the creek. Traveling would be quicker and safer with at least one torch to light the way.

Cotton thumped Albihere, waking the faces who complained loudly to me. "Because you managed to sneak under the master's blind eye does not mean he will not come a-looking. We have the light of God and our ancestors to guide us, but we will not be safe until we pass through the Great Dismal Swamp. That is when you can feel the warmth of fire again."

He led the way, walking downstream in the creek until its black water was up to my waist. I walked beside him, my usual place, Albihere whispering warnings and guiding my steps around sharp stones and deep pockets. We exited the creek with women carrying the youngest on their backs, followed by the older children, and lastly Pappi and the other men guarding the rear. Isaac and Nate were with Pappi, being long past the age of childhood. I looked back to make sure Sara, my sister, was okay. She was carrying one of the Marcus twins, walking between their mother and mine.

The moon was still at our back when we reached the blackness, the border of the Swamp.

Albihere said, "Horses."

For the first time, I heard all the voices speaking as one and saw through their eyes.

Pappi caught up to Cotton. "There are lights behind us. Still a good distance away."

"They ride though," Cotton said with certainty, "it will not be long before they catch up. Take a couple of men and go back a half mile and start spreading the extra food to the east. Then come back here. We will wait."

"No, you and the rest continue into the Swamp. We will catch up."

"We go as one," Albihere said to me.

"We must stick to the plan if we want to reach freedom," Cotton pointed Albihere back past the group. "The wind will carry the scent away from us and the dogs will follow. It will give us all the time we need to reach the path."

Pappi and two of the other men gave their red checkered handkerchiefs to their wives. "Aggy, I packed a little sweet bread in here for Sara and Sonny. To sweeten the sorrow if I don't make it back.

"Don't talk foolishness." Aggy stroked his face. "Now, get going, we don't have all night."

The three men ran off with their black handkerchiefs in hand. Seconds later they were lost to the darkness, and their footsteps faded even quicker.

What came next, I saw through Albihere's eyes.

Abram came to a small clearing on the path and began rolling on the ground.

The other two men looked on in bewilderment.

"Don't just stand there, help me lay down a scent track."

His two companions rolled with him through the clearing towards the east. A hundred feet in that direction they got up and ran, purposely rubbing against trees and brush as they went. They came to another clearing and the lights from the torches were visible enough to count.

"Eight torches, maybe a dozen men," Abram said. "Hear that?"

The pair nodded.

"Dogs are not far off. Let's spread the food in these bushes and get back to our families."

They headed back the way they came, again leaving their scent on the way. Before they reached the path each man broke off a Hickory branch and swept away their trail, rejoining the group when the moon was at its apex.

Pappi placed his hand on my shoulder as I sat with Cotton. "It is done. Let's get a move on."

"You men take a moment to rest," Cotton replied.

"No time. If the dogs do not pick up the false trail, they will be on us quickly."

"The dogs head east." I repeated what Albihere whispered.

Abram looked at me holding Cotton's walking stick in my lap, but I stared into the Swamp's blackness, still as a stone.

"This place holds powerful magic," Cotton whispered. "The ancestors know our plight; they guide our footsteps. It is easiest for the old ones to speak to the young ones."

"The dogs have found the bread soaked in Devil's Weed. They cannot resist its smell." My trance scared the others, but they closed in to hear my intoning. "The young ones have no sense of danger. Their parents are wiser.

But they are drawn to the meats, and the White Snakeroot therein. The men and their horses have arrived."

Again, the eyes of Albihere showed me what I needed to see.

Stephen Godwin watched his tracking dogs writhing in pain. His horse dipped its head and bit into an apple on the ground beneath a bush. The other horses milled about looking and finding the treats left for them. Then the youngest of the hounds vomited a white trumpet flower amongst the half-digested bread.

Ben Skinner, the head overseer, didn't need to see anymore, "Get the horses away from here. It's a trap. The food left here is poisoned." But he was too late, as his horse collapsed under him, kicking in obvious pain. Two more horses succumbed to the poison before the rest could be pulled away. "This is a false trail. Those runaways are heading for the swamp."

"You mean the Great Dismal Swamp," Robert said. He was young, sixteen and a few months, and was on loan from the Red Mill Plantation this growing season. "I'm not going in there. My father said never to set foot on that ground. It be full of Indian spirits and other devilish things. No sir! I am turning back right here."

"Okay." Ben took the reins of his horse. "Then you won't need your horse."

"Of course, I will!" Robert tried to pull the leather straps away, causing his steed to dance back and forth. "It is much too far to walk."

"You will not be walking," Ben drew his pistol. "I'm about to shoot you right here. And the same goes for anyone turning back." He took the boy's horse, making him walk with the others whose horses had eaten the poisoned fruit.

I held Albihere and walked alongside Cotton. I just knew where to go, although I'd never entered the Swamp. This night I'd gone as far from the plantation as I ever had. For most of my people this was as far from their homes as they had ever been. Yet, I had no fear of the darkness that enveloped us. The crescent moon beamed a single shaft around the group. Everywhere else, blackness was but an arm's distance away.

The night had a stillness, a stifling quiet that absorbed the sound of footsteps. No insects, no hooting owls, not the sound of one's own heartbeat escaped the darkness of the Great Dismal Swamp.

Still I saw with many eyes—mine and so many others.

"This ground is much too soft," Isaac said to Father, his voice as soft as the mud beneath his feet. "We are leaving tracks anyone can follow."

"No, we are not," Pappi answered, pointing behind them. They were no longer walking in a double line. They had bunched up in an undiscernible mass of huddled bodies. With so many feet trampling over the same ground, and the wetness of the swamp, their footprints vanished as quickly as they could be formed.

"Pappi, we do not have to keep running. Nate and I and a few others can lie in wait for the slavers. Surely, we have the numbers now."

Pappi took Isaac's hand and put his other on Nate's shoulder. "May be that we outnumber our pursuers. But they have guns and whips. And we have the women and children to think about. It is best that we all survive this night."

"Survival is good," Nate said, "but not if it only leads to being hunted down and returned another night."

"Your time for fighting will be here soon enough, Young Wilsons." Cotton had stopped and let the group pass him until he was side by side with Pappi and my brothers. "Our numbers grow by the night and more join each day. You speak the truth Isaac, we cannot outrun this beast, but neither can we beat it one on one."

"Who is at the lead?" Nate asked.

"Who do you think?" Cotton smiled.

"Sonny?" Nate twisted his neck to look between the bodies ahead. "But he's only twelve."

"How old do you think I was when I took the staff and walked the path to freedom?" Cotton laughed as he watched the young man trying to figure out his age. "It has been nine decades for me, seventeen fifty-four, on a night much like this. It is time for the next one to lead."

"But why Sonny?" Pappi asked but not in a questioning manner.

"Albihere chooses who it chooses. But if it comforts you, I will return to its side. Do not fall behind, we have not reached the path yet." Cotton stopped walking.

Before the three could utter another word Ol' Roy's white, cotton-topped head was at the front of the pack. He looked back and smiled.

Stephen Godwin's horse whinnied and bucked at the edge of the swamp. Stephen kicked and leaned forward then patted the side of the animal's neck. "It's alright boy, let's go."

The horse went two steps forward then back another five. He danced around in a circle, coming close to trampling those on foot.

Ben Skinner dismounted. "They will be of no use to us in there."

"See, it's like I said," Robert agreed, "the horses have better sense than to go into the Swamp. Like my daddy said—"

"Shut your mouth, boy! We can't ride in there because the ground is unfirm and the horses know they will get stuck in the mud. It has nothing to do with what foolishness your father told you. We go on foot. Now, let's hurry."

"How do you know they went this way? How do you know which way to go, Uncle Ben?" Stephen asked with a boyish tone.

"I lived my fifty years right here on this land," Ben said so all could hear, "I know every stone and stick here, and where they should be. They went this way." He pointed his torch ahead of him. But the light did not travel far into the Swamp.

When Cotton and I stepped into the light of a clearing, an old Indian sat on a log. The forty with us were glad to be out of the darkness. Ahead, Cotton and the Indian shared a few words nobody understood. I looked hard at the old Indian and recognized his face, but didn't know why.

As we left the clearing on the only path, Albihere spoke: "Do not stray from the path of freedom."

It was the face of the old Indian, on the walking stick, who spoke.

We all disappeared back into the darkness of the Swamp, guided by the faint light of the moon ahead, and me.

A few minutes later the lights like fireflies caught the old Indian's attention.

Ben approached the man. "You be Nottuwea? I thought all your people were dead and gone from this land."

"Your kind have pushed us from our homes, but you cannot rid this land of our spirit. We are the trees, we are the rain, we are the wind."

"We are looking for our slaves. Tell me which way they went," Ben demanded.

"They follow the path to freedom." The old Indian stood. "You will not find them."

"Why not?" Stephen stepped forward from the dozen men with him.

"They follow the path to freedom. Your path leads to the darkness of your hearts."

A loud boom filled the clearing. The old Indian fell back onto the ground. A small dark red circle covered his jacketed chest. Wind blew in from every direction.

"What did you do that for!"

"He was trying to delay us, Stephen." Ben turned to the men, gun still smoking. "There is only one path out of this clearing. It's that way." He pointed his torch ahead.

"Where did the Indian go?" asked Robert.

"He ran off."

"How? You killed him!"

"Let's go!" Ben shouted, just as he would for any questions he had no answers for. "We keep moving."

Stephen followed Ben past the log and into the darkness once more. The other men reluctantly fell in behind. Robert looked at the ground one last time where the Indian had fallen and noticed there was no blood. He lagged behind the group.

The men held two torches together to brighten the flame. But the light shone no farther; they could see a yard ahead and no more. The solid ground showed no footprints, it was smooth and undisturbed.

Stephen spoke up. "Are we sure we're on the right path?"

One of the overseers stumbled and left the small circle of light. He screamed.

The others turned to see him up to his thighs in black ooze. Two men stepped forward, reached their hands to pull him out. But other hands reached up his legs and pulled him down deeper. He screamed for help, but his friends retreated in fear.

"It is quicksand, boys," Ben warned. "Step back or it will pull you in too." Meanwhile, the black hands pulled the man under. "Let's go," he continued. "And watch your step, they don't call this place the Great Dismal Swamp without reason."

Robert lingered longer, as if his fears had been confirmed.

The rest went only a few more yards, only a few minutes, when a loud roar broke through the silence. A dark mass barreled into the group. In a flash, one man's midsection was ripped from his body and another was carried off. Two others fired their rifles into the blackness.

Robert, frozen, stared at the man's severed body.

"*Bear*," Ben hissed. "*Bears!* Let's go. Those slaves are getting away."

He quickened his gait, causing the others to do the same.

Robert picked up the torch that had been carried by the man who disappeared into the Swamp and waited a few seconds before following. "No safety in numbers," he whispered to the night. "Not here."

A swarm of mosquitoes was drawn to the light of the torches. The men swung their flames wildly trying to fend them off. Robert watched as black lines traced the veins of the men who were stung. Their faces swelled quickly and they fell.

Ben, moving fast, too fast not to show his panic, set fire to the five dead men. It drew the bugs away from him. Suddenly, he eyed Robert hanging back and drew his pistol.

Robert saw it just in time and tossed his torch onto the heap of burning flesh. Then he disappeared into the darkness, running full out as shots like dull drumbeats sounded. He could not see where he was going but the ground beneath his feet was solid, so he kept going.

Stephen, off from the others, heard the growl of wolves, the war cries of Indians, and a thousand angry voices. He could not see his Uncle Ben. Or any of the others. They'd been swept away by the blackness or plucked out of existence—there was no other way to describe it.

Out of nowhere a faint glowing figure approached.

Stephen drew his pistol with shaking hands. "Who are you? What do you want from me?"

"Freedom," I said, hearing myself speak through the lips of Albihere's faces. "It is all we ever wanted."

"I was good to you. Not like my father. I played games with you."

"You wanted to play with me, you had no one else to play with." I stood inches from him, but my voice sounded like we stood across a field. "I had to play with you. I had no choice."

"Don't you think I wish I could be free? Not have to look after you. I didn't want this."

"You can walk away, anytime you like. We have to run."

I paused.

We paused.

"But don't take too long," we said. "Your chance for freedom is fading. And we will be back to take ours."

I left, fading from Stephen's view, but we watched for a long time while he stumbled in the darkness.

KEEP IT CIVIL

Clay McLeod Chapman

1906

"Some time ago The Journal advocated in its columns the erection of a monument to the living and dead soldiers of this county who responded to the call of Virginia and the South and followed the fortunes of the Confederacy from Manassas to Appomattox. Each one of these heroes, many of whom sleep in unknown and unmarked graves, is entitled to a high place in the affections of the people of Mathews and their heroic deeds should be commemorated by the erection of a fitting monument to their memory...

Confederate soldiers of Mathews, awake and respond to the sacred duty resting upon you to pay the deserved tribute of a shaft of marble to the memory of the comrade who slept by your side in winter's cold and summer's heat, and who fell under the rain of the enemy's bullet with his face to the foe, whose life blood baptized the soil of our mother State and who died in defense of his country's honor, with face as calm and smile as sweet as patriot ever wore.

Sons and daughters of the Confederacy, arise in the strength and beauty of your youth and proclaim to the world your pride in the splendor of courage and wealth of self-sacrifice shown by your fathers upon the battlefields of Virginia, and honor their deathless valor and their unexampled patriotism by lending your youth and your strength to the erection of this monument."

– The Mathews Journal, March 8, 1906

2020

They're toppling our monuments. Ripping our history right on down. Look at what those rioters are doing in Richmond. They've laid siege to that city—the goddamn heart of the Confederacy—singing and dancing in the streets as they tear down every last statue.

First, it was General Williams Carter Wickham in Monroe Park.

Then it was Jefferson Davis on Monument Avenue.

Now the city itself removed ol' Stonewall. Got one of those telescoping boom cranes to roll on in, cinching its winch around the General's bronze horse and hefting them both off their pedestal while all those protestors cheered, snapping off selfies with their goddamn phones.

Those statues have stood for well over a hundred years and their mayor's got the gall to pull them all down? Whose statue are they coming for next?

Not our monument, no sir.

We only got one stop light, but Mathews County sure as hell ain't sitting back and watching our one and only statue get torn down like they've done in Richmond. We're not turning our backs on our heritage. You damn well better believe we're protecting our legacy.

A group of us boys have taken it upon ourselves to stand watch, keeping vigil over our Confederate memorial, just in case any looters decide to take a little road trip here to Mathews.

Go ahead. Try knocking our monument down, I dare you. Let's see how close you get before you're whistling Dixie through your freshly ventilated chest. Open-carry is legal here in Virginia, last time I checked, so you better think twice before coming after our statue.

Our militia is strictly volunteer. Ain't nobody getting paid to stand watch. We consider it our civic duty to protect our monument. Let's see, there's myself. Walt Tompkins. Hank Reynolds. Jimmy Litch. Ben Pendleton bailed on us after the first few nights, so he's out.

We're taking six-hour shifts. Day and night. Seven days a week. We gotta dance around each other's work schedules, which ain't that hard for me, considering I'm in between jobs at the moment. Walt's the only one with a nine-to-five, while the rest of us gentlemen tend to take work wherever we might find it. Makes it easier for us to commit to our call of duty.

Our memorial might not look like much compared to the big boys on Monument Avenue, but it's all we've got. We give our statue the respect he deserves. Back in 1906, the Daughters of the Confederacy put out the call for *a monument that commemorated the men of Mathews*, those boys who responded to the battle cry of the South and *followed the fortunes of the Confederacy from Manassas to Appomattox*. Each one of them boys were heroes—*our heroes*—many of whom *still sleep in unmarked graves* to this very day. Damn straight they're entitled to *a high place*. They deserve to be on a pedestal overlooking courthouse square.

It's a fitting tribute, if you ask me. A shaft of marble reaching twenty feet straight up in the air. Nobody knows who that reb standing on top is. He's no general. There's no name on the inscription. He's just some unknown soldier boy who once called Mathews home, a brother in arms *who slept in winter's cold and summer's heat, who fell under the rain of the enemy's bullet with his face to the foe, whose life blood baptized the soil of our mother state and who died in defense of his country's honor*. Us boys all call him Mathew 'cause—well, because this here is Mathews County. For as long as I can remember, ever since I was a kid, that's just what everyone around here called him—as in, *Hey, meet me under Mathew*, or, *Turn left at Mathew and just keep on driving till you hit Route 611*. It's a nickname that sticks. Our very own mascot.

I looked up to him. Literally.

As a kid, no older than eight or nine, I'd stand under the statue of Mathew and stare up at those bronze eyes of his, cast out cross the horizon. I always wanted to see what he'd seen on the battlefield. He's looking at it right now, always staring at the aftermath along the front, the outright carnage of it. I remember wanting to be like him, growing up and serving my country—most of it, at least—just like he had. How old was he when he went to war?

I'd talk to him. If nobody else was around, I'd end up asking: *What was it like? Believing in something so much?*

But Mathew never answered. Sometimes I imagined him talking back to me. Still do. Ain't like I'm the only one, either. Hank was convinced he'd conversed with Matthew one night a few years back, but that was after a twelve-pack of Pabst, so nobody's buying his ghost story.

What I wouldn't give to see the things he'd seen.

I've lived here my whole life. Mathews is my home. Mathews is my people. I've been taught to respect where I come from, even if it's fallen out of fashion. To hell with what the history books say. Teachers are whitewashing whole battles out from their lesson plan. Kids these days don't even know what war's been fought right under their feet. Who died on this very ground that we're standing on now.

This statue is all the history I need. The erection of this here monument is a tribute to the *courage* and *self-sacrifice our forebearers showed on the battlefield, honoring their deathless valor and patriotism*. It stands as a testament to the Confederate sons of Mathews County who gave their lives to the cause. If that ain't worth protecting, then what the hell is?

I pull the midnight shift.

Walt is asleep in his Chevy when I come up on him, so I give that boy the scare of his life by pounding on the hood, thunder rumbling all around as I shout—"Antifa are attacking!"

You should see the look on his face as he springs up in his seat, eyes wider than a pair of hubcaps. Probably pissed in his Pampers. I nearly keel over, busting my gut.

"The hell, man... I coulda shot you!"

"You'll have to wipe your ass first, after the crap you just shat in your pants..."

"Mattie's all yours, asshole," he mutters before turning over the ignition and driving off.

"See you tomorrow... Bring a fresh pair of underwear!"

There's a picnic table in the courthouse square, situated next to the monument, just under Mathew and his musket. Gives me a clear sight line between Church and Fisher Street.

I prefer keeping my vigil outdoors. Boredom settles in pretty quick behind the wheel. Ain't no surprise Walt dozed off. Luckily, it's not raining tonight. I got myself a front row seat to a jam session between the crickets and cicadas, sawing their asses off in the dark.

Nobody is awake at this hour. Just me and Mathew, standing our watch. He's leaning against his musket made of marble, its buttstock between his feet as he stares blankly out at the horizon—while I got my 9mm on the table, simply listening to the spring peepers. There's a slight breeze coming in from the Chesapeake, so I get a good whiff of salt water in the air. It's pushing one A.M. and it's still more humid than Hades right now. I can feel the mugginess cling to the back of my neck, summoning the sweat all across my skin, rising right out of me.

"Whaddya think, Mattie?" I ask the statue. "See anybody up there?"

Nobody's come for my main man so far. That don't mean either of us ever let our guard down. This vigil here is to hold the front line. We're letting the folks in Richmond know we won't sit idly by while these looters take to the streets and bowl over our legacy. There may be over a hundred miles between the state capital and our town, but we all know how these things go. I've heard all about their night raids, spray-painting statues across the state. Last I heard, defacing public property was a crime—and around these parts, the law still stands for something. It don't matter if it's a can of spray paint or a Molotov cocktail; they're carrying a weapon and nothing would make me happier than to show them the business end of my pistol.

"Ain't that right, Mattie?"

He don't answer.

Never answers.

We're taking a stand. The culture wars end here, my friends. If those protestors come marching our way, you better believe we'll be ready for them. I'm holding the line just like my great great great grandfather held the line over two hundred years ago. I even got myself a great aunt who disguised herself as a man and fought on the ground. That's how deep our roots go. So, you damn well better believe I'm here for the cause. Ain't nobody taking Mathew down.

But Christ, does it ever get boring. I've glanced at my watch five times in the last twenty minutes alone. Mosquitoes are downright murdering my ass, making a meal out of me.

It's the last hour of my shift. The sun will be softening the horizon before long. Once I see that egg yolk yellow seep through the trees, my vigil will be done.

I can't remember who's picking up the morning shift. Either Hank or Jimmy. They better not sleep through their alarm and leave me hanging like last time. To hell if I'm abandoning my station, though. Until one of them shows and relieves me of my duties, I'm sitting right here.

"You hear that, Mattie?" I ask. "Just you and me…"

Nothing, someone whispers.

I leap up from the picnic table. I grab my 9mm and circle the perimeter once, then twice.

Ain't nobody around. The streetlamps are getting battered by moths, but that's just about as much as I can see moving in either direction.

"Who's there?" I weigh the words down with enough concrete for this son of a bitch to know I mean business. "You got three seconds to show yourself. One…"

The streets are clear. Ain't no one hiding behind the pillar.

"Two…"

The safety's off. Finger on the trigger. I'm listening to the cannon blasts of my own heartbeat battering against my chest as I try balancing my breathing through my nose.

"Three…"

Silence.

There's nothing.

The voice sounds closer now. I can't put a bead on where. It's faint, more air than utterance, as if the word itself was exhaled from the mouth of whoever said it.

Sounds like they're right on top of me. Whispering from above. So, I tilt my head back.

The monument is empty.

Mathew is gone. As in, he's no longer there. The pedestal is empty.

I stumble back, away from the monument. I'm not looking where I'm going, so when I collide with whatever's behind me, it feels like hitting a brick wall. But this wall's got arms.

I spin around and find myself face-to-face with him.

Mathew's staring back at me with his chiseled eyes. Nothing but grey marble sanded down by a century's worth of bad weather, a pair of rotten robin's eggs settled in each socket.

Do you want to see? I swear I hear him say it, that sandpaper rasp summoning the word up from his marble throat. He's shaking his head as he steps closer to me. *See for yourself?*

Before common sense seeps in and I second guess myself, I hear myself answer...

"Yes." I want to know. I need to see.

See the war with my own eyes.

Mathew—this statue, this man made of stone—takes hold of his own face, simply gripping his eyes with both of his weatherworn hands and digging those brittle fingers into the sockets. The rock crumbles under his clutch as he pulls in opposite directions. Pulls at his face.

"Wait," I say. "Don't—"

The stone gives, brick flesh separating along the bridge of his nose. His fingers have plunged so far into his sockets he's able to break open his own skull, splitting it vertically in half like an arid coconut and now I see what's been hidden within the tomb of our nameless soldier's face.

Nothing, Mathew whispers to me as the halves of his head envelope my own. *There's nothing to see.*

Now I see it, too. See that vast greyness for myself. There's a brittle chill coming off it, a cloud cover of cataracts eclipsing my vision—and in the very moment his head seals up again, closing over my skull and trapping me inside, I don't know what's suddenly happening to my own eyes. I can feel the weight of them growing heavier by the breath, a pair of rocks settling into their sockets. Every time I blink, my eyelids scrape over coarse stone. Nothing's there anymore. Nothing to see. It's all gone grey for me.

ABOUT THE AUTHORS

Catherine Kuo is a graduate of the University of California, Davis, where she was selected as one of the winners of the 2010-2011 Prized Writing competition. She is a member of the Horror Writers Association and her other stories can be found in the *Bloodless* anthology, published by Sliced Up Press, and *Monstrous Futures* anthology, published by Dark Matter Ink. She currently lives in Arlington, Virginia.

Paul Michael Anderson is the author of the novellas *Standalone, How We Broke* (with Bracken MacLeod), and *The Only Way Out is Through*, as well as the collections *Bones Are Made to be Broken* and *Everything Will Be All Right in the End*. He lives in Northern Virginia. www.thenothingspace.net

Charles E. Wood writes horror, dark fantasy, and other light-hearted fabrications. Born in West Texas and transplanted to Virginia by the USMC in the 80s, he lives in Fairfax. He loves dark alleys, side streets in large Asian cities, abandoned houses, beer, and various combinations of those. In his spare time, he may be found in shadowy corners of taverns, speaking softly to small rocks and murmuring to himself. www.inadarkwood.com

William R.D. Wood traces his love of science fiction and horror back to a childhood filled with Space: *1999* reruns, visits to the *Night Gallery*, and a worn-out copy of *Dune*. His work has appeared in *Nature, Daily Science Fiction* and *Cosmic Horror Monthly*. A good day finds him on Virginia's Blue Ridge Parkway with a fully charged laptop and diabolical plans. www.williamrdwood.com

Margaret L. Carter attended the College of William and Mary and received graduate degrees in English from the University of Hawaii and the University of California (Irvine). She specializes in vampires and writes horror, paranormal romance, and fantasy, plus nonfiction on vampirism in literature. Recent releases include *Against the Dark Devourer* (Lovecraftian dark paranormal romance novel) and *Bunny Hunt* (contemporary fantasy short e-book). She has had stories in anthologies including the *Darkover* and *Sword and Sorceress* series, among others, and coauthored fantasy novels with her husband, Leslie Roy Carter. Please explore love among the monsters at Carter's Crypt: http://www.margaretlcarter.com.

Stephen Mark Rainey is a native Virginian, having grown up in Martinsville, in the foothills of the Blue Ridge Mountains. He is the author of numerous novels, including *Balak, The Lebo Coven*, *Dark Shadows: Dreams of the Dark* (with Elizabeth Massie), *Blue Devil Island*, and others. In addition, Mark's work includes six short story collections; 200-some published works of short fiction; and the scripts for several *Dark Shadows* audio productions, which feature members of the original ABC-TV series cast. For ten years, he edited the award-winning *Deathrealm* magazine and has edited several anthologies, including the upcoming *Deathrealm: Spirits,* due in October 2023 from Shortwave Publishing. www.stephenmarkrainey.com

Sonora Taylor is the award-winning author of seven books, including *Little Paranoias: Stories*, *Seeing Thing*s, and *Without Condition*. Her short stories have been published by Tenebrous Press, Rooster Republic Press, Cemetery Gates Media, Kandisha Press, and others. She also co-edited *Diet Riot: A Fatterpunk Anthology* with Nico Bell. She is an active member of the Horror Writers Association. She lives in Arlington, Virginia, with her husband and a rescue dog. www.sonorawrites.com

Ivy Grimes lives in Northern Virginia, and her work has appeared in *Vastarien, The Baffler, Ergot., Tales From Between, Seize the Press, Interzone, Cosmic Horror Monthly, Coffin Bell,* and elsewhere. She has future book projects planned with Spooky House Press and Grimscribe. Press. Find her on Twitter @IvyGri and at ivy.grimes/substack.

Nicole Willson's debut novel *Tidepool* (Parliament House Press) came out in August 2021 and was a finalist for the Bram Stoker Award and the Ladies of Horror Fiction Award. A Spanish translation of the novel is available from Dilatando Mentes Editorial. Her novella *The Shadow Dancers of Brixton Hill* will be published by Cemetery Gates Media in 2023. Her short fiction has appeared in anthologies by Cemetery Gates Media and Death Knell Press. She lives with her husband and a rotating cast of cats in Northern Virginia. www.nicolewillson.com

Michael Rook is not cursed. He was named after a ghost, doesn't sleep, and writes to release the thing in his head, but he definitely doesn't blame his parents. Originally from Ohio, he wonders (worries) what it'll take to become a true Virginian. Find his other stories in *Penumbric Speculative Fiction Magazine*, *Teach.Write.*, and *After Dinner Conversation*. Or check out his Instagram (@michaelrook10) and website: www.michaelrookwrites.com

Brýn Grover grew up when the Soviet Union was the enemy. "Bomb" drills were generally held as he ducked and hid under desks and learned to count 'flash to bang' times. Culturally, this was accented by B Movies of monsters resulting from 'atomic' problems and nuclear explosions. He grew to love those movies and the supernatural literary works of such authors as H.P. Lovecraft, Clark Ashton Smith, Lord Dunsany, and T.E.D. Klein. His horror stories and poems often have a dark, and perhaps fantastical, side. They are generally macabre or gothic in nature and do not generally result in happy endings.

J.T. Glover has short fiction in *Best New Horror*, *Pseudopod*, and *Nightscript*, among other venues. He's published nonfiction in *Postscripts to Darkness*, *The Silent Garden*, and *Thinking Horror*. By day he's an academic librarian specializing in the humanities, and he lives in Central Virginia. www.jtglover.com

Valerie B. Williams came to writing late in life but is making up for lost time. Her most recent publication was "The Tinker's Gift" in the *Refracted Reflections* (WordCrafter Press) anthology published in September 2022.

Her short story, "Wheels Against Wings" will appear in the *Vinyl Cuts!* (Scary Dairy Press) anthology in the spring/summer of 2023. Valerie lives near Charlottesville, Virginia, with her husband and two Golden Retrievers. When not writing, she can be found reading and drinking either wine or tea, depending on the time of day. www.valeriebwilliams.com

María Badillo: Born to tell stories that explore the shadows of humanity, María Badillo's award-winning writing has been featured in *Parhelion Literary Magazine's* Halloween Issue, *Lingering in the Margins*, *Style Weekly Magazine*, *Paranormal Daily*, and more. Badillo is a member of the Horror Writers Association and author of *In Her Bones* dark poetry chapbook. Spotted on numerous literary stages, including a special event for the Edgar Allan Poe House in Baltimore, Badillo has a deep love for travel both literal and metaphorical. www.mariabadillo.com

Sidney Williams is the author of the *Si Reardon* detective thriller series from Crossroad Press's Gordian Knot imprint. Titles so far include *Fool's Run* and *Long Waltz*. His body of work also includes traditionally published novels from Kensington Books and original titles from Crossroad including *Dark Hours* and the Lovecraftian thriller *Disciples of the Serpent*. Sidney's recent short stories include *By Side Saddle* in the anthology *Unknown Superheroes vs. the Forces of Darkness,* His short work has also appeared in the anthologies including *Under the Fang*, *Love Among the Thorns* and *Cat Ladies of the Apocalypse*. http://sidisalive.com

Joseph Maddrey is the author of more than a dozen books, including *Nightmares in Red, White and Blue*; *Not Bad for a Human*, the authorized biography of Lance Henriksen; and the two-volume *Adapting Stephen King*. He has written and produced over 100 hours of documentary television, focusing on true crime and the paranormal. A native Virginian, Joe lives in Midlothian with his wife and daughter. http://maddrey.blogspot.com

Querus Abuttu, or "Dr. Q.," writes strange dark tales, speculative fiction, and weird sci-fi. She is a midnight poet, savior of road turtles, and a solitary green-gray witch living on the wooded banks of Iron Shores. When she's not writing, Dr. Q. explores the wilds of Virginia and interviews interesting individuals for her next novel. She loves foraging for wild foods, edible landscaping, and trying to find 101 ways to thwart deer from eating her plants. You may find her at a local wine tasting or in a local pub drinking craft beers talking to random people and writing furiously in a tattered notebook that she keeps under her pillow at night. Visit her author website at QuerusAbuttu.com.

Sirrah Medeiros is a dark fantasy, horror, and thriller writer. She is a graduate of the University of Maryland, a Marine Corps veteran, and a former program manager and technical communicator. Her passions include writing, drawing, hiking, and travel. She is the author of the *Cristiane Bradford* dark urban fantasy series—the most recent in the series, *Secrets of Mother*, was a 2022 Pinnacle Book Achievement Award winner. You can see a list of her previously published horror short story works on her website https://sirrahmedeiros.com. Sirrah lives in Virginia with her family and two rescue dogs.

Bryan Nowak is an author from northern Virginia, where he lives with his family. He has written several horror novels to include *The App*, *Formula-12*, *Riapoke*, and *Crimson Tassels*. His earliest horror influences include the great monsters of old, cheesy B-movies, as well as the tales of Edgar Allan Poe and ghost stories he checked out from his local library. His goal is to entertain above all and he believes in the power of the pen to shape imagination. www.bryannowak.com

Brad Center lives and works in Fairfax, Virginia. He owns an IT consulting firm (Occam Edge Technologies). He has worked on Capitol Hill and served on the Fairfax County School Board. As a writer he tends to focus his efforts on suspense/horror, speculative and science fiction. Brad has written two books. His novel *The Unspeakable Heart of the Mangroves* received the Horror Novel of the Year award from The Writers Forum. Additionally, Brad published *Blurring the Lines* (a short story collection of horror and speculative fiction). Brad has had short stories published in magazines like *The New Accelerator* and *MetaStellar* and has contributed to anthologies like *Land of 10,000 Nightmares*.

D. Alexander Ward is an author and anthologist. His most recent novels are *Pound of Flesh* and *Beneath Ash & Bone*. He edited the Bram Stoker Award-nominated anthologies *Lost Highways: Dark Fictions From the Road* and *Gutted: Beautiful Horror Stories* (co-edited) as well as *The Seven Deadliest* (co-edited) and *Shadows Over Main Street*, Volumes 1 and 2 (co-edited). He is an Active Member of the Horror Writers Association and operates Bleeding Edge Books. He lives near the farm where he grew up and spends his nights penning, collecting, and publishing tales of the dark, strange, and fantastic. www.dalexanderward.com

James L. Hill, a.k.a. J L Hill, is a multi-genre author, currently working on a three-part historical fantasy *Gemstone Series*. *The Emerald Lady* is in publication. *The Ruby Cradle* and the third book, *The Diamond Warrior,* are due soon. The four-part adult urban crime series, *The Killer Series*, is finished. *Killer With A Heart, Killer With Three Heads, Killer With Black Blood*, and *Killer With Ice Eyes* have all received great reviews. The last two novels were runners-up in the *Killer Nashville's* contests of 2022. Then there's the psychological dystopian science fiction thriller, *Pegasus: A Journey To New Eden* for your reading pleasure. https://www.rockhillpublishing.com

Clay McLeod Chapman writes books, comic books, children's books, and for film/TV. You can find him at www.claymcleodchapman.com.

CONTENT WARNINGS

Dark Corners of the Old Dominion is a fairly "quiet" anthology of horrors. However, there are a couple of stories that may be triggering to some individuals who have experienced trauma. The authors have offered the following content warnings:

Domestic Abuse, Sexual Violence, Attempted Abortion:

"The Bride of Dream Lake"

Domestic Abuse, Suicide, Violence:

"The Wrong Time"

Made in the USA
Middletown, DE
29 September 2023

39625564R00137